Kaidenberg's Best Sons

ESSENTIAL PROSE 193

Canada Council for the Arts

Conseil des Arts du Canada

ONTARIO ARTS COUNCIL
CONSEIL DES ARTS DE L'ONTARIO

an Ontario government agency
un organisme du gouvernement de l'Ontario

Guernica Editions Inc. acknowledges the support
of the Canada Council for the Arts and the Ontario Arts Council.
The Ontario Arts Council is an agency of the Government of Ontario.
We acknowledge the financial support of the Government of Canada
through the National Translation Program for Book Publishing, an initiative
of the Roadmap for Canada's Official Languages 2013-2018:
Education, Immigration, Communities, for our translation activities.
We acknowledge the financial support of the Government of Canada.
Nous reconnaissons l'appui financier du gouvernement du Canada.

KAIDENBERG'S BEST SONS

A NOVEL IN STORIES

JASON HEIT

**GUERNICA
EDITIONS**
TORONTO • BUFFALO • LANCASTER (U.K.)
2020

Edited by J. Jill Robinson
Book designed by Grace Cheong
Typeset by David Moratto
Cover image: Peter Henry Emerson (British, born Cuba, 1856–1936)
A Stiff Pull. [Suffolk.], 1888, Photogravure 20.8 × 28.6 cm (8 3/16 × 11 1/4 in.),
84.XB.696.2.4, The J. Paul Getty Museum, Los Angeles.
Printed and bound in Canada

Guernica Editions Inc.
287 Templemead Drive, Hamilton (ON), Canada L8W 2W4
2250 Military Road, Tonawanda, N.Y. 14150-6000 U.S.A.
www.guernicaeditions.com

Distributors:
Independent Publishers Group (IPG)
600 North Pulaski Road, Chicago IL 60624
University of Toronto Press Distribution (UTP),
5201 Dufferin Street, Toronto (ON), Canada M3H 5T8
Gazelle Book Services, White Cross Mills
High Town, Lancaster LA1 4XS U.K.

Second edition.
Printed in Canada.

Legal Deposit—Fourth Quarter
Library of Congress Catalog Card Number: 2020942679
Library and Archives Canada Cataloguing in Publication
Insert CIP: "Title: Kaidenberg's best sons : a novel in stories / Jason Heit.
Names: Heit, Jason, author. Series: Essential prose series ; 193.
Description: 2nd edition. | Series statement: Essential prose series ; 193
Identifiers: Canadiana (print) 20200294121 | Canadiana (ebook)
20200294180 | ISBN 9781771836517 (softcover) | ISBN 9781771836524
(EPUB) | ISBN 9781771836531 (Kindle)
Classification: LCC PS8615.E375 K35 2020 | DDC C813/.6—dc23"

For Jacqueline, Odelia, and Oleander

Foreword

THE STORIES IN this book are inspired by the experiences of a small group of ethnic Germans, known as the *Schwarzmeerdeutsche* (Black Sea Germans), who settled the St. Joseph's Colony in western Saskatchewan in the early 1900s. My ancestors were among these settlers and I've woven what I know about some of their personal experiences into these stories.

I'd like to acknowledge that my ancestors and other immigrants were able to settle on the Canadian prairies because of Canada's treaties with First Nations. The St. Joseph's Colony was established on Treaty 6 land.

STORIES

THE FEUD
1907

In the late 1800s, large numbers of German-speaking farmers emigrated from the Russian steppe to find new fortunes on the American prairie. Many of these first settlers made their way to the Dakotas, but the prospect of better land took some of them further into the northwest frontier, up into Canada and the newly formed, as of 1905, province of Saskatchewan.

ه

I REMEMBER IT like yesterday. The smell of desperate, tired men lined up outside the small one-storey brick building grumbling in the summer heat waiting for the agent to arrive. The land titles building stood atop a hill overlooking the town of Battleford, Saskatchewan, and the junction of the North Saskatchewan and the Battle rivers. Young caragana trees made a rough perimeter around the building, stifling the already heavy air. The year was 1907. I, Jakob Feist, was only 19 years old, and while I was as excited as any of those men to get my very own quarter of land, there was another feeling that overtook me that day. Something much bigger and much darker than my excitement. It was an ugly feeling—like the way you get before a fist fight, with your guts tied in knots and everything

1

is nerves. My father, Kaspar, had that feeling too. I can still remember the look in his eyes. If eyes could growl, his would have growled, *Ich will das Land.*

And they would have growled at Bernhard Holtz too. Bernhard and my father had been at each other since we left North Dakota, but my father hadn't really figured it for much until he suspected Bernhard had his eye on a quarter section of land we planned to farm. It was good land, and one of only two quarters next to my uncle's that was still open for homesteading. You see, each man 18 years or over could get one quarter of land for ten dollars, which was a very good price considering it was nearly $500 to buy an extra quarter. Father planned to file a claim for one quarter and I'd take the other.

The thing about feuds is sometimes you can be in one without really knowing it. For Father and me, it started outside that land titles office in Battleford. For Bernhard, it started some years before in North Dakota. He blamed us for ruining his fingers, which I'd admit we had a part in, but so did Bernhard, seeing how he had a bad habit of putting them where they didn't belong.

We had a hard time making a go of farming in North Dakota. Father was at it eight years. Eight years too long, he'd say. We'd left good farmland in South Russia—not far from the Black Sea, with tall grass and plenty of rain—for America. I was only a young boy when we left. I liked the place—well, it was all I knew—but Father said the time to leave had come. We weren't welcome any longer. It'd been nearly a hundred years that our people were there—keeping to ourselves, in our own villages, and speaking our German language. Until one day someone in

Saint Petersburg snapped their fingers and said we needed to speak their language, go to their schools, and fight in their armies. No, that's not our way. So we went from Russia back to Germany and onward to America, from Philadelphia to Towner, North Dakota. And what we got was the late comings—land too sandy for grain farming. If there wasn't a flood of rain, the soil baked and the crops turned to dust. It was heartbreaking. Year after year we prayed for a good crop, and year after year we got more frustration and disappointment. We tried grazing animals on the wild grasses but we couldn't do more than a few head of cattle. The land just didn't produce—except for gophers. They were all over the place. Without crops, though, it was hard to put food on the table. It seemed our bellies were always aching with hunger. I remember before bed each night, the littlest ones bawling for a spoonful of molasses to fill the hollowness inside them. Living like that, you do everything you can to make ends meet.

First, we collected buffalo bones. They were everywhere and we got more than a few wagonloads. We sold them to traders; they'd turn around and sell them to some big shot fella in fancy clothes who'd haul them east on the train and turn them into fertilizer for the farmers back there. When the bones ran out, we took to trapping. Like I said, there were plenty of gophers. Father was always lamenting, "They're the only thing that grows in this godforsaken land." I think it had something to do with the buffalo being gone, because no land should be infested like that. If Moses had been around surely he would've called it a plague, but since there was no Moses in North Dakota, the county put a bounty on the tails. It was enough so we could buy a sack of flour, some coffee and sugar. That was in the summer.

In the winter, we turned to trapping weasels and jackrabbits.

Rabbit was good eating. Mother would cook it long and slow so the meat would fall right off the bones. We sure did eat a lot of rabbit back then, not so much nowadays.

Weasels, though, could make you a little money, especially in their winter coat. We had a few miles of traps running along the creekside between our two quarters and Uncle Sebastian's land. Those weasels would come off the creek looking for whatever food they might find and that's where we'd get them.

Father appointed me to the job of trapping the critters. I liked it. I was the right age for it, 12 years old. It was my responsibility to walk the line each day; sometimes my brother Anton would come along. He was a few years younger than me, so I was expected to show him how to set the traps and what to do with the weasel or the gopher depending on the season. He didn't like to touch them though. He was scared they might come back to life and bite him or run up his arm and under his clothes. It helped if we put them in a burlap sack so Anton didn't have to hold them by the tail or look at them, but the sack never got very full. On a good day, we'd get a weasel. It seemed to me that happened about once every five days. Maybe a week. It'd been better at the start but the more we trapped the fewer there were; then, for a while, there was nothing. It didn't mean much at first, but after a few weeks it seemed a little suspicious. Father got that angry look he gets when things aren't going right—his dark eyes narrowed and all the lines in his forehead turned to ridges.

"What kind of tracks did you see?" he asked. My father was always worried that we weren't checking the traps often enough and that a coyote or fox, maybe even an owl or something, would get there before we did.

"No tracks," I replied. "There was nothing there."

Father snapped his index finger against my forehead. "You *Dummkopf*. What do you mean there was nothing there?"

I rubbed the palm of my glove where he'd hit me on my forehead and stared off toward the soddie where mother and the other children were keeping warm. "The traps were bare. They hadn't even been set off."

"That can't be." He looked to Anton. "Is your brother lying to me? Have you boys been playing on the creek when you're supposed to be checking traps?"

"It's the truth, Father," Anton said. His voice was always so gentle, more like Mother's than Father's or my own. Father was quiet. Anton could settle the fight in him better than anyone else. It was his eyes; they never wavered.

"Show me," Father said.

The traps were just as I had described to him, but Father noticed something I hadn't—someone was walking our trail. You could see it every now and again: a boot mark that was too big to be from my foot and with a heel that was much more square shaped than mine.

"Someone's stealing from us," Father said.

"What are you going to do?"

"Teach them a lesson."

So, he sent me home to fetch a fox trap and the fur from the last weasel I'd skinned. He fixed the fur in the trap to look like its old self and set the fox trap right next to it, covered in a little snow and with the fur teasing its trigger.

"What happens when someone reaches for the trap?" I asked.

"If they're smart they'll see what's waiting for them; then, maybe, they'll think twice about stealing from others."

"And if they don't see it and the trap goes off?"

He shrugged. "That poor sucker's hand is going to hurt awful bad."

I wasn't happy with the idea of hurting someone, but I also knew that those weasels were more than a few dollars in my father's pocket: they put food on the table. When I started to think about Anton, Magda, Johanna, and Adam aching with hunger and Mother crying because of all the pain and sorrow she felt for our dear family, I couldn't help but think that maybe our thief was owed some pain of his own.

The next day, Father and I checked the traps. When we got to where the traps were, we found nothing—no bait trap, no fur, and no surprise trap either.

Father studied the ground. "He's been here."

"I reckon someone has. They took the traps," I said.

Father grunted and lowered down onto one knee. "Look here." He pointed to a blotch of red snow. "See how it moves from here to there and back."

"It cut him."

Father nodded. He stood up and surveyed the marks in the snow.

"Do you think he's hurt bad?"

He took a step to the side and picked something out of the snow—a bloodied piece of flesh, maybe part of a fingertip or a knuckle or something. The flesh was an ugly blue-white fused with crystals of blood. It made me sick to look at it, knowing some man or boy was missing a part of himself.

My father stood there shaking his head looking at it. "He must be some kind of idiot not to see that coming."

As it happened, we didn't find out who took the bait for quite some time. Father was a little sore that we'd lost two good traps, but for a while at least there was no more trouble from our thief.

❧

I remember it was in the fall of 1904 when the land agents came around and started to spread word of a new settlement for German-speaking Catholics up in Canada. Folks were wary. We'd already been offered plenty of cheap land and it showed. Still, it was hope and it got folks excited thinking of what could be. Father was one of those, but it was bad timing for our family—it was only a few months after Anton died. Pneumonia took him. There wasn't much talk about leaving North Dakota when Father mentioned the idea to Mother. She was set against it.

"You'd have us leave a child behind?" Her blue eyes teared.

"I don't want to, but we need to think of the future. Each year we stay here we have less money in our pocket. I wouldn't have Jakob farm this land. I'd tell him to go find better land somewhere else. We should take our own advice and put an end to this suffering."

"No," Mother said as she wiped her cheeks. "We need to have faith; next year might be better. God'll reward our faith and sacrifice."

"I could say the same thing for moving."

"Well, I won't go. There'll be no one to watch over him," Mother declared. I can still see her standing in the kitchen and trembling like an autumn leaf. She'd said her piece and Father put the idea away. For a while, life went back to normal.

Of course, that didn't stop other people from talking about picking up and starting over on cheap land. At that time, places like Canada and Saskatchewan were nothing more than strange words to us. It could mean anything—fortune, disaster, hope, disappointment—depending on the day and who it was doing the talking. It didn't take long though and our friends and neighbours were selling their land and whatever else they could and leaving for the unknown. Fourteen families left in 1905, including the Werans and the Eberles. Uncle Sebastian was ready to go too. I heard him and Father talking in the little clapboard shed where Father did his blacksmith work.

"We came here to build something for ourselves, something we could leave for our children, but this isn't it," Uncle Sebastian said. "This land is a curse."

"Please, don't go," Father said. His voice was low and desperate.

"I don't understand, Kaspar. This place has handed you and Margaret more than your share of suffering. Why stay?"

"The Lord brought us here to build a new life for our children; we must stay constant in our belief."

"Is it Margaret?"

Father was quiet for a long time. "We've buried a child here."

After that I never heard Uncle Sebastian say another word about leaving to my father. But, a year later, he left with Aunt Helen and their daughter, Mary, who was only a toddler and their boy, Ignaz, who'd only just been born.

Things seemed to shift then. Father's grief took hold of him and he retreated to the forge and the anvil. He was a fine blacksmith. Had he a different mind he might have used it to put a little more food on the table, but he was more given to trade his work for whatever a neighbour might have on him, which, in those days, wasn't much. A tin of coffee, a quart of wild berries or a piece of leather to mend a saddle was often the measure of his work.

Father found his hope again that spring day when he returned from town with a letter from Uncle Sebastian. He was so excited he ran straight into the house without unhitching his horse, Juniper, from the wagon, so he could gather us around the table and read us the letter.

February 24, 1907

    Greetings to you, dear brother, Kaspar, sister-in-law, Margaret, and children, from all of us, Sebastian, Helen, and children. We are all healthy and praying for an end to this long, cold winter. Helen tells me to write that Ignaz is walking and Mary sings to us each night.

    Brother, did you get my letter from last September? Please, you must not wait any longer. There is good farm land here. I broke ten acres of land last summer and the soil is a good, thick clay, not as rich or deep as the steppe, but it is an improvement from North Dakota.

    There are two quarters next to mine that have not yet been settled. As I wrote before, we are on the northeast quarter of the 24th section. NE24-36-21-W3. The other quarters are the southeast and northwest quarters of the section. These are both good pieces of land with no hills and a few sloughs for water.

    With this I will close my letter. Give my greetings to all, God keep you healthy and strong, and please do not wait to join us.

    Sebastian Feist

Father smiled. "Two quarters." He held the letter in his hand for a time. All of us children smiled to see him so happy, but on Mother's face I saw a worried look.

"Father, was there another letter from Uncle Sebastian?" Magda asked.

"Not one that I got," Father said. His eyes barely moved from the page.

"It might've been lost," Mother said, wringing her hands in her apron. "It's good to hear the children are growing fast."

"And the land is good," Father added. "Sebastian's right. We can have a new start—a quarter for us, and another for Jakob—"

"For me?" I blurted. I'd gotten to believing Father had forgotten about me.

"You're old enough," he said. He looked to Mother. "It's time we go."

"Kaspar, we mustn't rush—"

"No." His anger turned red hot and he aimed it at Mother. "I will not waste any more seed on this godforsaken land. This time we go."

Mother cried all afternoon. She didn't say it but I knew she was crying for Anton; there was nothing else to cry for. Father left the house. He had made a habit of leaving the house whenever Mother became grief stricken. I stayed with Magda, Johanna, and Adam, but from the window I watched Father slip away to his little blacksmith shed where he fetched his heavy hammer and a shovel and loaded them onto the wagon. It was late evening when he finally returned to the house; I listened to him and Mother from my bed but they barely made a sound between them. All I could hear was their whispering and then a muffled whimper.

Things got fixed up on Sunday. It was our tradition then to make a family visit to Anton's grave. The first thing I noticed when we got there was the wooden cross that Father had planted at the grave had been replaced by a strong iron cross— more than three feet high with all sorts of pretty bends and twists in the metal. Mother buried her head in the collar of Father's sheepskin coat and he held her close.

"You did this?" she asked Father once she'd composed herself.

He nodded.

"You didn't tell me."

"Some things are best seen rather than talked about."

She wiped away her tears. "Isn't he a good father?" Mother asked the little ones.

"Yes, Momma," said Little Johanna and Adam, and they each gave him a kiss on the cheek, and Mother did too.

ℰℴ

It was late June when we left the farm. Father had sold it and his anvil for the money we'd need to make our new start. The land went cheap with all the folks thinking the same way; we were lucky the anvil fetched a good price. I could tell Father was sad to see it go, but he was a practical man and didn't dwell on it too long, not like other things. We caught the train in Towner, North Dakota. I reckon there were at least a dozen families travelling with us and a few more that came out to see us leave. There were the Gutenbergs, the Dudenhafers, the Gereins, the Zerrs, and the Holtzes. There was also an agent from the land company who could speak both English and German there to make sure we had the right documents and that our passage would take us to North Battleford, Saskatchewan. My father and the other men gathered to make sure there were no folks competing for the same quarter. We'd heard the land where Uncle Sebastian had settled was filling up with our friends and kin, so finding a quarter or two that hadn't already been claimed was getting to be tricky.

Later, when Father and I had settled into the freight car—we rode in there with the livestock, our wagon, and everything else we owned, while Mother and the little ones sat up in one of the passenger cars—he told me Mr. Zerr and Mr. Dudenhafer had their eyes on the same quarter.

"What'd they decide?" I asked.

"Mr. Dudenhafer said he'd leave it for Mr. Zerr."

"But Mr. Dudenhafer has a family, and Mr. Zerr ain't got one."

"That's why he did it. Because the quarter's right next to Mr. Zerr's brother, Nikolaus."

"That was good of Mr. Dudenhafer," I smiled. Father smiled too and waved me over to the loading door. He slid the door open a bit wider so we could watch all the land coming and going. This was still many years before I'd watched my first moving-picture show, but the view from that door held me just the same.

The train stopped in Portal, Saskatchewan and again in Weyburn. Each time boxcars were loaded and unloaded and people went their different ways, coming and going as they do. It was something to watch.

In Weyburn, Father decided to take Juniper for a little walk. I stayed behind to watch the milk cows, which I did until a ruckus in the car next to ours caught my attention. Bernhard Holtz and his brother, Christian, were struggling to get their horse out of the freight car. Bernhard, a barrel-shaped man with a patchy beard, was drinking from a jug of moonshine with one hand and pulling the horse with the lead line in the other. But the horse refused to move.

"Give me the rope," Christian said. "You're going to ruin that horse."

"It's already ruined," Bernhard said. "It can only be fixed now." Then, to make his point, Bernhard tossed the rope at Christian, climbed the ramp and punched that poor horse on the side of the jaw. The horse lurched back and pulled Christian into the side of the ramp, knocking both the rope and the wind from him. The horse must've figured it had had enough of the Holtz brothers, because it bust down the ramp, narrowly missing Bernhard and sending him off balance in such a way that he had to jump from the side of the ramp in order to avoid an ugly fall. Then the horse bolted through the crowd and up along the track.

"Get the goddamn horse," Bernhard shouted at his brother. Christian picked himself up and ran, swearing and cursing, after the horse. I watched him chase after it thinking he'd need a miracle to catch that poor beast. When I looked back, Bernhard was taking a pull from his jug, which didn't seem very brotherly to me. I must've been watching him a little too long, because he gave me an awful stare as he wiped his face with his sleeve. "What are you looking at?"

I didn't answer.

"Ain't you Kaspar Feist's boy?"

I nodded and took a step back. I figured any man that'd punch a horse was twice as likely to hit another man.

"Where are you going, boy? I have a question for you."

"What sort of question?" I muttered.

"You scared of me?"

"No," I lied.

"Come here."

I stepped toward him, fearing I might be the next thing he punched, but instead of throwing a punch, he thrust the jug of booze into my hands. I might've had three or four inches on Bernhard, but he was as wide as any man I'd ever seen. His eyes were wild and bloodshot, like he'd starved them of sleep for days, maybe weeks.

"Take it," he said. I took it from him and held it while I considered what to do next. He answered that for me. "Drink it," he said. "Drink."

I took a pull from the jug. It was nasty stuff. Some folks call it potato wine, but it'd burn if you set a match to it. My insides turned in pain. I had a feeling that my stomach might bleed out of my chest. He only stood there and laughed at me as the drink made my eyes roll and my face twist.

"Your father's going to get a quarter section, huh?"

"Yeah," I coughed. "And I will too."

"Well, you can't do any worse than your father did back there."

I was raised to show respect to my elders, so I kept my mouth shut and handed him back his jug, but he wasn't finished.

"You know there's a curse on your father, don't you?"

"You're lying."

"I ain't."

I turned to walk away from the man, but he grabbed me by the shoulder and spun me around.

"Ask him about my cousin, Claudius Volker. He died about the same age as your brother did. Drowned in a well back in the old country, no thanks to your father."

"Why should I believe you?"

"Don't need to believe me. It's true." He paused. "I only hope your father doesn't leave another dead boy in this country." Then he let loose his grip on me.

I should've left then. I knew there was something wrong with Bernhard, but I wanted to know about the curse. "What's your curse?" I asked him.

A mocking sort of smile flashed across his face. "I reckon I pick the wrong neighbours."

"But you farm next to your brothers," I replied.

"So, you understand the problem."

"No."

"Your father don't knock you around?"

"Nothing bad."

"Lucky you." He raised his jug and took a pull, then wiped his chin with his sleeve. "I hear your father plans to set up next to your uncle?"

I nodded. "Uncle Sebastian says it's good land."

"That so." He grinned. "And which quarter you going to take?"

"Father thinks I should get the south quarter. He's going to take the one to the west."

"Ha! Do yourself a favour and get a quarter at least two miles from your nearest kin. Take it from one who knows better."

"Jakob!" I heard from behind me. It was Father calling. "Did you milk the cows?"

"Ha! Speak of the devil," Bernhard said. "Better go milk those cows, Feist. When you finish up, come get yourself another nip from my jug. It'll put hair on your chest."

"No thank you."

"I'd take it as an insult," he replied and a strange sort of smile took over his face. I know now it was a drunkard's smile, a mean one at that, but back then I didn't know those things so well.

My face tightened. I didn't want to look at him any longer.

"Jakob!" my father called again. This time I hurried back to the stock car.

"What did he want with you?"

"Wanted me to drink with him."

Father shook his head. "He's a troubled man. Don't let him poison you like he does himself."

"I won't."

"Good. Now get to those cows before we have sour milk on our hands."

I didn't give our conversation much thought after that. I thought I was indulging a loud and careless drunk, but I was wrong.

15

❧

The next stop was Regina, Saskatchewan's capital. It was dusk when we arrived so I didn't see much of the town except the rail yards and the profiles of some nearby brick buildings, warehouses I was told. The older men organized a card game in one of the stock cars. The game was *Juckerspiel*, a trick-taking game, like the Kaiser game the Ukrainian settlers played. It was a good turnout. There were more than a dozen card players, enough to have three games. My father partnered with his friend, Johannes Gutenberg, and they took up opposite ends at one of the makeshift tables. They were playing a nickel a game, so I sat back in the hay pile and closed my eyes while Mr. Dudenhafer played his accordion.

A thumping sound woke me from my dreaming. Bernhard was pounding at the floorboards as he kicked up his foot and tried to climb inside the freight car.

"Give me a push," he called to someone behind him and he rolled inside. He picked up his bottle of booze from the floorboards and staggered forward. Behind him, Christian pressed himself up and kicked his legs off the ground and into the freight car with all the strength and grace his brother was lacking.

"What is it, Bernhard? Still looking for your horse?" Mr. Gutenberg teased.

"It's not here," shouted another voice, and we all laughed.

"Found the damn horse," Bernhard said. He swung his arm back toward Christian. "Didn't you?"

"Yeah," Christian said. "And thank you, Mr. Dudenhafer, for your help."

Mr. Dudenhafer nodded and kept on playing his accordion.

Bernhard cast a squirrelly-eyed gaze across the room. "I'm looking for a rat." He stopped on my father. "Kaspar Feist."

"What do you want?"

"Let's play a game," he said, and he waved his half-empty bottle of booze in a sweeping gesture.

"You're drunk." Father tossed his last card onto the table.

"Play me." Bernhard leaned in toward my father. "Play me and I'll make it worth something for you."

Father counted the tricks and tossed the cards to the centre. "We made eight. Your deal, Johannes."

"I'm talking to you, Feist."

"What have you to wager, apart from that runaway horse?"

"This." And he reached for his collar with his left hand and fished out a little rope from around his neck. He pulled the rope loose to reveal a patch of fur hide. He held it out like some trophy, but it sure was nothing fancy. It was an ugly old weasel hide —stained with blood and yellowed from dirt and sweat. He slammed the thing down on the table.

I felt sick to my stomach.

"You remember it." He tapped it with his left hand.

From what I could see, and surely Father had a better view, his hand wasn't as it should be. His middle finger was cut short at the nail and his ring finger was puffed like a mushroom.

Father huffed. "You can keep it."

"No! You took something of mine. Now I'll take something of yours." And without the slightest warning, Bernhard smashed his bottle against the table's edge. Glass exploded everywhere. Father barely had a chance to cover his eyes, then the room went quiet and we all focused on Bernhard and the jagged bottle-neck he gripped in his beaten-up hand—we waited for God, or

Bernhard or someone to decide what might happen next. It was Christian who moved first. He grabbed Bernhard around the shoulders and pulled him away from the table. Then my father stood up and grabbed the stool he'd been sitting on and clubbed Bernhard's hand, sending the bottle flying from his fist.

"*Scheisse!*" Bernhard bellowed as he shook the pain from his hand.

"Get him out of here," Mr. Gutenberg shouted. Two or three other men went to Christian's side and carried Bernhard away. Father was quiet but he was boiling under his skin.

"Seems you have a new friend," Mr. Gutenberg said. "How did that happen?"

"I trapped a thief," Father replied. "A dumb one at that."

"Be careful, Kaspar. God only knows what that one might do next."

Father spat on the floor. "He's nothing but a lazy-born drunkard."

☙

The next day the train travelled north, and stopped in Saskatoon around mid-morning. The day was warm and sunny, and folks had plenty to talk about as we stepped off of the train. News had spread that a priest had come to offer us Mass, and there were all sorts of stories going around about the card game and Bernhard's threats to Father. Mother was upset.

"I think we need to pray," she said.

"Absolutely," Father replied.

"And ask the priest for penance."

"But I did nothing wrong."

"You hurt the man."

18

"I defended myself; I didn't kill him."

"You did a violent thing," Mother said. "And the Lord says, 'what ye have done to the least of my brethren, ye have done onto me.'"

Father shook his head. "That's not how it goes."

"Well, it's the spirit of the scripture."

"I'm right with the Lord, and the Lord's right with me."

Mother frowned and looked to the little ones to remind him of his place. "People have been talking," she said in a hush. "You need to set a good example for the children."

He shook his head in frustration. "Let's go then."

The Mass was outside, not far from the rail yard, in the place where the immigrants camped before going off to find their quarter sections and commence building their homesteads. The priest had a tent there to cover him from the sun and rain; inside it was a fine cross painted gold and an old kitchen table, likely abandoned by some passing traveller, which served as his altar. Plenty of people had shown up, mostly German-speaking immigrants like us. The men stood with their hats in their hands, while the young mothers tried to keep their toddlers from running about the place. One little boy kept breaking loose. Twice he made a dash for the priest's tent, but each time a friendly arm swept him up and returned him to his mother. Bernhard was there, in his own way, sleeping off the drink or giving everyone the impression he was. Whatever he was doing, his presence stirred up an anxiousness inside of me that no sacrament could put to rest. If Father saw him he didn't say a word, and the whole thing passed without the excitement from the night before.

We loaded up again after the Mass. It was the movement of the train that lulled me back into a sense of ease. The gentle rocking of the freight car, side to side, as it rolled along. Ca-thunk, ca-thunk. I watched the land from the side door as my father read the letter from Uncle Sebastian once again and checked it against the map the land agent had given him. This was a ritual I had watched him perform on each leg of the trip; he was always a little happier for it.

"It won't be long now," I said.

"Yes, and then the real work begins."

"But Uncle says it's good land."

"Thick clay. No more sand."

"And the work will go easier with Uncle helping us."

Father nodded. "We have to watch out for our family. In the end, that's all we have."

"I wish Anton was here."

"He's with us."

"I know," I said, but there was still something on my mind. Something Bernhard had said that was eating into my thoughts. "Father—"

"What is it?"

I felt myself choking on the words. "I overheard some folks talk about a boy from the old country; his name was Claudius Volker. Did you know him?"

Father was silent for a time. "He was a friend of mine," he said. "He died playing a silly game."

"How?"

"Claudius always wanted to be the last one found. I figured he was hiding in the well; there was a little ledge..." he spread his thumb and index finger about two inches apart and stared into the space. "But I pretended he went home and we kept playing. Then I started to believe that he really must've gone home or he'd have come out." My father stopped; I could tell he'd said as much as he cared to, maybe more.

e◊

At North Battleford we opened the freight door for the last time. I'll never forget that view. The land seemed to open up below us, rich with lush prairie grass and fringed with aspen and brush where the two rivers—the mighty Saskatchewan and the meandering Battle—cut through the valley bottom before they joined together, and square between them was the original town of Battleford, the fort, the buildings and the people. Further away, on the western horizon, the land rose up above us and I could only imagine that somewhere not so far away might be the Rocky Mountains and the Pacific Ocean and other places I never imagined knowing or seeing when I had been a child. Life had moved so fast since we left Russia and the Black Sea, so much had happened for us to move halfway across the world, and still more needed to happen before we could make a home.

Yet, when we got off that train, a giddy sense of celebration and accomplishment had set in, and while there was still work to do—stock cars to unload and rivers to cross—there was not one person without a smile on their face. It was like a dream. At the river crossing, which was marked by a pair of stone cairns on each bank, Mr. Dudenhafer played a waltz on his accordion as the women and children boarded the ferry to Battleford, and he kept playing as the first few wagons crossed the river. The North Saskatchewan was an impressive river—broad and with well-treed banks and thick sandbars blotting its flow. There was little in the way of trouble. The oxen were stubborn and needed some encouragement to get into the water, and Mr. Zerr lost a fry pan and a sack of old potatoes from the side of his wagon; otherwise, the river crossing was a success.

From there we rode to the Mounted Police fort and the

barracks where they put us immigrants until our papers cleared and we had our land patents in hand. The music played and there was more than a little dancing. I think we made an impression on our new Canadian friends because a few brave officers joined in our merriment and even played some of their songs for us.

Over supper, Father told us his plans for tomorrow. "Magda, you'll milk the cows in the morning, while Jakob and I get our land."

"Yes, Father," Magda replied.

"And help Mother with the children."

"I will."

"Can we trust the people in this place not to steal our things from the wagon?" Mother asked.

"Do you mean Bernhard?" I said.

"There are all sorts of people in these camps. Many of them far more desperate than our drunken friend." Father took a drink of tea from his cup. "Best I sleep in the wagon tonight," he continued. "And tomorrow while we're away, Magda, you'll keep an eye on it. If something happens, tell Mother or someone you know. These people don't all speak our language."

"You won't be too long? Will you, Father?" Magda asked.

"Not too long dear, but don't worry, thieves are fearful types, they won't do anything if there are people around."

"Have you seen Bernhard?" Mother asked.

Father shook his head. "He's probably sleeping under a wagon, or gone to find himself a bottle of something."

"I feel sorry for that man." Magda crossed herself.

"Don't waste your prayers on Bernhard," Father said. "If you want to pray for someone, pray for his brother, Christian. He's the one stuck cleaning up Bernhard's messes."

I have to confess that, all these years later, I often wish we'd been more like Magda. A little compassion could've spared our families so much unnecessary pain. Such is the wisdom of hindsight.

❧

Father woke me sometime after dawn. "Come along," he said. "Something's not right."

I jumped down from the bunk and followed him out of the camp. We hustled toward the big hill in the southwest, the one I had admired earlier from the rail yard. We'd heard the land titles building was atop it. We crossed a small wooden bridge over the Battle River.

"What's wrong, Father?" I asked.

"I don't trust the man."

"Bernhard?"

"I thought he'd try to steal from our wagon during the night, but he didn't show. I spoke with Christian and he doesn't know where he is either."

"I don't think he wants to farm with his brothers," I said.

Father shot me another worried look. "Why do you say that?"

"He said something about it when their horse ran off."

"What else did he say?"

"I don't remember; he just gives me a bad feeling."

"If he's up there, Jakob, we can stop guessing what his plans are. He's going for our land."

I got an awful guilty feeling in my gut. Ashamed, I hadn't told my father everything Bernhard had said to me earlier. If Bernhard took our land, we might end up farming something just as lousy as we had before. I'd like to tell you I raced up that hill but, honestly, I didn't want to see who I figured might be up there, so I kept pace with Father and prayed to God that Bernhard was elsewhere. Once we'd come within a stone's throw of those red-brick walls, I knew my prayers were too late—Bernhard was sitting cross-legged at the foot of the door. When he saw us, he smiled and raised his jug of moonshine. Father clenched his jaw and marched towards Bernhard, and I followed on his heels.

"What are you doing here, Holtz?"

Bernhard picked himself up off the ground. "I figured I'd get the first pick of the day."

"You know we all got an agreement not to go after another's claim."

"Who's we? You and Gutenberg?"

"Your brother, Christian, and Mr. Zerr, Mr. Dudenhafer—"

"Ha! I ain't made no agreement."

I'd say Father was doing his best to stay civil with Bernhard, but I could see he was heating up around the collar. "Tell me, why are you wasting good land by trying to farm it?"

"I could ask you the same thing, Feist. What kind of farmer can't feed his own family?"

Well, that did it. Father turned as red-hot as a cattle brand. He charged Bernhard and slammed him into the wall of the land office. It was a powerful hit that knocked the wind right out of Bernhard. He choked to get his breath back but Father punched him square in the jaw before he'd the chance. Bernhard's eyes rolled and Father hit him again. Blood poured from Bernhard's lip, and my father showed no sign of letting up. I figured he was about to give Bernhard the beating of his life. I don't know if I was more worried he might kill him or someone might see us, but I grabbed Father by the shoulders and tried to pull him away. Bernhard used the moment to his advantage and punched Father low in the gut. Father dropped to the ground nearly taking me with him. He landed on all fours and didn't get up. He just moaned and swore whatever he could think to say. I was worried that Bernhard might try to get him while he was down, so I got between them. I was tall, taller than Bernhard, but I wasn't very broad. I certainly wasn't a threat to him, but I was ready to make whatever stand I could.

"Get out of my way," he said.

I clenched my fists. "No."

He laughed at me, but the laughing seemed to hurt him some. So, I pushed him in the chest and waited for him to hit me. I didn't care. I wanted to hurt. I wanted my outsides to feel like my insides. But he didn't bother hitting me; he just turned to fetch his jug.

My father wasn't looking so good—his eyelids were pulled shut and his face was all twisted in knots. He wasn't fit to fight any more; he'd enough just bearing the hurt. So I helped him to his feet. We stood there—Bernhard with his bottle and his sore jaw, and Father holding his pain in stillness—I couldn't say how long. Not too long, I suppose, because there were more men approaching. I could tell from the sound of them they weren't from our group—they were speaking English. Not to mention, they looked too pretty to be farmers. These three fellas were wearing bowler hats and white collared shirts and carrying their coat jackets over their shoulders by the hook of their fingers. I'd say they figured themselves big shots. And, by the way they looked at us, they must've thought we were animals in our dirty, old clothes and our eyes seeing red. And they'd have been right to think so in that moment.

Their presence put our little war on the back of the stove. Father and I gathered a little closer to the door, a little closer to Bernhard. I put myself between them, if only to dull the glares.

I didn't feel good being stuck between them with the English-men there and knowing our plans had gone up the spout. A sick feeling came over me. My guts tightened and my body lurched. I tried pretending I'd only meant to spit, but I saw one of those Englishman shake his head at me like I was some leper or some-thing. I didn't look to see how Bernhard looked at me.

Thankfully, it was around that time that more of our kind began to show: Mr. Gutenberg, Mr. Dudenhafer, and others. Mr. Gutenberg stepped aside from the Englishmen, meaning to chat with us without crossing their place in the line. He looked to Bernhard and my father. "Did you two scrap again?"

Father kept quiet.

"They did," I said.

"Yes, and Jakob, here, has been playing the role of protector, even for his new friend, Bernhard."

"What else would you have him do?" Mr. Gutenberg asked.

"Know his place."

I was the one who kept quiet now. I knew too well Father's habit of lashing out at others when he was under attack and I didn't want to be next. I checked the line behind us. It had grown to 20 men or more and nearly all of them had shed their jackets in the heavy heat. Some of them were watching us, oth-ers were talking among themselves, and some of them just kicked the dirt, anxious to get moving. I noticed another one of our group approaching. It was Christian. I watched him take his place at the end of the line; he looked distracted, but when he spotted Bernhard he straightened up and came around to have a word. "I've been looking for you all morning," he told Bernhard. "I'd given up, figured you passed out under some wagon."

"I was never lost, brother." Bernhard grinned. Then he pulled Christian in close and whispered something in his ear.

Christian pried himself away from his brother's grasp. "Don't be a fool!"

"You have to take the things you want in life."

"Listen to you speak; you sound like our father," Christian said. Bernhard shoved him in the shoulder. "You—you're turning into him. If you do this, you'll have everyone against you." He back-stepped away from Bernhard, stopping next to my father. "I'm sorry," he said.

"He ain't no angel either," Bernhard snapped at Christian. "What he did to cousin Claudius—"

My father winced at the sound of that name. He turned to me. "Is he the one who told you?"

I nodded, but I couldn't bear to look him in the eye. The next thing I knew, I was falling to the ground and when I looked up, Bernhard and my father had locked horns—grabbing and twisting each other for some kind of advantage. When they finally spun apart, Bernhard hit Father with a strong punch that cut him across the brow.

He smirked. "You're bleeding, Feist."

Father growled and swung a right fist at Bernhard, hitting him on the chin, before Christian and Mr. Gutenberg pulled them apart.

That was about the same time another pair of men in bowler hats and dress coats approached the building. The tall one said something I didn't understand, but whatever it was it sent the other group of Englishmen laughing. These new fellas shook their heads at my father and Bernhard as they sidestepped the wrangle. The short one pulled a key from his pocket, opened the land titles building, and shut the door behind them.

My nerves were on fire. These land agents weren't going to fix things. They didn't care that Bernhard and Father were fighting; they'd only made a joke about it. I looked at Mr. Gutenberg holding Father around the shoulders while Christian backed Bernhard up against the brick wall, and all I could think about was getting on the other side of that door. So I went up and knocked on it. Bernhard got right angry. His eyes turned to dark coals set against a bloody red. Fortunate for me, Christian held him off long enough that I got clear of the door. Mr. Gutenberg also tried to come to my aid, which set Father loose, and the whole group began unwinding. The Englishmen stepped in, making sure Mr. Gutenberg and Christian understood they weren't to use this as an excuse to cut in line. Others too began crowding towards the door. Mr. Zerr. Mr. Dudenhafer. The whole bunch of them started spinning in on each other—people shouting and speaking all kinds of languages. And, in the middle of it, Father and Bernhard just stared at each other. No more words.

A few moments later, the door to the land titles office swung open and the tall land agent came out and stood at the entrance. He didn't say anything at first. He just stood there looking us over with his cold cat-like eyes. Most folks quieted right down. A couple of would-be scrappers kept stoking their fires until they realized the moment had passed. When they'd settled, he said something I didn't understand and the other agent, the shorter one, came forward and the tall one went back inside. The short one said something about ten dollars and documents; then, he said something to the Englishmen and one of them pointed to Bernhard.

"You." The agent waved Bernhard forward. Bernhard smiled and let out a smug little laugh as he stepped into the office.

After that folks began finding their places again. The land agent stood watching us from the door, making sure folks took their places without all the commotion from before.

Mr. Gutenberg clapped Father on the shoulder; then he went and took his place in line next to Mr. Dudenhafer. Christian too disappeared to the back of the line. That left just me and Father.

He didn't say anything to me. He just pulled out the map he'd been carrying since North Dakota and shook his head at it.

"Where will we go?" I asked.

He looked up at me with tired eyes. "How could you be so—" He was right to be mad at me: I was still wet behind the ears. I didn't know what angry people might do to make other people hurt like them. I moped around kicking at the dirt for some time before Father grabbed me by the shoulder and gave me a shake so I'd look him in the eye. "You'll take whichever quarter is left next to Uncle Sebastian. He'll be happy to have your help—"

"No, you have it," I said. I didn't want to make things hard for Mother and the little ones.

Father's jaw tightened as he shook his head. "No. This is the way it has to be. Or would you prefer I take the land Mr. Gutenberg or Mr. Zerr plans to farm?" He sighed. "I don't intend to make more enemies this day."

He was right, of course; he'd find no peace living next to that man. So I agreed and let him get back to figuring where he'd settle Mother and the kids. It was hard standing there watching Father trying to find some kind of hope on that map, while on the other side of the door Bernhard was changing our future on something as small as a piece of paper. I wanted to tear down that door and tear down Bernhard while I was at it. I imagined him begging for mercy and handing me the title to the land he'd stolen. Then the door opened and Bernhard stepped out. He looked over to me and Father and smiled. "Fine day, Feist. Fine day. I figure this about settles it for us."

I lunged at Bernhard and nearly had him by the collar, but Father held me back.

"It's too late, Jakob." Father steered me inside the office. Once more, my father and Bernhard fixed eyes on each other, but this time when Father spoke there was an eerie calm in his voice I'd never heard before. "You're going to have a very short and difficult life, Bernhard, and when it's over, you will regret this."

Maybe it was the look in Father's eyes or maybe Bernhard's heart finally heard through his hate, but that smug grin washed clean off his face. It didn't last more than a second or two, yet it said plenty.

I don't know if it had something to do with the way Bernhard's look changed when Father spoke to him that last time, or the fact some promises are just too big to be kept; either way Father didn't repay Bernhard what he was owed. And while there are some folks that think he did, they're wrong. In the end, any revenge my family might've taken came from my hand—in a roundabout kind of way—and whatever satisfaction I got from it faded fast.

I reckon someone else can tell that story. I take no pleasure in it.

The Horse Accident
1909

NELS EBERLE FIXED the collar of his sheepskin jacket against the cold wind as his heavy horses, a pair of black Belgian mares, carried him east to Frank and Katherine's farmyard, which, from his vantage, was nothing more than a few dark mounds of earth against the pale morning light. Swirls of fresh snow kicked up against the sleigh like dancing spires, bringing a smile to his face. He considered taking a pull of moonshine or whiskey—he'd packed both, along with his axe, bucksaw, chains, ropes, blankets, oats for the horses, and the box of food his wife, Aggie, had set out for him—except his sister, Katherine, might smell it on his breath. Nels worried about her. She was pregnant with her first child, which according to the midwife would be here before May seeding, should all go well. He'd worry less if it weren't for her husband, Frank, always sitting on his hands until the very last minute. The woodpile was proof enough. Nels had noticed it was light back in December, had warned Frank that if the winter turned cold they'd be in trouble, but Frank was stubborn and didn't take well to others telling him what to do. "Ah, there's still tables and chairs in the house," Frank had told Nels. Sure it was a joke, but January had brought a biting cold and weeks bound inside the soddie watching the firewood dwindle. Had the cold spell lasted another week, Frank might've eaten those words.

Nels was close now. He could smell the woodsmoke from their stove and see the yellow lamplight through the window pane. It'd be dawn soon. Precious daylight. This time of year, February, you could get about ten hours of good daylight; they'd need all of it today to get where they were going.

In the yard, Nels tethered the sleigh lines to the hitching post and made his way to the two-room sod house; knocking twice, he opened the door. "Katherine." He smiled. His sister was packing parcels of food into an apple crate. She wore an ankle-length dress, faded lilac-blue, with an apron tied loosely around her pregnant belly.

She shuddered a moment. "You startled me, Nels." And, just as quickly, she turned away from him to sweep her thick mane of dark hair forward over her right shoulder. "I thought you'd be out there helping Frank get his team ready."

"I'm sure he can handle them." Nels pulled off his mitts and wiped off the ice crystals that had fused to the long bristles of his dark-brown moustache. "I wanted to see you before we leave."

Katherine passed him a closed-lip smile as she cleared the dirty plates from the table and placed them in the wash basin. He hadn't remembered Katherine being so tense: shoulders up towards her ears, the crisp tone in her voice, even her smile was rigid. He took a seat at the kitchen table and wondered what was troubling her. "How's the baby?"

"Kicking like a horse," she said, wearily.

"Bet it does." He breathed into his cupped hands.

Katherine set a cup of coffee next to Nels and took a seat at the table. "How's Aggie and the little ones?"

"They're good." He chuckled. "You should see them race to steal my part of the bed when I get up to do chores." Nels held the cup between his hands to collect its warmth; he looked into her green eyes. "You'll see; it won't be too long now. God bless." She lowered her gaze. He took a sip of coffee and studied his sister's face. It was strange that she appeared so sad when she was so close to having the child she'd always longed to have. "What's the matter?"

"Why must you take Frank with you?"

"He says he wants to do his share."

"I could use him here."

"I told him the same thing. Joseph, Peter, and I can cut enough firewood for all of us." Katherine's brow knit tight. Gauging her response, Nels was doubtful Frank had shared his offer with Katherine. "Isn't Frank's father coming to help with the chores?"

She raised her eyes to her brother's. "Kasimir? Oh, he'd come stinking of booze, talking and talking... No, I'll do the chores—"

"Be sure to let him."

"Aagh!" she cried. "None of you listen." And covered her eyes with the palms of her hands.

Nels stared at her. "Listen to what?"

Katherine exhaled a deep sigh as her hands fell to her lap. "I hate being alone with the quiet. The sound of the wind—it gets into my head."

It was Nels, now, who averted his eyes; softened his expression. "This land is too big," he said, restraining his words. Not the right time to tell her about its ghosts—the many voices, buffalo, Indian—hiding in the open, like rocks buried in the clay. How each spring he heard their cold whispers carry on the wind as he worked the plough turning the sod, breaking the soil. "I forget Aggie has the children to keep her busy." He reached to hold her hand but instead rapped his on the table. "Don't worry, we'll be back in a few days. I promise."

"Remember the steppe? I miss it. I miss having people near me. I'd step out the door and the whole village was waiting for me." Katherine eked out a smile.

"You were still a child." He smiled. A strand of Katherine's hair fell to her cheek; he reached to brush the hair aside, but Katherine pulled away. "What's wrong?"

"It's nothing."

"We could take you back to our place; the kids would be so excited to see you."

Her eyes fluttered shut. "No, I'll be fine. I'm just not myself."

He stood up and leaned towards Katherine, trying to get an eye on her neck. There, along the collar of her dress, he saw the blue and yellow hues hiding behind her thick hair. "Did Frank do this? Did he grab you?" he said, his voice hushed.

She opened her eyes and stared at him, but she kept quiet, simmering. It seemed at any moment she might bare her teeth at him and growl. He studied the cuff of her dress and wondered what other marks were there. His jaw tightened. "I'll talk with him. Set him right."

"He's not one of your horses, Nels."

"Yeah, a horse wouldn't do such a thing." He turned for the door.

Katherine stood up. "Nels, stop. Frank's not like us. Kasimir wasn't a good father."

Nels lifted his hand from the door handle and looked back to Katherine. "Would Kasimir hurt you?"

"No. Never. Frank wouldn't allow it."

Nels had always known Frank to be loud and aggressive— not the type of man to back down from a fight. That was something he'd liked about Frank, even before the man had married Katherine. "You're right. He'd probably—"

Then the door opened and Nels was face to face with his brother-in-law. Frank wiped away the snow and ice beads frozen to his brow and the lashes of his deep-set eyes and clapped Nels on the shoulder. "Staying warm? Before we go freeze our nuts off?"

"I was just speaking with Katherine—"

"Aggie and the kids might visit in the cutter," Katherine said.

"Good," Frank said. "Now all your little worries are taken care of." He took her by the arm with one hand and caressed her long hair with the other.

"Yes dear," she murmured, tensing, not looking at the hand clutching her arm.

Outside, Nels marched to his sleigh. Katherine was wrong, he thought. He could fix Frank. A man is no different from a horse: only worse, only crueler and more manipulative. It was as their father had said: Horses know their place in the herd and how they relate to one another; while men seldom know their station among others. That's why Frank, like so many men, is troubled; he just needs some reminding, Nels thought. Taking the driving lines into his hands, he flicked them so that neither line rustled a hair upon the horses, and the sleigh glided forward.

Nels and Frank drove on to Nels's uncle's farm, where his cousins, Peter and Joseph Eberle, joined them. The brothers drove their father's sleigh pulled by a Percheron mare and a gelded Morgan; ahead of them was Frank with his team of quarter horses and Nels, in the lead, with his big Belgians. They took the main trail north—a thin band fragmented by drifts of fresh snow in a cold white desert, running long and straight over the top of the land. Further along, the trail crooked east, where they'd cross the coulee and the frozen lake below. From there, it'd be about 15 miles before they reached Aggie's uncle's farm, where they'd stay the night.

The mid-morning sun shone weak through the low clouds and it seemed the wind had let up from earlier. Nels turned to check on the others and found them keeping pace. It was good that his cousins had joined them; they were hardworking young men and they'd be a buffer between him and Frank. Peter, the older, was 21, the same age as Katherine. They had been best friends, sweethearts even, until the horse accident about four years ago. After that, Peter no longer smiled or spoke as much as he used to—not surprising, considering he'd had his jaw broken and half his teeth knocked out. Joseph, on the other hand, was a talker, always smiling and filled with laughter.

They stopped at the top of the coulee: a scar running through the table-top prairie, some 60 or 70 yards deep and nearly a quarter mile wide. The coulee's slopes, cushioned in powdery snow that clung to thickets of wild rose and patches of wolf willow, were barren of any tree or shrub thicker than a man's fist. Joseph started a cookfire in a shallow pit along the coulee's edge, close to the brothers' sleigh. The others were busy tending their horses. Slowly, the men gathered around the fire, taking turns to stretch their cold limbs over the flames in a sort of dance. "How's Katherine doing with the pregnancy?" Joseph asked Frank.

"Good. She's nearly eaten the cellar bare."

Joseph smiled. "You must be happy to be a father soon."

"It's been a long wait." Frank backed away from the flames and took a swig from Nels's jug of moonshine. "Always seems to take quick for the cows and pigs." He leaned towards Joseph and lowered his voice, "I think it's in the mounting."

Blushing, Joseph tittered and shook his head in mock disapproval. He wrung his hands over the fire, taking in the warmth. "I wouldn't know."

"Don't tell me you haven't—" Frank made a circle with his thumb and index finger, the jug of moonshine hung from it, and directed his mitted hand toward the circle.

"No!" Joseph smirked.

Nels removed his fur hat so he could better hear Joseph and Frank. "What are you talking about?" he asked.

"Not even a sheep?" Frank persisted.

Joseph shook his head, no.

"Forget I asked," said Nels.

"What about handsome Pete there?" Frank asked Joseph, his voice louder now.

"I think you've been drinking too much, Frank," Nels interjected.

"Probably," he replied, and he took another pull, then let loose a long breath. "Strong stuff, Nels." He handed Joseph the jug. "It's good to be here. It's good to get out of the house and have a drink with other men."

Joseph smiled and took a swig from the jug.

"You could have stayed home and done that," Peter croaked. The right side of his jaw bulged where the bone had broken, accentuating the hollowness of his jowl.

"I'm not one to sit by the fire drinking coffee and reading the Bible," replied Frank.

Peter folded his arms and pulled his sheepskin coat tight around him. "I wouldn't be leaving Katherine by herself."

"Peter!" Joseph chided his brother.

Frank glared at Peter. "I think it's best I pull my own weight. I know Katherine feels the same."

Nels spat into the fire. "I ain't so hungry," he muttered. He left the jug of moonshine with the others and went to check on his horses.

After lunch, Nels asked Frank to ride along with him. They tied the lines of Frank's team to the back of Nels's sleigh and pushed on. Nels sat quietly, thinking out what he wanted to say to Frank and how he planned to say it. It was awkward being so close to Frank—the two of them sitting on the small sleigh bench with their coat sleeves brushing up against one another— he hadn't anticipated that. It pushed away the words which had seemed so much more certain this morning. Now, he didn't know where to begin. He worried his words might miss the mark; and, worse, that they might lead Frank to respond with some new vengeance against Katherine. Sure, there was a chance of it, but there was nothing to be gained from idleness. He just needed to begin.

A mile and a half up the trail, Frank leaned forward folding his arms over the front rail of the sleigh. He stared at Nels. "What's this about?"

Nels eyed Frank. He could smell the moonshine heavy on his breath. "You and Katherine."

"Yeah. What do you got to say?"

Nels shot a round of spittle to the snowy ground moving below them. "I saw the marks on her neck. You hurt her."

"I don't know what she told you, but I didn't—"

"Don't lie."

"I'm not lying," Frank stared off toward the east. Like everywhere around them, there was an expanse of snow and sky that seemed to meet at some indefinite grey border 20-odd miles away. He turned to Nels. "You know she goes for a piss nearly every twenty minutes."

"What?"

"Because she's pregnant, right? Well, that's what happened. She was trying to find the lamp in the dark and she tripped, caught the back of the chair around the throat. Good thing it wasn't lower is all I can say."

Nels looked Frank in the eyes. They were dark and cloudy with only a trace of light shining through them, like nail holes in an old roof wanting for shingles. Nels grimaced.

Frank snickered. "You must learn to trust, Nels."

And how do you trust a liar? Nels wanted to shout back; instead, he calmed himself, wiping the corners of his moustache with his mitted hand. "You should be minding Katherine and taking better care of the farm."

Frank scowled. "I'm a good husband, Nels, and I'll be a damn good father too. Damn you and Pete. You watch me."

Nels huffed. More words.

❧

The four men and their sleighs made it to the Landgrafs' before sundown. Aggie's uncle stepped out from the warmth of the soddie to greet Nels and invite them all in for supper. The men settled their horses—fed, watered, and checked them for cuts and sores—before joining Mr. Landgraf and his family for the meal. Nels brought a bottle of whiskey to the house, and Frank insisted on bringing a jug of moonshine. Inside, the men and their hosts gathered around the woodstove as Nels poured them each a whiskey. They raised their cups to Mr. and Mrs. Landgraf for their kindness. Karolin, the Landgrafs' youngest daughter and the only child still living under their roof, raised her cup too. The girl was pretty with thick bright lips that barely hid what seemed an everlasting smile. She blushed as her fingertips wiped a drop of the liquid from her chin. Nels noticed Peter look away from the girl, turning his gaze to the cup of whiskey in his hand, while Joseph and Frank stole looks at her—Frank more boldly.

"How old are you, Karolin?" Frank asked.

"She'll be seventeen next month," Mr. Landgraf answered.

"You must have all types of suitors." Frank smiled.

"You recall you're married to my sister, don't you?" Nels quipped.

"Of course," Frank snorted. "But don't forget, we have two of Kaidenberg's best sons with us—Pete and Joseph Eberle." He clapped Peter on the shoulder.

Joseph blushed and flashed Karolin a warm smile—wide and toothy. Next to him, Peter's shoulder tensed from Frank's unwanted touch.

"Peter doesn't smile much," Frank said, "but you should hear him whistle a tune."

Joseph choked down a laugh as Peter brushed Frank's hand off his shoulder and shook himself clear of Frank's reach. He lowered his head and turned it slightly to the right, so as to hide his protruding jaw.

"Don't be modest," Frank said.

Nels glared at Frank. "This ain't the time to be picking fights."

"I only tease, Nels."

Nels snorted his protest and considered telling Frank to shut his mouth.

"If you don't mind me asking, what happened to your jaw?" said Mrs. Landgraf, who was standing across the stove from Peter.

Peter stared at the floor. "Horse kicked me."

"Oh my," breathed Mrs. Landgraf. "When did this happen?"

"Four years ago July," Joseph interjected. "Right?" Peter nodded to his brother, before shrinking back from his place at the wood stove. "It happened while we were at the immigrant camp in Battleford, when we first got here," Joseph continued. "Father had gone with Nels and Uncle Johannes to scout for the best land. There'd been a bonfire that night and, well, you can imagine, everyone was in such fine spirits with all the excitement of being in a new country. I don't think I'd have ever been able to get to sleep with all the noise and celebration." The smile on Joseph's face softened as he turned to his brother. "I can't remember whether it happened that night or at chores the next morning?"

"It happened at night." Peter lifted his gaze to meet his brother's. "You don't remember because you got drunk on moonshine and Mother had to milk the cow the next morning."

A nervous laugh peeped from Joseph. "Oh yeah, I forgot."

"I'd say God was watching out for you, son," said Mr. Landgraf. "It's a miracle you're still among the living. "

"It happened so fast I didn't even see it coming," said Peter.

"Oh my," Mrs. Landgraf said again. "But, perhaps, that's for the best—not seeing it coming."

"Does it still hurt?" Karolin asked, wincing. Her own hand stroked her cheek.

"Like a bad toothache, throbbing all the time."

"Pour him some more whiskey, Nels," said Mr. Landgraf. "Dull his pain some."

Nels splashed another ounce into Peter's cup. "I remember hearing about it when we returned; I'd never seen Katherine so upset, barely eating for days. Father said it was a bad omen for a new beginning, and he wanted to take the train further west but I convinced him we should stay."

"Why was Katherine so upset?" asked Mr. Landgraf.

Nels looked to Peter, who seemed uninterested in reciting the details of that painful evening. "I believe she was the one who found you. Is that right?"

Peter nodded. "She went for help."

The room fell quiet, a heavy mood weighed on the Landgrafs and their guests, except for Frank who broke the silence with a poorly stifled giggle.

"What's so funny?" asked Peter.

"Oh, I was just wondering why you decided to pay a visit to the livestock at such a late hour," Frank smirked. "Most of us were happy enough enjoying a fine evening by the fire."

Peter's face twisted into a grimace and brightened crimson red. Nels clutched Peter's shoulder. "Stay calm."

"Mr. Weran," gasped Mrs. Landgraf. "That sort of humour is not fit for my home, nor is it kind to young Mr. Eberle."

Mrs. Landgraf's reaction reminded Nels of something Aggie had once said about her, how she'd never taken any nonsense from her husband or their four sons. Now, it seemed she wasn't going to take it from Frank either.

As Frank turned to Mrs. Landgraf his smug grin was replaced, for an instant, by an indignant scowl. "Hmm. I suppose you're right, Mrs. Landgraf." Nels noted the irritation in Frank's voice as he put on a softer, more penitent tone. "What I said wasn't suited for the company of women or your warm home. I'm sorry for my rudeness."

Mrs. Landgraf puffed her cheeks. "A piece of advice, Mr. Weran, if you care to keep your wife happy, put a smile in your voice when you apologize to her."

"I'll try to remember that," Frank said in a muffled voice.

Suppressing a chuckle, Nels took a sip of whiskey and smiled. That had turned out better than expected, he thought.

After supper, Mrs. Landgraf and Karolin cleaned up the dishes while Nels chatted with Mr. Landgraf about their crops and, later, when Mrs. Landgraf had returned to the conversation, how their other children, the married ones, were doing. He knew that Aggie would be interested in knowing. Peter listened for a time, then excused himself to get some fresh air. Amid it all, Frank and Joseph stole looks at Karolin as they talked among themselves. Their conversation and laughter turned louder and louder as they exchanged whiskey for moonshine. Nels was surprised to see Karolin returning Joseph's looks with her own coy glances. Thoughts of matchmaking tickled his imagination—he could ask the young pair to join him in a game of cards, or maybe put a bug in old Mr. Landgraf's ear about his cousin's prospects —but this wasn't the right time. Frank had made too rough an impression on Mr. and Mrs. Landgraf and he feared Joseph might be painted with the same brush.

Nels had sufficiently put away any thoughts of a matchmaking when Karolin returned from the kitchen to ask her father to bring out his accordion.

"It's getting late."

"Please, Father, just one song and I'll sing," she said, her eyes gleaming. A smile crept across Mr. Landgraf's face and he left the room to fetch his accordion.

Joseph smiled at Karolin, the booze bright in his cheeks. "What are you going to sing?"

"Sing 'The Fox and the Rabbit,'" Frank said.

"I was thinking 'Home on the Steppe,'" Karolin said.

"That's a fine song," Joseph said, and the two exchanged smiles.

As Karolin sang 'Home on the Steppe', Nels felt himself ease back into his chair. The words brought to mind memories of his youth—of him and his cousins playing hide and seek in the orchard as the older girls sat under a cherry tree singing songs and braiding each other's hair. When Karolin and her father had finished, the men applauded and Mrs. Landgraf asked her husband to play a waltz. Frank grabbed Karolin's hand. They danced around the table; on their return, Joseph cut in, taking his turn with Karolin. Nels offered his hand to Mrs. Landgraf and was surprised by her spry steps. Shortly after, the door opened and Peter snuck in as quiet as a church mouse. He leaned against the wall watching his brother dance. Nels saw the trace of a smile, closed-mouthed, lighten Peter's face.

There were a few more songs and drinks before the men said their goodnights to Karolin and Mrs. Landgraf. Mr. Landgraf insisted they have one more drink before they laid out their blankets on the floor to sleep.

In the morning, Peter managed Mr. Landgraf's chores while the others readied the horses. After a quick meal of coffee and porridge, they rode out.

❧

Twenty-seven miles later they arrived at Battleford, with daylight on their side. They stabled their horses at the livery, went to the General Store, and bought the things they'd been told to get from those at home—coffee, tea, sugar, salt, fabric, lamp oil, whatever was on the lists.

They stayed in a bunkhouse above the livery, where they ate their evening meal. Frank passed around a jug of moonshine,

Kasimir's recipe. Nels took a swig. His face twisted as the liquid went down. "Harsh stuff." He wiped his moustache clean of the liquor.

Joseph held out his hand. "I don't mind it."

"Because you don't know better," Nels teased.

"What do you think of Karolin?" Frank asked Joseph.

Joseph laughed a little nervously and took a swig from the jug. His cheeks flushed red—but likely not from the drink, thought Nels.

"She's very nice."

"And?" Nels rolled his finger as if he were winding a string.

Joseph looked to the jug in his hands. He had the worried look of a child about to enter the confessional for the first time. "There's another girl I'm sweeter on. I've been talking with Margaret Dudenhafer after church." He passed the jug back to Nels.

"You like her?"

"I think she's very kind—beautiful too."

"Good hips," Frank said. "You'll want that."

Peter huffed.

"I'd like to marry her," Joseph confessed.

Nels and Frank smiled.

"I could speak to Margaret's father about a matchmaking," Nels said.

"You'd do that?"

"I've done it a few times before."

"It's his ticket to the wedding feast," Frank teased.

"That's also true," Nels agreed. He took a pull from the jug. It was better on the second draught.

"I remember asking Johannes for Katherine's hand," Frank said. "I nearly froze, turned to stone, but I had to make Katherine my wife. I knew I'd never be able to live with myself if another man married her first."

Peter grabbed the jug from Nels. He took a deep swig, slow and deliberate, as though he were cleansing his mouth of a bitter taste. When he finished he leaned back against one of the livery's support beams and took another pull.

"Do you have any marriage prospects, Pete?" Frank asked.

"The only woman my brother loves with any true devotion is our mother," Joseph chuckled. Nels and Frank laughed along with him.

"No," Nels said. "You're too young to remember, but years ago on the steppe, Peter and Katherine would hold hands and walk through the fields together. They were quite love-struck." This set off another round of laughter.

"I'm sorry I stole your true love," Frank said.

Peter took a drink from the jug and capped it. He closed his eyes and clenched what remained of his teeth. Nels stopped laughing. He wasn't too sure why he'd started in the first place. The moonshine, probably. Joseph eased up; Frank too, but not before he let out one last snicker. The room was quiet except for the fire crackling in the wood stove and the heavy sounds of horses breathing through the floorboards. Peter opened his eyes and exhaled.

Frank swaggered over to Peter. "You think you'd have a wife now if you had your teeth?"

"That's plenty, Frank," Nels said.

"It's fine," Peter said. "We don't have to dance around it..." He stared at Frank; his eyes narrowed. "Sure, I'd be married, but you might not."

Frank turned red with anger, grabbed Peter by the coat

sleeves, and pulled him close. "Take it back or I'll knock out the rest of your chompers."

The jug of moonshine swung loosely at Peter's side. He shook his head. "Do it."

Frank cocked his fist at Peter, but hesitated just long enough for Nels to grab him by the shoulders. "Hit him, Frank, and you'll have to deal with me next."

"Let me be," Frank snarled; he shot a piece of spittle at Peter's feet. Nels manhandled Frank towards his bunk. "Fine," he acquiesced. "He ain't worth it."

❧

The sounds of Frank's and his cousins' snoring droned in Nels's ears as he lay awake thinking about Katherine. She'd been sad ever since they stepped off the train from North Dakota—not that she'd reason to miss the place. None of them did. Yet it seemed silly to think all her sadness was from Peter getting his jaw broken by that horse. Sure, that probably played some part, but if he was honest the real fault lay with him. He was the one who'd encouraged his sister to marry Frank after their father had told her it was time to pick a husband or join the convent. He could have found others to court her; there were plenty of widowers and old bachelors around. Any of them would've been happy to call her wife—she was pleasant to look at and hard-working too—but Frank had been there waiting, helping them build cattle fences in the summer of '06 and checking in on Katherine and the family through the following winter. Yeah, Frank had put on a good show. Not so much now.

Nels got up from his blankets to add a piece of wood to the

stove. In the soft light of the flame, his hands stumbled upon the jug of moonshine; he slipped two fingers in the neck handle and took a swig.

"Ahem," coughed one of the others.

To his right, Nels made out the silhouette of Peter sitting up in his bunk. He passed him the moonshine. Peter drank and let the jug fall to his lap—both the jug and Peter seemed to slump toward Nels.

"Katherine's not like she was on the steppe or in the Dakotas," Nels said, his voice hushed. "She doesn't talk like she used to—doesn't share. Sometimes I wonder if seeing that horse kick you changed her somehow."

"I think she has her own grief," Peter said, quietly. He took another pull from the jug.

"Would you have married her?"

"I would have asked."

"You didn't."

Peter passed the jug to Nels and sank into his bunk wrapping himself in his blankets. Nels poked the fire once more. He'd never really considered Peter and Katherine in that way, not seriously. They'd seemed so young then. Nels closed the stove door and returned to his bunk. In the darkness, the glow from the red-hot stove coals lit up the back of his eyes. He wanted to wish something better for Katherine, but what that was, he didn't know.

❧

They got up tired. Frank and Peter stayed to their sides of the room as they ate their breakfast and drank their coffee, casting silent glares at one another. Joseph tried to ease the silence and make conversation with Nels, but Nels wasn't interested in small talk.

About three miles west of Battleford, they stopped at the bottom of an east-facing hill loaded with trees—aspen and birch—and made their rough camp, and then the men set to work felling the largest trees in the stand. Swinging and chopping a path northward along the edge of the bluff. As the hours passed, their forearms grew thick and their bodies warmed from the effort.

Nels led his mare through the packed snow and the silvery wolf willows toward the biggest of the fallen trees. He wrapped his chain around a pair of trees and hauled them to where Frank and the brothers bucked them down and loaded them onto the sleighs. Their muscles had become tired and their bellies tightened with hunger. After they'd finished loading the brothers' sleigh, Peter volunteered Joseph to return the loaded sleigh to the shelter of their camp some 40 yards south and get some food ready while the others kept working.

Nels was chopping the thick branches from the fallen trees when Frank stopped to rest against the stack of wood loaded onto his sleigh. He eyeballed Peter trudging toward him carrying a big 12-foot birch log across his chest; Frank started to whistle, 'The Fox and the Rabbit'. "Do you like my tune, Pete?" he called out. Peter spat into the thick snow. A sly grin crept across Frank's face as he stepped away from the sleigh toward Peter until there was a half-dozen feet separating them.

"Get out of my way," Peter warned.

Frank laughed, then faked a quick move to tackle Peter.

"Damn you!" Peter swore and he heaved the log at Frank. It landed at Frank's feet. He tried to skip over it but the toe of his boot caught the log and he tripped, landing face first in the snow. Frank brushed the snow from his face and hurriedly picked himself up.

Peter laughed. No more than a few short puffs, but it was enough. The first punch hit him below the eye, as did the second; the third knocked him into the foot-deep snow. Frank fell on top of him, straddling him, holding down his forearm with one hand and washing his face in icy snow-beads with the other. "Katherine never wanted you," Frank hissed. "She's happy I stopped you."

Nels ran toward them, tossing his axe to the side.

Blinded, Peter struck out wildly with his free hand. Frank punched Peter again, hitting him on the jaw before Peter folded his arm over his face to shield himself; still, Frank pressed him deeper into the snow. "I would've killed you, if you'd touched her."

Nels grabbed Frank under the armpits and pulled him off Peter. A flurry of elbows thrashed to the left and right of Nels; he firmed his grip. Crouching down, Frank slid his foot behind Nels's and drove him backwards into the snow. Nels's grip loosened and Frank rolled free of him. Scrambling to his feet, Nels leapt upon Frank and was met with a punch to the ear that blotted his thoughts and turned his vision to a red haze. Nels countered, punching Frank across the jaw, once, then twice; he cocked his fist back and held it ready. This was his chance to really hurt Frank—he understood this like he did the pain in his ear. "Aagh!" Nels hollered as he released his fist, dropping his arm to his side. He'd resolved to keep Frank pinned in place until everyone had settled, but that didn't pass. Instead Frank raised his knee, striking Nels in his crotch. The pain shot through his guts and Frank took advantage, rolling him to the ground. Once again, Frank had turned the table, straddling Nels. He looked for Peter.

From the corner of his eye, Nels saw something flash behind Frank. He heard Joseph shout, "Stop!" A bone snapped, and a sound like a drowning calf poured from Frank's mouth as he crumpled over Nels. Nels could feel the heaviness of Frank's body weighing him down and in his ear a panicked scream pierced his thoughts. He pushed Frank away, rolling him onto his back. The hairs on Nels's forearms and the nape of his neck pricked up like a bucket of ice water had washed over him when he saw Peter standing above him, his chest heaving and his body trembling as he gripped Nels's axe.

Frank's scream had softened to a low bellow as he smacked his fists into the white snow; Joseph kneeled down next to him and stared at Peter. "Why did you—"

"It was him." Peter pointed the axe at Frank, accusingly. "He was there. He—"

"Drop the axe, Peter," Joseph shouted, before the sound of Frank attempting to stay his puffy breath turned his attention. "Where are you hurt?"

"*Scheisse. Scheisse.*" Frank moaned.

Careful of the dull pain in his lower body, Nels got up slowly, wiping away the ice crystals that'd attached to his eyebrows and moustache, and scanned the trampled snow around them. "I don't understand," he said. "There's no blood." He looked to Peter. "What did you do?"

But Peter's attention remained focused on Frank while his hand still held tight to the axe handle. "I know it was you."

"I can't move my legs," Frank's voice quaked. He uncovered his eyes and looked to Peter. "Goddamn it! Goddamn it, Pete!"

"Listen, Frank—" Nels started.

"The hell with you, Nels."

"Listen—"

"I know you were there," Peter swore.

"He hit me with a goddamn axe!"

"The hammer end."

Nels grabbed the axe from Peter and threw it in the snow. "Get out of here." He pushed Peter in the chest. "Shut up and go."

Peter pushed back. "You don't know what he did."

Nels waved Peter away. "This ain't the time." Returning to Frank, Nels lowered down next to him, opposite Joseph. "You have to stay calm." Frank was anything but calm; his breathing was short and fast, like a chugging train. "It might just be a passing thing," Nels continued. "I've seen it happen before. When Andreas Stolz was a kid he fell off a horse and broke his back and he's good now, but you have to calm down." Frank caught a breath and nodded fast. "Good." Nels surveyed their surroundings. "We'll need to carry him—"

"What if he's bleeding?" Joseph asked.

Nels had forgotten to check. He unbuttoned Frank's sheepskin coat and reached under his back. Frank's shirt was wet and sticky against his skin. "Get some rags," he told Joseph. "Whatever you can find."

Joseph nodded and ran back to the cook fire.

"Will you help us?" Nels hollered at Peter.

Peter sat, shoulders hunched, on the birch log he'd heaved at Frank; his teeth chattered uncontrollably. "He—he doesn't deserve our help."

"You hurt him bad, Peter."

"Good. He hurt me and Katherine bad too."

"Hell no!" Frank grimaced through the pain. "I saved her from you."

Nels looked from Frank to Peter. "What's he talking about?"

Peter stood up, took a half-step toward Nels and Frank. "It

wasn't a horse that broke my jaw, wrecked my face. It was that bastard."

"Liar," Frank cried.

"You were there. I know it."

"You don't know shit."

"You just said to me you stopped me from being with Katherine." He paused. "But we didn't tell anyone we'd planned to meet."

Joseph returned with a kettle of water and a scrap of cloth from an old flour bag. He knelt down next to Frank and commenced pulling Frank's arm out from his coat sleeve.

"I don't understand," Nels said.

"The night when I had my head bashed in. It wasn't no horse."

"Ahh!" Frank cried in anguish.

"Enough, Peter. Either help us or get out of here," Joseph demanded.

"Damn you!" Peter spat in the snow.

Joseph shook his head in disapproval before turning his attention back to Frank, who had shut his eyes and seemed to be bearing down on the pain. "Help me turn him over," he told Nels. Nels grabbed hold of Frank at the shoulder and waist, rolling him onto his side, while Joseph pulled up Frank's shirt so he could put the cloth to his wound. Squeezing his eyes shut, Joseph looked away.

"Lots of blood?" Nels asked.

Joseph shook his head. "It's the bone."

Frank groaned.

"Let him bleed," Peter muttered.

Joseph glared at his brother. "God forgive you."

"Hold the cloth tight against him," Nels told Joseph before turning to Peter. "Tell me what this is about."

"That night Katherine and me... We planned to meet and watch the northern lights. It was already dusk when I left the bonfire and I was nearly at our meeting place, a grove of choke-cherry trees, when I heard something behind me. I remember turning to see what it was, then nothing. I was knocked out. When I came to I was seeing stars and the pain—it hurt bad!" Peter pointed at Frank. "He knows what it's like now—"

"Then why lie about the horse?" Joseph asked.

"I couldn't talk then, so Katherine spoke for us. She told Mother it was a horse because she was too ashamed to tell folks what really happened."

"Because you'd planned to lie with her," Frank panted.

"No," Peter said, shaking his head at the accusation. "We didn't think that way."

"The hell you did! I saw the way you looked at her at the bonfire; you had plans for her." Spittle dripped from the corner of his mouth as Joseph braced him on his side. "I might die here, Nels, but I'm not going to let this whiny ass say what I did or didn't do. I stopped him. Knocked him out and stomped his—" Frank's chest heaved as he panted for air.

"See!" Peter rushed toward them looking as though he might pounce at any moment. "He admits it."

"Slow down, Peter," Nels growled. "What were your plans with Katherine? Why was she ashamed?"

And just as quickly Peter drew back. "Nothing, Nels." His hand went to his cheek. "She was hurt too. When I came around I heard something rustling in the bushes and other sounds, too, like someone choking. The sounds were close but it was so dark I could barely see. I tried to scare whatever, whoever it was away..." He growled at Frank. "It was you. Wasn't it?"

Frank didn't respond. Joseph lowered him onto his back and

inched away from him. Now, he lay in the snow working to catch his breath, drawing quick short puffs through his nose.

Peter continued. "After he ran, I found Katherine blacked out. I stayed with her till she woke up around dawn. She didn't know who did it and neither did I; she made me promise not to tell."

"Bullshit," Frank groaned, recovering his breath. "Pete's got it half right. I bedded Katherine and she knows I did," he smirked.

Clenching his fists, Peter dropped down next to Nels; the two of them knelt in the snow only inches from Frank. "No. No, you didn't. You raped her. Knocked her out like you did me."

"Ha! Ha!" Frank laughed. "Ow!" he moaned, shriveling from the pain.

Nels's guts were tied in knots. He wanted to be sick—all of this, it was all too disturbing, too grim. The one night he and his father leave Katherine alone and the most terrible thing happens. He wanted to undo it—push time back and shove Frank down a deep hole. He tried ordering the pieces Peter and Frank had placed before him, but they were all mixed up inside. "You married her; and I vouched for you."

"She wanted me," said Frank. "Even back then." Then he pawed at the snow scooping a handful to his mouth.

Nels tried to steady himself, his impulses, but he could feel the blood rushing through his veins moving his body in a pulsing motion. "You're a monster."

"She's my wife, Nels. My wife! And I did nothing wrong. In fact, I did right by her. So, go ahead and say I'm a monster but she loves me and if you don't bring me back to her and my baby that blood will be on all of you."

"Goddamn you to hell!"

"You're sick, Frank," said Joseph, stepping away from the others. "I don't—I can't look at him."

"Suit yourself," said Frank. "But just do me one goddamn little thing before you leave and fetch me some of Nels's whiskey."

Joseph looked to Nels for a sign. "Check by the campfire," he replied, and Joseph trudged off in search of the bottle.

"Goddamn, if one of you don't kill me the pain will do it," Frank moaned. "How about it, Pete, gone this far; show me you're not a whiny little ass."

Peter grimaced and looked to Nels. "What are we going to do with him?"

"You know, Pete, when I told Katherine what I did to you that night, she laughed."

"There's no way, you bastard!" Peter clenched his fists and hammered the ground next to Frank.

Frank smiled weakly. "Well, Nels, Pete seems to lack the balls to finish what he started. How about you?"

Nels grabbed Frank around the neck, pressing his weight down on Frank's throat. He felt Frank's Adam's apple sink deep into his windpipe, forcing a swallow that squeaked from his mouth. "This ain't no game, Frank." Panicked, Frank's eyes widened as his face twisted fiery red. Nels squeezed. "Admit you raped her." Frank managed a nodding twitch of his eyes, and Nels loosened his grip.

A dry retch poured from Frank's mouth. "Damn it," he muttered. "Kill me and you'll rot in hell for an eternity."

"Then it'll be me and you." Nels reached under Frank's back and found the cloth Joseph had used to cover the wound.

"What are you doing?"

"You don't need this anymore." Nels pulled the cloth out from underneath him.

"To hell with you." Frank coughed. "She's carrying my child."

Nels gnashed his teeth and punched Frank in the nose; then he forced open the man's mouth, stuffing the bloody cloth inside.

Blood gushed from Frank's nose as his eyes filled with icy tears; he swung his fists but his punches landed weakly, hitting Nels in the chest and the arms. Nels covered Frank's mouth and nostrils with his bare hands and pressed down. Still, the words lodged in the back of Frank's throat came muffled through Nels's hands, demanding that he stop and cursing him to hell.

"You don't have to do this," Peter said. "We can take him to a doctor. It's my doing; no one else has to be involved."

"No way he's going back to her."

Frank's fingernails clawed into Nels's hands, pitting the flesh like a piece of fruit. While next to him, Peter continued to plead for Frank's life, but it was no use. The more Peter talked the more Nels realized he'd no other choice. He pressed harder, careful not to look Frank in the eyes; instead, he looked off toward where he'd last seen Joseph. He spotted him at their camp rummaging through the supplies for the whiskey bottle. Good, he thought, keep looking. A tremor pulsed through Nels's hands setting his forearms shaking, until soon his entire body rattled from exertion. Yet Frank's fingers still grasped his hands. He prayed for it to end soon, for Frank to die. Nels closed his eyes and swallowed hard.

By the time Joseph returned with the whiskey, Nels had pulled the cloth from Frank's mouth and tucked it in his pocket. "We can't tell Katherine what happened," he told the brothers, his breath still heavy from the effort. "She can't know about any of this—for her and the baby."

Peter wiped his face with his coat sleeve and looked away.

Joseph nodded and stood there quietly staring at Frank's body. "I figured he'd be dead by the time I came back. I didn't want to be here for it, and I don't want to know which of you did it." Tears stained and froze to his cheeks. "Just tell me what we're supposed to tell folks when we get home."

"We'll tell them it was his horse," Peter said. "It kicked him. Broke his back."

"Sounds right," said Nels.

∾

They'd pointed their half-loaded sleighs southward and hurried to be gone from the place—to be home and out of sight. Like before, Nels took the lead, now followed by Joseph in Frank's sleigh, and Peter in the rear; while Frank's body lay wrapped in a blanket atop the stack of wood behind Nels. It seemed they'd barely set off when Nels caught sight of a rider on the crest of a sparsely treed hill about 400 yards to the west. The horse and rider picked their path down the hill favouring a snow-swept flank where the frost-bitten ends of the prairie grass peeked through the white cover. Together they melded—the horse's dark mane and the rider's black braids chest-length over a tan blanket with a wide blue stripe that framed the rider's shoulders and the lengths of his arms, draping the buckskin horse—into something ghostly and soothing, a sort of reaper.

Joseph called out to Nels, "Is that an Indian?"

Nels ignored the call and kept his eye on the rider. The Indian was joined by another of his kind. The two riders stopped on the hillside and watched the men. Surely, they could see Frank's body lying behind him. It was probably better to be found out by an Indian than an Englishman, Nels told himself; then, he snapped the lines and his big horses quickened their pace.

Later, when darkness came, the men stopped in the middle of the cold prairie and set their sleighs in a half-ring. They built a snow wall at the base of the carriages to protect them from the wind. Joseph built a fire and heated up some food; they ate quietly. Afterward, they didn't talk. Joseph sobbed to himself, while Peter huddled up next to the fire, his head dipping from time to time and then snapping back to place. Nels wondered about the Indians. They'd seen a dead man being hauled home—nothing particularly odd about that. And who would they tell anyway? As for the brothers, they had their share in the matter, even Joseph in his way.

Nels reached into his pocket and pulled out the bloodied cloth. He looked it over. Things were better, now, he told himself. He'd made a good choice for Katherine and her baby; they'd be free of that devil. He tossed the cloth into the fire, closed his eyes and tried to sleep.

The next day, they carried on before dawn's light, continuing their push south. Nels faded in and out of a nightmarish sleep. Still, he held the lead position, knowing his Belgians would keep to the trail and find their way home. As the day passed, he grew more and more tired until he no longer heard the sounds of the horses and the sleigh running through the layers of snow —powder, crust and hard pack. Those sounds—the crunching squeaks, the heaving breaths—were inside him. And, on the woodpile behind him, Frank whispered into his ear: *to hell with you, Nels; she's carrying my child.*

The setting sun bled red and blue through the flesh of the evening clouds as Nels set his eyes on the farm. A grey spool of smoke unwound itself from the chimney pipe of the house Frank had built. He couldn't remember what he'd planned to tell Katherine. He hoped something would come to him.

He knocked on the door. Katherine opened it and shook her head at him. "Where is Frank?" she asked, her voice raw.

The words circled him: *It was the horse. It was the horse...* But he couldn't get them out; they'd frozen like everything else.

A Turn West
1909

TRADITION DICTATED THAT Frank Weran's body lie in wake for three days prior to the funeral. Peter had intended to go alone to pay his respects to Katherine, but Joseph caught up to him as he gathered the horses from the corral.

Joseph slung his arms through the sleeves of his sheepskin jacket as he hurried along the trampled snow trail. "Where are you going?"

Peter looked up from his work fixing the harness to the black Percheron mare and shook his head at his brother. "Katherine's."

"I should go with you. Make sure you don't say the wrong thing."

"What would I say?"

Joseph shrugged and started fixing the breeching to the mare's hindquarter. "Something about Frank."

Peter huffed. "Like the truth."

"We gave our word to Nels."

"Trust me. I won't say anything. I wouldn't hurt her."

"You need to make a confession, Peter—ask for God's forgiveness. It'll ease your burden."

Peter spat into the snow. He didn't need Joseph telling him what to do. His brother didn't know the full story—had refused to hear it. Sure, he might've wanted Frank dead, but it was Frank who'd gone after him and it was Nels who'd killed him. It wasn't his sin to carry. Not alone.

"I've heard you in your sleep," Joseph continued. "Calling out for her."

Peter looked down, ashamed. It was true he hadn't been sleeping well—his dreams kept bringing him back to the darkness of that night when Katherine was raped and his jaw and teeth were broken. He hadn't been able to call out her name then and now the memory haunted his dreams and his waking mind. "You can go later," he mumbled to his brother.

Joseph hitched the mare to the shafts of the cutter. "No, I'm going with you."

The brothers arrived sometime before noon, but they were not the only ones at Frank and Katherine's farm to pay their respects. Frank's father, Kasimir, and Frank's sister, Teresa, were sitting with Katherine; across from them, set on a pair of sawhorses, was the box with Frank's body. The only other seating in the room was a four-foot-long bench running parallel to the coffin. The kitchen table had moved from its usual place near the wood stove to the wall opposite the door to allow for the setup. Kasimir greeted the brothers at the door with a firm handshake and a wafting cloud of moonshine. Katherine poured them fresh cups of coffee which they gladly accepted, and Teresa offered up her chair, as did Katherine, but the brothers declined.

"It's fine." Katherine's hand gently stroked her pregnant belly. "I need to stretch my legs and there's always the bench for us."

Peter's eyes locked on her belly—his jaw tightened and that old venom pumped through his veins. He hadn't expected to feel this way. Hadn't expected to see Katherine so very pregnant with Frank's child. A part of him wanted to tell her then— wanted to pull her aside and tell her the terrible lie Frank had held over her—of the evil she carried inside her. But here she was, tired, her green eyes turned red and puffy, and offering him her chair. Peter bit his tongue and buried his anger.

"Yes, yes," Teresa agreed; her nose twitched with each word. She had always seemed a mouse-like creature to Peter.

The brothers relented and took seats on the offered chairs. Teresa thrust a plate of *Kuchen* at Peter. He stared at it, then took a small piece; Joseph reached for a couple pieces for himself before Teresa could attack him with the plate.

After he'd washed the cake down with coffee, Peter turned to Kasimir and then Katherine, and realized they were waiting on him or Joseph to say something. Peter looked to Joseph, whose mouth was full of cake, and rolled his eyes.

"Mr. Weran. Teresa. Cousin." Peter looked at each one in turn. "I'm sorry for your loss."

"Thank you." Kasimir belched.

It was a disgrace to see the old man drunk at his son's wake. Peter felt embarrassed for Katherine, Teresa, and in a strange way even for Frank—despite all the horrible things he'd done, this minor offense seemed to be its own ugly violence. He couldn't imagine his own father behaving this way. Peter fumbled as he tried to think of something he might say to Katherine that would counteract Kasimir's foul presence. But he couldn't bring himself to say the things that are usually said: *He was a good man; He loved you.* So, he sat there with his troubled thoughts.

"It's sad that he won't have the chance to see his child," Joseph said, breaking the awkward silence.

Peter noticed Katherine's lips purse. "I apologize for my brother," he quickly said. "He should be more careful with his words. It's a painful matter."

Kasimir waved away the comment. "Ah! He speaks what we

all think." He reached for the jug of moonshine next to his chair, pulled out the stopper, and poured an inch of clear liquid into three glass jars.

"Father's been waiting for someone to have a drink with him," Teresa said. Peter took a jar from Kasimir; he passed it to Joseph with a look that said don't say a word. "You're the first to arrive today," Teresa continued. "Yesterday there was a good many."

"We're happy to keep your company," Joseph said.

"Where's your cup, Daughter?" Kasimir said.

"Oh, Father, perhaps, this one can just be for the men."

"No, this is special. These are the men that shared Frank's last hours. Katherine, you too." Kasimir spat in the pair of empty coffee cups he held between his fingers and polished their insides with his handkerchief before pouring two more shots of liquor. He passed the cups to the women, picked up his own jar, and raised it up.

"To a good son and husband—may he never be forgotten. God bless him and give peace to his soul." Then the old man put the jar to his lips and guzzled the drink down.

Peter took a sip. He didn't like drinking in the morning. His insides weren't ready for it.

Joseph finished his drink and the old man refilled their jars; he splashed an ounce into Peter's drink as well. Joseph raised his drink. "To Frank, to his family, may God love them and keep them strong."

Kasimir raised his drink and emptied it just as fast; he splashed more moonshine into his jar, and topped up the women's cups too.

Peter shook his head. The old man was his own worse menace, but Joseph certainly wasn't helping matters—he was being far too gracious for Peter's liking. Joseph didn't seem to appreciate that there was a certain amount of bitterness that was owed to Frank and his father. And Joseph's warmth was making his own contempt all the more conspicuous. Peter could feel the old man's eyes on him, willing him to raise a toast. He coughed and turned to Katherine. "I should say something," he said.

Katherine tried to smile. "That would be nice."

Peter lowered his head as he looked for the words. "Frank was a strong man," he started. That was true enough. "And when he wanted something, he'd do anything to get it." Peter's eyes met Katherine's as he felt Joseph's elbow in his ribs. He continued: "I'll never forget that about him—who he was as a man and what he did with his time here." He paused as he noticed Katherine dabbing the corners of her eyes with a handkerchief; then raised his jar, "To Frank." The words tasted sour in his mouth. He drank and the others followed.

"Thank you," Kasimir said.

Peter nodded and sank back into his chair, sipping the liquid fire. He had made a mistake coming so early. He'd imagined speaking with Katherine, comforting her, saying something just for her. Now, he realized he'd have been less conspicuous in a packed room with the old man drunk on his booze and folks' flattery for his son. Peter resigned himself to the notion that they'd stay until the next visitors came to show their respects. That was before Kasimir sidled his chair closer to him, clapped him on the shoulder and leaned in close. "You don't mind me saying those were some sweet sounding words for a man who ain't hardly got no teeth."

Peter clenched his jaw, turned to Kasimir, and searched the drunk for some spot of remorse, but all he saw was a darkness that wanted to spread itself. Peter pulled away from the man's grip and stepped towards the door.

"Where are you going?" Kasimir said.

Peter turned to Katherine and Teresa. "Perhaps I should take Mr. Weran home. I'm sure there are chores he needs to take care of."

"*Nein*," the old man grunted.

"Sure there are," Peter said. "You can bring your jug to keep us warm."

"Aah, I'll stay with my boy."

"Father," Teresa said, "I think it's best. I'll fetch you later this afternoon."

"Help me, brother," Peter said, and the brothers grabbed the old man and hauled him outside before he could put up more of a fight. They had Kasimir half way to the cutter before he called out for his jug.

"It's too bright," the old man complained as the brothers hoisted him in.

Teresa brought Kasimir's sheepskin coat in one hand and his jug in the other. The brothers forced the coat onto him, then Joseph planted the jug in Kasimir's thick hands as Peter took the lines. The old man tipped back the jug.

"Stay here with the women," Peter said to Joseph. "I'll be back soon." He flipped the lines and the horses stepped through the soft, sticky snow.

The old man took another pull from the jug and pressed it against Peter's side.

"I've had enough," said Peter.

Kasimir hugged the jug to his chest as if he were holding a small child, then took another draught and set the jug down on his lap. "You should be married," he muttered. "My Teresa needs a husband. She ain't as pretty as most, but neither are you."

Peter looked straight into the old man's pearly black eyes; he had a feeling that if he stared too long he might also fall into that same darkness. Frank's darkness.

"A man needs more than a pretty face," Kasimir continued. The old man took a final pull then corked the jug and let it fall to his feet. "He was my only son." Peter stayed quiet. Some hundred yards later the old man slumped to the side of the cutter's bench.

Kasimir was still asleep when they got to the Weran farmyard. Peter grabbed him by the coat and hoisted him over his shoulder; he carried him through the open door of the soddie and dropped him on the straw mattress. The old man was passed right out. Peter stared at Kasimir—he had the same deep-set eyes as Frank although his eyebrows were twisted, thick and long with age—it seemed Frank had inherited plenty from the old man. Peter sighed. Perhaps, if he'd had a father like Kasimir he'd have hurt people too. The man had that kind of effect on people. Peter could feel that darkness inside him now—it would be easy to stifle the life from the old man. He shook his head. God forgive him. That was a truly terrible thought. Peter knelt down on one knee and pulled off Kasimir's boots, then covered the old man with the blankets. He added some wood to the stove, enough to keep the place warm until the man woke up.

Outside, Peter checked on the animals. He had a feeling the old man might not get to his chores until the next morning, so he took up the job of feeding the livestock and milking the cows. When that was finished, he grabbed a half pail of Kasimir's oats and fed it to his mare. Once the horse had eaten its portion, he went back to Katherine's.

The soddie was now packed with nearly a dozen visitors— neighbours and family—Sebastian Feist, his wife and children, Nels and Agatha and their boys, Jakob Feist and Joseph. The young men had gathered next to the door, which they'd opened to let in the fresh air. A small remedy against the fetor of Frank's corpse. They reminisced, telling old stories, some involving Frank but most of them not, while the women sat in the chairs talking of pregnancy and the things that followed. Someone handed Peter a coffee and he took it and found a place against the wall. It happened to be next to the coffin box, which had been moved to accommodate the growing crowd. He looked down at Frank's upside down face and torso and closed his eyes to re-member it. He wondered which memory of Frank would survive the longest—this one of Frank, grey and motionless, or the last one of Frank, desperate and suffocating to death at Nels's hands. Peter turned away. He knew the answer.

Nels picked his two-year old son, Lambert, off the floor and tossed him in Joseph's arms, then grabbed his jug and tin and weaved his way to Peter. "Katherine told me what you did."

Peter felt a bead of sweat break on his brow. What did Kath-erine say, he wondered? All of a sudden, he wanted to get away from Nels.

"You did us all a favour getting the old man out of the house." Nels poured a shot from his jug into a tin and handed it to Peter.

Peter swallowed the liquor down in nervous relief and wiped the dribble from his chin. The liquor was much smoother than the fire-starter Kasimir had poured him. Peter felt the warmth grow inside him as he handed the tin back to Nels. "I've met oxen with more charm than that man."

Nels snickered.

"Where's the daughter?" Peter asked. "Teresa?"

"Resting in the other room. Too much to drink."

Peter nodded, unsurprised. "And how are you?"

"I'll be happy once he's in the ground." Nels twisted the corner of his moustache.

Peter agreed. There had been some good in what happened to Frank and he needed to remember that—this wake was a lie. He felt insulted by the ignorance of those around them. And while he was bound by his word to keep quiet, it only made him feel like an imposter in this place. He supposed Nels felt the same.

"What about Katherine?" he asked Nels.

"She'll stay with us until the child is born and the snow has cleared. I've convinced her of that much."

"That's good."

"Afterward she wants to stay here with the child."

"She's a strong woman."

Nels's eyes shifted to his sister. Katherine sat surrounded by the other women, a hand on her belly, the other holding a cup of tea. Peter ran his tongue along the smooth curvature of his lower right gum until it found the worn edge of his left lateral incisor. The muscle washed over the broken tooth as he thought of Katherine sitting, pregnant. In his most secret of dreams, he'd wished for this to be his life. Forget a mouthful of teeth. He'd gladly trade them all for this—a small house and a life with Katherine. How strange to be jealous of a dead man.

"I pray that child takes from its mother," Nels said. The words tore Peter from his fantasizing. "A girl would be best."

Peter nodded. He shared the same thoughts. Nels poured some more liquor in the tin and offered it to Peter. "I better not," he said. "I should get Joseph home. We have chores to do."

"For the ride home." Nels handed Peter the tin.

Peter took it and downed the liquid. He felt the liquor taking hold in the base of his mind—the room took on a fuzzy shape, his thoughts slowed—he knew it was time to go. He found his brother and, after some trying, got Joseph to finish his drink. Katherine saw him off at the door.

"Thank you for coming," she told Peter. "And for taking Kasimir home."

"Well, for that, you owe me."

She nearly smiled. He felt the corners of his mouth pull up.

"Don't let him overrun you," he told her.

"He's better when he's not been drinking."

Peter nodded.

"We'll talk more next time?"

"Yes."

෧

The day after next was the funeral. Peter never doubted that he'd attend the service, but it was more than a surprise to him when Nels pulled him aside and, on behalf of Katherine, asked if he'd be one of the pallbearers.

They stood outside, along the south wall of the sod church, protected from the cold northeast wind. It was a modest church, running east and west, with a gable roof; a cross mounted on the east side of the building welcomed the congregation. A short distance from the church was the graveyard, where a handful of metal crosses marked the community's deceased.

"I know it's a lot to ask," Nels said. "She wants me to ask Joseph too."

Peter shook his head.

"I'm doing it as well. I don't have a choice in the matter."

"Maybe we should tell her," Peter said.

Nels's eyes sharpened on Peter as he shortened the distance between them to a thin channel. "Are you so selfish, Peter, that you'd ruin her life and the child's to avoid a passing thing?" His voice was low, assertive.

"No. But when does it stop?"

"With this," Nels said. "I promise."

Peter studied Nels's eyes. No, this wouldn't be the end of it. Maybe it'd slow for a time, but one day it'd start up again. The child would want to know about its father, and the lies would pile on. Peter also understood the only other choice was not a real choice. Not today. Peter shook his head. "Lead the way," he told Nels.

In church, Peter's mind spun through the events of the last few days—the old man and the wake, the long trip home staring at Frank's frozen corpse on the back of Nels's sleigh, Katherine pregnant and surrounded by friends and family, Frank's confession, the fight in the woods, watching Nels choke Frank to death and not doing a thing to stop him—and it seemed to him that they all deserved much less than this. Frank didn't deserve these tears and fond memories. He deserved a shallow hole cut in the prairie, no marker, no remembrance.

Peter stepped in time with the other men as they carried Frank's casket out through the doors of the church. He was happy to be leaving. He'd felt the weight of God's disappointment heavy on his shoulders. They'd disrespected God, themselves, and Frank too, disguising themselves as good men as they processed the man they'd killed in and out of the church. They'd be judged for this, and God would reject them. They'd burn. He would burn for his silence. For never having the courage to speak out. It was fitting that he should have his teeth knocked out, since he only ever spoke out when it was too late, or when he had to save his own skin.

They loaded the coffin onto the back of Kasimir's sleigh, and Peter took his place alongside it with the other pallbearers. He couldn't bear to look at that box any longer and searched the small crowd of 50 or 60 people for Katherine. He spotted her at the head of the funeral procession, walking alongside Nels, and weeping into the collar of his jacket. He wondered, would she still be crying if she knew what he knew? Maybe, but for different reasons.

 భ

After the funeral, a quiet noisiness echoed through Peter's thoughts. Work was his only escape. He busied himself sawing the logs they'd hauled from Battleford into one-foot lengths and splitting them into pieces. Joseph offered his help but Peter refused it. This was his work. His contrition. He swung the axe with fury until his frustration and dark cravings wore raw through his blistered and peeling hands.

Yes, he wanted God's forgiveness; but, more so, he wanted to close his eyes and not see Frank in a rage or dying in front of him. He wanted to forget, to run far away, yet he didn't want to leave. He still wanted Katherine. He still loved her; and maybe she loved him too. This could be their chance. It might even be God's will, he thought. But how could they ever build a future together on a lie? Katherine should know it was Frank who had raped her. But he feared telling her and tainting whatever little bit of good might've come from her life with the man. There was another problem too. Telling the truth about Frank meant telling the truth of how he died, and that would mean admitting what he'd done. What Nels had done. The thought made Peter wither—it would be the ruin of them all.

As for Joseph, he was finding his own obsession in the form of Margaret Dudenhafer and the promised *Koublien* that Nels had arranged with her father. Joseph had already met the family once for coffee and a chance to talk with Margaret and was preparing for a return visit. This time for a family dinner.

"If it goes well and if you like the girl's company, then don't wait around for the foxes to come and check your traps," their father, Konstantin, said as he stirred sugar into his afternoon coffee. "Isn't that right, Mother?"

Johanna finished pouring Joseph's coffee. "As I remember it, it was you that played the fox." She winked at her husband.

"That might be true." Konstantin smiled, first at his wife, then at Joseph. Peter sat at the table quietly thumbing through a deck of cards.

"So, when do I ask Mr. Dudenhafer for Margaret's hand?"

Konstantin set his spoon on the wood table. "Best to wait a few days. He'll have questions for you and you'll need to have your answers."

Peter noticed a passing glance between his parents. It was easy to see how much they were enjoying this moment. They'd only ever been on the other side of the proposal—with his sisters, Barbara and Magda—losing daughters to families miles and miles away. Peter shuffled the cards into the palm of his hand, faster and faster. He'd given up hopes of marriage years ago, but he'd not prepared himself for Joseph to take his place.

"He'll want to know where we'd be living."

"I've given that some thought," Konstantin said. "We'll build a new house on the west quarter."

Peter slapped the cards onto the table. "That's my quarter."

"Yes, and we'll build a good wood house with windows and a room for you and one for your mother and me. Joseph and Margaret will take the soddie." Konstantin turned to Joseph. "You can tell Dudenhafer that she'll be well taken care of."

Joseph smiled.

"But do you have the money for that, Father?" Peter asked.

"I think so. We've managed to tuck a little away since we left North Dakota. And the crop looks promising this year. What else do we have to spend our money on?"

A warm hush fell over the table, and perhaps the talk would have circled back to wedding plans and happier things, if it weren't for Peter's brooding thoughts. "Why are you moving so quickly, brother?" he asked.

"Why should I wait?" Joseph said.

"Out of respect for our cousin."

"What happened to Frank is all the more reason for me to marry Margaret. Life is too short to wait."

"That's right," Konstantin said. "Sometimes you have to take the bull by the horns."

"Like Frank did," Peter said.

Joseph looked at him with a troubled expression.

"What do you mean by that?" their father asked.

Peter shook his head. "Nothing."

After that, Peter never again questioned his brother's path. Yes, life must go on, but, for Peter, which path life had for him never seemed less clear. When he heard the news a week later that Katherine had given birth to a baby boy, and that Joseph's proposal had been warmly accepted by both Margaret and her father, he began to question what was left for him in this place. He saddled his mare and set out for Nels's farm.

The spring sun was at work thawing the icy puddles on the trail. When Peter arrived he found Nels outside trenching the melting snow and water away from the soddie. Peter grabbed a shovel and gave Nels a hand with the work. They worked quietly for a half hour or more; by that time, Peter's boots and wool socks were soaked from the thaw.

"Joseph is going to ask for Margaret's hand," Peter said.

"That's great." Nels smiled. "She'll make a good wife and mother."

"You don't think it's too soon?"

"Life moves on. You don't expect time to stop when someone dies, do you?"

Peter shrugged.

"It doesn't," Nels said, and he dug his shovel into the ground. The icy water pushed forward as he loosened another clump of cold earth from the path.

"Do you regret it?" Peter asked. "What you did?"

Nels turned to the soddie. They were alone, some 30 yards from the house. He stabbed his shovel into the soft, wet snow, and looked to Peter. "Do you regret swinging that axe?" he asked, in a low voice.

Peter looked down. After he'd done it—after he'd swung the axe—he'd been scared that something inside him wanted more. He had never imagined that hurting someone, really hurting someone, might feel so good. Even now, the thought of it made him tremble. "I don't know."

"Do you think he regretted attacking you? Attacking Katherine?"

Peter dashed his shovel in and out of the soft snow. "No. But don't you think there might've been another way."

Nels's face reddened with agitation. "What do you think would've happened if he came home to her, even as a cripple? You think he wouldn't have told her what we did? Think of the lies he might've told her. The lies she might've believed."

Peter massaged his cheek. He knew Nels was right; still, he wasn't convinced they'd done the right thing.

"You know he'd been hitting her too?"

Peter shook his head. He hadn't thought much of their married life—had never wanted to—but he believed it. The thing with Frank he'd learned is that it piled on in heaps. "I didn't know."

"She's forgotten all about him hitting and pushing her. It's like he's a saint in her mind." Nels turned quiet. "You ask what I regret. That's what I regret. That's what I figure I'm meant to bear. Don't burden me with your second thoughts. I've got plenty to think about." Nels stamped the shovel blade into the frozen earth.

Peter's mind wandered. Why did she still love Frank so strongly after all the pain he'd caused her? Was it possible that love could be made from fear? "Why did she marry him? Why did Johannes allow it?"

Nels pulled a whisker from his moustache and flicked it to the ground. "It's easy now to see that Frank was no good, but it was harder then. Katherine wasn't happy and our father gave her the choice to marry or to go to the convent, but even in her sadness she knew she wanted a child. So it was Frank."

A sound came from behind them and Peter turned back to the sod house. Katherine appeared outside the door holding a small bundle wrapped in blankets. He swallowed. The baby was real. He realized he didn't want to see the child.

"Speaking of," Nels said. "Why don't you go see her for yourself."

Peter started toward the house as Katherine picked her way from one snowy footing to the next, avoiding the mud and the afternoon puddles.

"Wait there," Peter shouted.

"Mind what I told you," Nels said.

Peter nodded and made his way to Katherine. He moved carefully across the patchwork of snow and frozen puddles.

Nels's words settling in his mind. Katherine had the child she wanted although the cost seemed too high. Still, it was best Frank was dead. He would've told the tale to his benefit. Turned everything on its head.

He held his arm out to Katherine as she neared him. She steadied against it for an instant as her footing shifted; she smiled at him. Her eyes, like wolf willow leaves fluttering in the summer sun, revealed something like contentment.

"I'm happy to see you, Katherine."

"It's good to see you, Peter. I see you've been helping Nels. Is Joseph here too?"

"No, it's just me. Joseph has his head in the clouds."

"Really?"

"He's like a bee buzzing around a flower, and it's all Nels's doing."

"Yes." Katherine smiled. "Nels mentioned the Dudenhafer girl. They're getting on well?"

"They are," Peter replied. "They plan to marry this summer."

"That's wonderful. They must be very happy."

"Maybe not as much as Nels, now that I've told him."

"It'll be another feather in his cap," she said. She looked to the bundle in her arms.

Peter nodded and rested his eyes on the child. "A boy?"

"Yes," she replied. "Frank, like his father."

Peter cringed.

"Is something the matter?"

"Only I would've thought, Johannes, after your father."

"Well, he'll be christened Frank Johannes Weran."

"Perhaps, you might give some thought to Johannes Frank Weran," he countered. He could see frustration growing along Katherine's brow.

"Are you trying to be funny?"

He saw that he was on the cusp of offending her in some irrevocable way, but he also felt that he might be protecting her. "I only think with Frank's misfortune perhaps the name is tainted. Johannes is a fine name and nothing evil ever befell your father." He paused. "He lived a good life."

"I've never known you to be superstitious."

"Well, I'd never name a son of mine Peter, nor would I have any of my siblings do such a thing." He offered one of his closed-lip smiles.

"Perhaps, you might also warn them against naming their daughters Katherine as well."

"Now that you mention it, yes, I would warn them against it," he said, playing along. "Then again, perhaps, each name has an unknown misfortune attached to it." He paused. "And the baptism is this Sunday?"

"Yes."

"So, you have time to think about it."

"You confuse me, Peter. Frank was good enough for his father; it'll suit our boy fine too."

Peter sighed. He could end it all now. He could tell her the awful truth, although Nels would make him pay. That he could handle. But Katherine would never forgive him and he wasn't brave enough to live without her love. Yet some part of him believed that Katherine's and the boy's fate were tied to her knowing.

He took a step closer to Katherine and carefully pulled the wrap away from the baby's face. Deep set eyes, thick lips, dark hair—he was his father's son. "Yes, I suppose it will."

Katherine smiled as the baby turned away from the light and

pressed his face towards her chest. "I should take him inside. I
don't want him to get a chill."

Peter nodded and watched Katherine make her way back to
the soddie with baby Frank in her arms.

ᘓ

If there was one thing the baptism showed Peter it was that
there was no burying Frank Weran. He just kept coming back.
Things could've been worse. Katherine could've asked him to be
the child's godfather, but he was sure his comments about naming the child had removed any such idea. And, of course, Nels
and Agatha would make fine godparents. A new truth seemed
at hand: whatever wishes he'd had to do right by Katherine
seemed an impossibility now. She held onto Frank too closely.
The child's name was proof of that. Perhaps, if it had been born
a girl.... No, that wasn't it. There was only so much he could tell
her, and only so much that she'd hear from him. And the truth
lay outside those borders.

He would've been happy that day to have put his hat on after
church. To saddle his horse, and leave, ride off for some distant
place. He felt then that he was done in Kaidenberg, but it seemed
the obligations were only beginning to pile on, with his brother's
upcoming wedding and a new house that needed building.

He pushed through the rituals of seeding—horse and plough
clockwise around the field—the furrows turning as they had
year after year. Once he'd finished, he went to check on Katherine. He found her working the land with her team of horses
hitched to the double plough and the baby swaddled to her back.

"I'll come back with my horse and plough," he said.

"Please don't," she said.

"It's fine. I have nothing more to do."

"No, Peter. I want to do this myself." She was quiet. "It might sound strange, but he feels closer here."

There wasn't anything he could say to that. He had helped to destroy the monster, but the ghost was proving much stronger than Peter could ever have imagined. As he rode back home, he cursed God for ever making a man like Frank Weran.

℘

It was the middle of June when he found extra work building the rail bed for the tracks that would link Kaidenberg to the main line. He wasn't the only one. Most of the young farmers had jumped on the opportunity to earn a few more dollars. As he bent over his shovel, piling dirt for the embankment, Peter began to think seriously about going west. He'd heard men telling stories of panning gold and trapping grizzly bears, though none of them seemed to have done it themselves. Except for one of them, a foreman, Karl Ziegler, who hailed from Baden, Germany. Ziegler shared stories about his work laying rail through the mighty Rocky Mountains, felling trees as broad as a man and building trestle bridges spanning wide mountain chasms.

"They're giant mountains," he said. "Even the biggest, loudest man is humbled in their shadows."

It was that sentiment that attracted Peter. If there really was a place where men were humbled by the greatness of nature, of God's creation, he wanted to be there. He wanted to see it while it was still wild and untamed by men. The prairie was vast, seemingly endless, yet settlers were filling every corner, taming it with wheat, oats and barley. But the mountains, whole ranges of them covered in forest and ice, a man could get lost there and never be seen again.

He worked four weeks and earned $20. Ziegler asked Peter to stay on longer. "It's hard work," Ziegler said. "But if you want to be in nature, see the beauty of the land, I always need another good worker."

But he had to turn him down. He'd promised to help Joseph and his father build the new wood-frame house for their mother and father.

The idea of leaving Kaidenberg, of going west and starting a new life, became more and more deeply rooted in Peter's mind as the walls of the house went up. It made him happy to think his life needn't be one long straight line. He kept these thoughts to himself until the Sunday before Joseph's wedding. On the way home from church the family stopped at the house to show their mother, Johanna, their work. It was nearly finished—only the windows and doors were missing.

"It's beautiful," she said, as she climbed down from the wagon. "You've done such good work."

"It'll be a good house," Joseph said.

She kissed Joseph on the cheek, then Peter.

She stepped inside the three-room house. "This will be our new home." The men followed. "Wood floors!" she sighed. She examined the new wood stove and flashed them an approving smile.

Konstantin took her by the hand and walked her to the room closest to the stove. "This is our room."

"Very nice." She smiled. Then she peeked her head into the other room. "Oh, Peter, you have a window too. I'm so happy you will be living with us."

Peter shook his head. "I don't know, Mother."

"What don't you know?" Her forehead creased with worry.

"If I should want to live here."

"Don't be ungrateful," Joseph said.

"I'm not ungrateful."

"Well, you can't stay in the soddie."

"I don't want to."

"What's this about?" asked his father.

Peter looked down. "I'd like to keep working on the rail."

"On the rail. That's fine," Konstantin said. "Now that the house is done you can go back, although there's only a week or two until harvest."

"And don't forget your brother's wedding," Johanna added.

Peter shook his head. "Not here, Father, I want to go west. I want to see some new country."

"How far west do you mean?" Konstantin asked.

"Alberta. The mountains."

"No, you can't go," Johanna sobbed. "You might be hurt. Those are strange places with strange people."

The room took on a quiet heaviness. His father chewed on his lip, as Joseph tried to comfort their mother. Peter caressed his jaw where the bone had fused, misshapen. He regretted his timing. He'd stolen a piece of his mother's happiness and, perhaps, tainted her future memories of this house and this day.

"Please, Mother, don't cry. It's just a thought."

"You mustn't go," she whimpered. "We're getting old. We need you too much."

"Don't talk like that," Konstantin said. "He might be your boy, but he must be his own man."

Peter nodded. Relieved his father understood.

"You say this is just a thought," Konstantin said, his eyes studying Peter. "Or maybe it's more than that. But for your mother's sake and for mine too, stay with us until the harvest is done. Afterward, if you still want to go, you'll have our blessing and we'll put some money in your pocket."

Peter looked to his crying mother then back to his father. "I will."

⌘

The wedding celebration had more than its share of good food and drink, and there wasn't a guest who found complaint with Mrs. Dudenhafer's banquet spread—a tender pork roast with roasted potatoes picked fresh from the garden. Nor could anyone wish for better music to mark the celebration. Mr. Dudenhafer's accordion and Mr. Zerr's fiddle incited a frenzy of dancing among the young and young at heart. Even Peter was caught up in the whirlwind. Margaret had obliged him to share a dance with her and afterward quickly passed him from one sister to another, until, he found himself hand in hand with Katherine and, forgetting his disfigurement, he smiled as he had years ago. When the dance was finished he held her hand in his for a moment longer.

She gave his hand a squeeze and closed her eyes.

He felt his world pulled into the quiet place she inhabited. What was behind those eyes? Not Frank, he prayed, as his smile faded.

She let go of his hand and opened her eyes. "I should check on the baby."

"Of course."

Those brief happy moments echoed in Peter's thoughts through the long days cutting and stooking the wheat, and the longer days when the rain came and every moment was spent waiting for the sun to reappear and dry the crop so the work could start up once more, and when the grain was good and dry, and it was time to pitch the stooks into the threshing machine, even then, he could close his eyes and retrieve the sound of the music and the smile on her face as they went spinning around the room.

Then, one day, it was done. He tossed the last sheaf of wheat into the steel beast. It turned and flailed out straw from one end and grain from another, then rolled to a stop. It took him another day to realize the harvest was over and he was free to go. There was nothing holding him to Kaidenberg but himself. In his 22 years of living, he'd never had to make a decision like this before. He'd never chosen a course of action for himself alone; nothing that'd take him away from his family. His guts clenched. He couldn't eat. His insides ached for him to make a decision. In the background, his mother's pleas for him to stay persisted and in his weakness they seemed more and more reasonable, but it was his father who finally pushed him to take his next step. They'd been doing the afternoon chores in their usual silence when Konstantin clapped him on the shoulder and told him to set down the feed pail.

"It's hard to leave what you know," Konstantin said. "I couldn't do it again, but I'm older now."

Peter listened quietly.

"This life here is far from what I'd imagined all those years ago. It's better in some ways and in some ways it's not." He paused. "There's no certainty to these things."

Peter nodded.

"So, if you're going to do this, you should get at it while you're young; while you have the stones to do it. And if you have a change of heart, or it doesn't work out, there'll be something here for you to come home to." Konstantin put his hand on Peter's shoulder.

The weight of it made Peter weak. He swallowed. "Thank you," he said.

After that, there was no delaying things further. He planned to ride out the day after next, taking what little he owned and 'borrowing' the things he'd need to get by. There was one last thing he had to do before he left.

ೲ

The next day, he saddled his horse and rode east to Katherine's. About a half mile from her farm he saw a figure leaving the yard on horseback and rode towards it. A few hundred yards on he recognized the figure on the horse as Bernhard Holtz. He'd heard that Bernhard had helped Katherine and Nels bring in the harvest. Peter began to wonder about the nature of Bernhard's intentions.

When they were some 50 yards apart, Peter shouted, "Holtz."

Bernhard rode closer. "Out for a ride, Eberle. Where are you headed to?"

"My cousin's—Katherine's."

"I just came from there. I'm sure she'll be happy to see you."

Peter had never known Bernhard to be so warm and pleasant. It reminded him of Joseph's cheery behavior during his courtship of Margaret. Peter spat on the ground. It was too early for Bernhard to be courting Katherine; it'd only been six months since she was widowed. And Bernhard of all people—the drunk, the thief—what good could he bring her?

"She's been wondering about you and your family," Bernhard added.

Peter's horse turned away from Bernhard, as if to say: *move on.*
But Peter circled him back.

"She got the harvest off," Bernhard said.

"Yeah, I heard you helped."

"I did. Along with Nels and Agatha. We managed to get it
done."

"No help from Kasimir?"

"No," Bernhard replied.

"I should've expected," Peter said. "His promises seem to end
at the bottom of a whiskey jug."

Bernhard nodded and made no comment.

Peter couldn't help but feel some small satisfaction knowing
his remark had touched Bernhard. It was well known that he
had his own problems with the bottle. "She deserves better than
what she's had in the past."

Bernhard stayed quiet.

Peter's mind flashed a picture of Frank dying in the snow. He
shook it off.

"She's been a friend to me," Bernhard said. "I ain't got any
others."

Peter nodded. "She has a good heart."

"She does."

Peter leaned back in his saddle; perhaps he'd been too rash in
his thinking about Bernhard. In some ways, they really weren't
so different.

"I won't keep you." Bernhard tipped his hat and steered his
horse to the side.

"Wait." Peter said, and Bernhard turned his horse back around
to face him. "I guess you know she doesn't take help easily."

"I've noticed. She's a proud woman."

"It's good you were there."

Bernhard nodded. "Thanks."

Peter tipped his hat to Bernhard, then put his heel to the horse's side and continued on to Katherine's.

She greeted him at the door, cradling baby Frank in her arm, as he hitched his horse to the post next to the house. She wore her long hair up, revealing the length of her neck. It was as strong and fine as a stem of golden flax. But it appeared the stresses of her life had begun to catch up with her. There were bags under her eyes and a slight hobble in her step.

"Peter, what a nice surprise. Come inside. I've got some coffee brewed."

Peter followed Katherine into the sod house. Inside, Peter took off his hat and ran his hand through his dark brown hair. "I passed Bernhard Holtz on the way here."

"Yes. Mr. Holtz's been a helping hand through the harvest."

"He says you bring out the good in him."

Peter noticed the slight blush on Katherine's cheeks as she poured him a cup of coffee. "I know he means well. And I think we all deserve the chance to have another start."

Peter feigned one of his closed mouth smiles. Those words—*another start*—coming from Katherine's lips were, to him, some kind of snake oil. A weak balm at best. The old impulse to tell her the truth about Frank twisted in his mind like red hot steel in the blacksmith's forge. But what would be gained by that? He took a swig of coffee and swallowed it down. He set the cup on the table and noticed baby Frank reaching his tiny hands toward the cup as his tongue protruded from his wet lips.

"You want to hold him?" she asked.

"I don't know," he said. "I don't have much experience with

babies." He wondered if some dark part of him might awake and dash the child's brains out. He felt a chill run through him. No, he shook himself, what a terrible thought.

"He won't bite," she chuckled. "Well, he might but it won't hurt none." She took a step closer and placed the baby in his arms. "My shoulders could use the rest," she said, under her breath.

Peter bounced the baby in his arms as the child waved his tiny fists and blew spit bubbles from his mouth. "He's happy."

"Now he is," Katherine replied. "He likes you."

Holding the child, it struck Peter that this would be the last impression he'd leave Katherine with, for God knows how long, and he felt an overwhelming need to be extra careful not to upset or disturb the boy. Just as he thought it, the baby tensed and squirmed, Peter shifted the little one into a cradle hold and rocked it from side to side. Baby Frank settled.

"You're good at that," Katherine said. "Maybe one day, you'll have one of your own."

"Ha," Peter huffed. "I'm not so sure about that."

"There are many women that would be happy to have you as their husband. I saw the way Margaret's sister, Adolfa, looked at you at the wedding."

"There was a time, I thought—" he looked at her, then stopped.

"We were young," she said.

He wondered if his thoughts were always so plain to see or if it was her special gift to read them as though they were written on his face. "Yes," he said, "but it doesn't change the way my heart works." He couldn't do it any longer. He stood up and passed the child back to Katherine.

"Are you going already?"

He lowered his head and stared at the earthen floor. He

thought of asking her about Bernhard, whether she liked him, if they were starting a courtship, but it didn't seem to matter. Whatever would happen, would happen, and him being around wouldn't change it.

"You've always been special to me, Peter. You filled my young heart with fun and laughter. I only wish it would've ended differently for us."

He fixed his eyes on her. "Do you blame me?"

"No, no," she said. "Never. But sometimes I feel there are too many reminders."

He nodded. "More than you know."

She looked at him curiously.

"I'm leaving," he continued. "I'm going west to find work."

She closed her eyes. "How far?"

"I'd like to see the Rocky Mountains," he said. "Maybe even the Pacific Ocean."

She opened her eyes. It seemed they spoke their own language. Slowed the current of thought moving through the pools of his mind.

"Oh, Peter." She paused. "When are you leaving?"

"Tomorrow."

"Is this is the last time I'm going to see you, then?" she said. "How long will you be gone?"

"I don't know. Maybe a year. Probably longer. I can't say."

Katherine stood up from her chair. She stepped toward him and wrapped her free arm around him; he returned the embrace, mindful of the child she was holding. He felt her nuzzle her cheek against the collar of his jacket. "Write to me. Tell me everything you see. Then, when I read it, it'll be like I'm standing next to you."

"I will," he said. He held her in his arms. Her green eyes

steadied him. Fooled him into thinking that this life, her and the child, might be his. "I'll imagine you're standing next to me." He closed his eyes and hoped to remember this feeling. Then he let her go.

She followed him to the door.

"God bless you and the baby," he said.

She kissed him on the cheek. "You'll be in our prayers."

He smiled for her. A real smile. Then, not knowing what else to do, he unhitched his horse and turned west.

Fireworks Over Kaidenberg
1917

I

FATHER SELZ WAS beloved by his parishioners. Not only was he young, barely 30, with boyish good looks—round dimpled cheeks with little trace of facial hair—he was also conversant and knowledgeable in the ways of his farm brethren, especially if the topic centred on the new technologies that were reshaping farm life. But his passion was photography. He was a true enthusiast, and owned several cameras both large and small. He was fascinated both by the mechanics and the chemical miracles of the craft—for him the camera seemed to be an apparatus of divine intelligence. Yet he knew not all in his flock were keen on the new inventions that were changing their everyday lives.

This impression became quite distinct when he first arrived in the community in the autumn of 1915. After his first Mass, he was approached by a handful of the grey-haired congregation led by Mrs. Stolz. They were adamant that the mechanical binders used by their grown children to cut and bind sheaves of grain were possessed by the devil. How else could this magic be performed so quickly before their eyes?

"Father, we pray that you warn our sons against using the

devil's tools to harvest their grain," Mrs. Stolz said. "No good can come of it."

"Those demonic contraptions will surely bind their eternal souls to Lucifer's dark heart," Mrs. Zerr interrupted.

"Please, Father, they won't listen to us," continued Mrs. Stolz. "They're blinded by the devil's magic. He feeds their sloth—"

"And promises them riches."

Father Selz smiled with child-like innocence. "Good mothers," he replied, "I pray you believe me when I tell you these are not the devil's tools. They are made by good Christian men, and used to the benefit of the Lord's earthly kingdom. There is no need to fear for your children's eternal souls, especially as it concerns the use of the binder or any similar device."

Of course, the old church mothers received his message with the courtesy owed to his position, but he knew that there was little hope of changing the hearts and minds of such folk. Their beliefs were born of ignorance and superstition and were thereby immune to logic and even his own authority. However, Father Selz, being both a man of the cloth and a repudiator of ignorance, gradually extended his pastoral mission to include challenging technological superstitions of this sort. It's true he caused a sensation when he became the first in the community to purchase an electric plant to light his parish house, but it was the events and spectacle of the parish picnic of 1917 that his congregation would never forget and, for different reasons, neither would he.

Father Selz wanted to bring the young community together to celebrate its many achievements. In little over ten years, it had grown from a grid of survey markers in the prairie to a growing concern with a railroad, a scattering of prairie schoolhouses, two grain elevators, three general stores, a butcher and two lumberyards. The settlers had even constructed a large wood-frame church to accommodate the growing congregation; like the old sod structure it replaced, the new church was built next to the cemetery, a little more than a mile from town. Yet, over all these years, the townspeople and the farm folk had not come together to mark their successes. Father Selz knew the answer lay in the character of the people. Although they loved to sing and dance, they had become accustomed to poverty and this had made them modest. If he could show them a truly unforgettable event, perhaps, he could help them enjoy richer spiritual and communal lives. To do this, he knew he'd have to dream big and employ all of the tools at his disposal. There would be games, of course, and contests—the men loved to compete—but he wanted more. He wanted fireworks. Yes, he thought, that would be good. He'd be surprised if any of them had seen such a thing, perhaps some had while in America; many had passed through—some had even settled in the Dakotas—before coming to Canada.

He had his own memories of America. He had landed in Boston along with Father Trimbach, his friend from seminary. He remembered the heat of the city in the summer, how the air was thick and heavy, and still the people bustled here and there, always working. What a relief it had been to find the Cathedral of the Holy Cross, and to commune with the Heavenly Father behind those stone walls. In the evening, he had taken a walk down Washington Street. He followed a group of young men towards Franklin Square. He turned on a side street. The sounds of men singing a merry tune poured out the doorway of a three-storey brick building. On the street, a group of young boys raced by him, chasing a friend down the sidewalk, while a young woman of refined appearance walked alongside a distinguished-looking older man, likely her father as there was some family resemblance. Then, to his right, swarms of young people piled into a little shop. He stuck his head in the door. The folks took their seats on long wood benches after depositing their three pennies in a jar. An apparatus not unlike a camera stood behind them. His curiosity had overtaken him, and he himself dropped three pennies in the jar and took a seat next to a pale-faced, red-haired man. Once the room filled, the windows were shuttered and a young man with greasy skin started up the apparatus, while a piano player struck up a pattering tune. Light from the machine projected onto a large canvas tacked to the wall. He felt his heart jump in anticipation of what he was going to see. An image of a title, the words in English, appeared before them. And then the picture moved again. It was like a black and white photograph that had come to life. Two men in hats and armed with revolvers entered a train office and tied up the clerk. Outside, a gang of men boarded a steam train and attacked the crew with their guns. They killed a man. Father Selz leaned forward. He was sweaty, nervous, his heart pounded with excitement. The gang hijacked the train and robbed the passengers before fleeing into the woods. It was unlike anything he had ever seen, and he was completely swept up in the story. He didn't know whether he wanted the gang to run free or receive some sort of divine justice. The tempo of the music accelerated as the gang fled into the woods, and the music pulsed, trilled, became sombre and exciting in turn. A fiddle player had joined the pianist, but Father Selz couldn't say at which point in the film this had happened. Next, a posse was formed, the outlaws were tracked and hunted down—a final gunfight and the outlaws were slain. The crowd applauded. Father Selz applauded too. He put his hand to his heart. Never before had he been transported in this way. It was like a dream cast into being. He felt his spirit rise. He left the nickelodeon and walked the streets in a kind of enchantment, deciphering the scene he had seen before him. This was something new. Something that would change the world, and that thought terrified him a little.

Now, as he planned the community picnic, it was the remembrance of that feeling—running like a current of electricity from his head down to the base of his spine—which swayed him.

Yes! That's it. That's what he needed for the picnic. If he could bring that feeling to the people of Kaidenberg, if he could jolt their lives in that way, maybe they'd see something bigger in these stories and understand something of God's nature in those moving pictures. He himself had said as much to Father Trimbach.

"It has led me to a better understanding of the Holy Trinity," he told his compatriot the next day.

"What do you mean?"

"The image. The film holds our spirit not unlike God holds or extends one or more parts of His three-fold nature unto this world."

"But God did not make this film. Men made it. And there is nothing to stop them from using these tools to blaspheme against the Lord," Father Trimbach countered.

"Man can blaspheme in stone if he so desires. What I see in this new machine is more revelation than proof—"

"And what is your revelation?"

"That each man and woman imparts something of their soul or essence onto this world. We can see clearly in photograph and moving pictures that the spirit is animated; in this simple way, man can impart something of himself through his words and actions that extends beyond his place and time. Therefore, even the atheist must recognize that just as the moving picture pulls the image of men from the world, so too will God call upon the spirit of men, through Christ Jesus our Lord, and grant them the gift of everlasting life in his Heavenly Kingdom."

His explanation had quieted Father Trimbach's objections.

In the weeks and years that followed, he had relished the opportunity to discover more moving-picture shows during his parish stay in Berlin, Ontario, before moving west for his next assignment in Humboldt, Saskatchewan. He especially enjoyed the films of Charles Chaplin. Chaplin's simple, well-meaning characters were amusing and generally created havoc in the lives of miserly aristocrats, arrogant strongmen, and anyone else who might try to dominate the little guy. And, for Father Selz, this was just fine. He was sure his parishioners would love the Little Tramp too, and if it all contested the views of dear old Mrs. Stolz and Mrs. Zerr and their lot, so much the better.

Father Selz took special care in his selection of organizers. He charged Sebastian Feist with organizing the men's baseball game, as Sebastian owned several baseballs and was known to make good wooden bats. He asked Fredrich Gerein to organize the family contests: the tug-o-war and the three-legged races. "And add something for the young men too," Father Selz said, with a telling grin. Fredrich, an avid card player and helpless gambler, smiled. "I have some ideas," he said. Joseph Eberle jumped at the opportunity to orchestrate and set off the several dozen fireworks that had been purchased as the evening's finale. And, as it was Joseph's way to embellish his duties, soon the whole town was abuzz with rumours of cannon fire and explosives and hot air balloons raining confetti and ribbons from the sky. Andreas Stolz, a man who loved the attention of a crowd and always had a joke that hadn't been heard before, was assigned the role of talent-show organizer. Soon the local shopkeepers were adding to the fun—Mr. Ball promised Coca-Cola and Orange Crush to the winners of the contests, and Mr. Fetsch promised a piece of chewing gum for every child, while for the grand prize in the raffle, Mr. Zahn donated a single shot .22 caliber rifle with a thumb trigger. And, since his plans for the day would stretch beyond the afternoon and late into the evening, Father Selz commissioned the parish women to prepare not one but two meals to sustain the merriment of the day's festivities. For this, he consulted with Mrs. Gutenberg and Mrs. Feist, whom he knew to be capable and earnest task managers. However, when it came to his most exciting plans—showing the first moving-picture show to his flock of German-speaking immigrants—Father Selz made the arrangements himself.

ço

The church overflowed. The pews were packed and in the aisles it was standing room only. The windows and doors swung wide, carrying the sounds of the prairie birds and crickets and the crackling rustle of sun-dried grasses through the room as a light breeze teased the sweaty collars and foreheads of the gathered faithful. There were nearly 300 of them. Word had travelled far and wide and people from as far as ten miles away had dressed their families in their Sunday best and hitched their wagons to make the morning Mass. There were two rows—more than 60 wagons—parked on the open prairie, and others were scattered along the roadway.

Father Selz was thrilled by the turnout. The room buzzed with excitement. The normally reserved and reverent folks passed each other frequent and jolly looks. There was a tipsy sense of impending disorder that revealed itself in more than a few suppressed laughs, a handful of elbows to the ribs, and more than a few dozen winks. Father Selz was not immune to the giddy and impatient current of the day and somehow managed to dispense with nearly 15 minutes of the Latin Mass. The church emptied in a rush, the littlest ones hoisted from the ground by their siblings and parents to save them from the trampling path of the herd.

Outside, Mrs. Gutenberg and Mrs. Feist took charge of things. Their husbands had, before the service, dutifully set up the long serving tables, and now shifts of women loaded them with fresh bread, roasted meat, cheeses, sauerkraut and pickles. Father Selz blessed the meal, and the men, women and children ate the picnic meal among their kin and neighbours—some in the shade of the church and others sitting on blankets in big circles on the summer grass.

After the midday meal was over and the plates and dishes had been cleared away, Father Selz set up his camera to take the first parish photograph. It was nearly an hour in the making. The children running helter-skelter were eventually corralled toward the church steps and lawn. The young women called out for their husbands, making sure that they had not slipped away at the last minute.

The men's choir took its place on the stairs of the church, and the rest of the congregation sprawled out below—the single men stood to the back, in front of them were pockets of married men and women and some of the elders (minus Mrs. Stolz and Mrs. Zerr and their husbands), and, spreading out and onto the grass, the children took their places in descending order of age, some wearing newly handmade suits or summer dresses as they sat or kneeled in the grass and the sun shone down on them all. The breeze blew fresh enough to keep the men and boys in their Sunday jackets. Father Selz beamed with pride. This gathering was no small feat, but he—they—had done it. He took one last mental image of his flourishing happy congregation before hunkering down behind the camera. He focused the lens.

"*Ein, zwei, drei!*" Flash!

II

Bernhard Holtz felt the soft coolness of his daughter's tiny hand in his own rough, sweaty misshapen paw. Elisabetha's small fingers explored his hand for the severed finger. He watched her trace the wound as Father Selz went on about something from his lectern. The three-year-old looked up at him with sad, caring eyes and pulled on his hand in that way that signalled she needed to whisper a secret into his ear.

"Does it hurt, Daddy?"

Each word tickled his ear with a kind of crisp heat. He smiled and shook his head. "Not any more," he told her. "You made it better." And he truly believed it.

He'd been an angry kid who turned into an angry man who found all sorts of trouble—fighting and stealing, but fighting, mostly. He'd inherited his anger, just as he'd inherited his barrel chest and his big nose, from his father. At ten years old, he'd stood up to his father's aggression, coming to the defense of his younger brother, Christian, while his older brothers sat quiet. Later, they taunted him for his bravery and the lashes on his backside, but he knew their secret: they were cowards. It was only his mother and Christian who showed him kindness in his suffering, and he'd never forgotten it. The beatings stopped just before he turned 14, when his father died quite suddenly from a bad heart. Perhaps if he'd had the chance to properly fight his father it might've calmed his spirit. Instead his anger seemed to flood out in all directions.

His drinking hadn't helped things either. If he was alone he was fairly harmless, lost in his own dark thoughts, but if there were people around his temper was sure to flare. Over the years, he had managed to offend more than his share of the farm folk—first in North Dakota, and, later, here in Saskatchewan— and those he hadn't offended were either friends or kin with the rest of them, and therefore held him in no higher esteem.

Still, he had changed, mellowed over the years, although he knew there were some who would never believe it. He'd had no other choice but to change. He had gone as low as he could without dying. It had been a slow turnaround. Meeting Katherine had strengthened him, given him the determination to slow his drinking, but it was their daughter Elisabetha who gave him the fuel he needed to carry on. Without his wife and daughter, he knew with certainty that his loneliness and frustration would bring him back to the bottle, and after that he'd be lost to his old ways. No one wanted that, least of all him.

⁓

Bernhard couldn't bear the wait. It seemed the priest would go on forever blessing the congregation and saying this and that about the festivities to follow. He sighed. Then, as the men's choir sang the last verse of their closing hymn, Bernhard picked Elisabetha up in his arms and carried her outside. Seeing that he'd lost Katherine and young Frank in the hustle and bustle of the folks streaming from the church, he set Elisabetha on the ground and turned back to scan the crowd. The congregation had broken into little groups, with the young men to one side kicking stones and stealing glances at the young women who pretended not to notice; while the married men laughed at each other's jokes as their wives chatted free from their children, who were busy chasing each other through and around the rings of adults.

"Daddy, I play with the kids," Elisabetha said.

He looked to the girl and shook his head. "Wait, my little mouse. We need to find Momma first."

He eyed the crowd for Katherine and crossed the cold stare of Kaspar Feist's son, Jakob, aimed at him through the crowd. Bernhard tried to ignore Jakob's glare and focus his thoughts on finding Katherine, but the look on Jakob's face took him back ten years to another July and what was probably the lowest point in his life.

Bernhard had just arrived in Canada along with about 40 other settlers from North Dakota, most of whom were either neighbours or kin. He'd been drinking nearly the entire trip. Angry at his failure to make something good from that land and at the land grabbers who'd offered him such a paltry sum to take it off his hands. At some point, he got it in his head to beat Kaspar Feist to the land titles office and take the quarter section of land Kaspar was wanting to farm for himself. He was still bent on revenge against the man: Kaspar was the one who'd set the fox trap that had mangled his hand. So he did it. He beat old Kaspar to the land. And yet, even as Bernhard left the land titles building with the coveted patent, he wasn't satisfied; rather, he was immediately overwhelmed with regret. Even in his drunkenness he knew he'd gone one step too far. The days and weeks that followed were among the worst of his life. He had embittered himself to, and made a lasting enemy of, Kaspar Feist, and Bernhard's whole family had become an object of scorn among their group of settlers. Even his brother Christian distanced himself from Bernhard. "I warned you not to do it, but oh no, you had to do it anyway. You've dug your own grave, and there are plenty who'd be happy to see you fall into it," were his brother's only words to him on the trail south to the homestead.

He knew he'd ruined his chances to make a clean and honest start on new land, yet he was too stubborn to make amends—had he traded his land to Feist the next day or the next week everything might have changed. But he hadn't taken that step.

So, he worked his ill-gotten land, cleared the rocks from it, fenced it, and watched his neighbours grow their fields and families and realized how much of life and living he misunderstood, and had been shut out of. In time, he befriended his brother Christian and his older brothers, Peter and Markus, whom they had followed north. Friendship and affection began to trickle into his life again after their forgiveness, and he started to think of himself as a better man than what most others thought of him.

The news of Frank Weran's death came as a great surprise to Bernhard and all of the settler families. It wasn't the first death in the community, but it was the first to leave behind a new wife and expectant mother. Bernhard had paid his respects to Frank at the wake, and thought little more of the whole thing. That is, until spring when, riding by the Weran farm, he saw Katherine with her sleeves rolled up, working the riding plough with her newborn child swaddled behind her. He had never imagined such a sight—a woman with her baby on a riding plough driving a pair of horses down a dirt field—nor had he ever seen a woman look more beautiful than she did, even with her face caked with dirt from the dust kicked from the horses' steps' mixed with the sweat of her brow. It must be difficult to control the riding plough while wearing a dress, he thought. He approached her almost shyly, and offered to help, but she tried to send him away. She told him it was her land to farm, and farm it she would. But he insisted.

"I've already sent my brother away," she told him.

"I have less land to farm than your brother. Let me help you."

"No thank you," she said once more.

He tried a different tack. "If Frank were here, he wouldn't want to see you working with his newborn tied to your back."

"He ain't here," she said curtly. Then she whipped the team of quarter horses onward.

"You're going to scare away all your suitors if you keep this up," he teased, calling back to her.

"Good," she hollered back at him as her plough cut through the prairie.

He made a point of riding past her farm on his way to or from town. He'd invent some reason to make conversation and she'd send him away again and again. But somewhere in their game of back and forth they softened toward one another. He no longer stressed the virtues he could offer or dared to call her stubborn or hard-headed, or chastise her for spoiling her feminine virtues by doing men's work, and she'd entertain his hunting stories and listen to his helpful advice on how to clip the horses' hooves or butcher a pig and humour him by not telling him she already knew how to do those things. Because they'd both come to realize they needed someone to talk to and to share the small parts of their day.

During harvest, he put his own field work on hold and helped her. She told him to go back to his own work, but he turned a deaf ear and leveled his sickle against the crop. She let him be and they worked quietly together and apart. With help from her brother, Nels, and his wife, Agatha, they finished with plenty of time for Bernhard to return to his crop, and with the help of his brothers he was no further behind. The following spring, she took him up on his offer to help with the seeding work. In the summer, she invited him to have dinner with her and her toddler, Little Frank, or Frankie, as she called him. He brought a young kitten for her and the boy. It was the most handsome of the new litter, a black long-haired cat with a splash of white running down from its nose to its chest. They named it Scratch, as that was the first thing it did when Bernhard handed it to Little Frank. The child dropped the cat and scrunched up his face as though he might cry, but he didn't. He just patted its head, one, two, three, times as if he were telling it, "No. Bad kitty." Bernhard and Katherine laughed as the boy disciplined the kitten, then Katherine touched Bernhard's wrist and held his hand in hers. Her touch rendered him speechless for a time, turned him into a bit of a smiling fool. He couldn't remember the last time he'd smiled for that long.

They had three more dinners over the course of the summer and to Bernhard each one seemed better than the last—she laughed at his jokes and teased him when he offered her advice on farming. He'd put away the bottle, didn't need it like he used to. He felt good. She was seeing him at what he knew was his best; God willing she'd never see him at his worst. Then harvest came and they combined their efforts first on her crop and later his, and once harvest was finished she invited him to dinner again.

"This time to celebrate," she said.

"I'd be happy to join you." He smiled.

She didn't know it yet, but it would be a special night. He had been waiting for an evening like this to ask for her hand in marriage. He knew it was risky. There was no telling how she might react, since he didn't really know how she felt about him other than that she liked his jokes. He certainly hadn't kissed her; although he'd imagined it ever since the day he saw her working in the field. As far as he could determine, it was a coin toss as to how she might feel about the prospect.

It was easier for him to imagine what others would say. They'd say he didn't deserve her, which was probably true. But he'd never relied on what other people told him when it came to doing or not doing something. Mostly, he'd just been foolish and impulsive, like with the quarter section, but this felt more calculated—maybe because he was scared. Or sober. In truth, he couldn't tell whether he was more scared she'd say, "yes" or "no." If she said "yes," he had a wife and a little boy to take care of, and if she said "no," he'd go back to his lonely life without the neighbourly visits, finding some companionship with his old friend, the bottle. It was a frightening feeling either way, but he had to do something.

He waited until the meal was over and they had cleared the table and washed the plates. She poured coffee and he waited for her to take her seat. He smiled nervously as he bent down on one knee and took her hand in his. "I'm not good at asking for things, Katherine, but I need to ask you if you'll marry me."

It seemed to Bernhard her face had filled with a mix of terror and surprise at his words, and it shook him. He stood up, embarrassed. "Forget I asked." He turned to leave.

"Wait!" She grabbed his arm; held it tight. He turned to her and slowly her grip loosened; her hand fell to his wrist. "You surprised me."

A shiver ran up his spine. It was terrible—how much he loved her.

"Will you let me think about it?"

"How long do you need?"

"I don't know."

A week later she gave him her answer. "Frankie keeps his father's land and his father's name," she said.

"Of course." He was halfway to the moon.

They were married before Christmas. Two years later, Elisabetha came to them, and he was happy all over again.

Outside the church, Bernhard shook off Jakob's scowl and scanned the crowd again. Katherine wasn't there. Fixing his eyes on the church door, he felt his chest tighten. It eased but only for a moment as she stepped out of the building followed by a man, the elevator agent, Charles Harrison. He remembered Harrison from the Zerr wedding a month earlier. He'd noticed the young man eyeing Kathrine from a distance. His long looks had irritated Bernhard more than any nasty look Jakob Feist had ever directed his way, and he'd have done something about that too, if Katherine hadn't asked to leave. Bernhard had put it out of his head until now, but seeing Harrison's big toothy smile infect Katherine had brought it all back like a steaming locomotive. She said something to Harrison and smiled in a way Bernhard had rarely seen.

"Let's go to Mother," Bernhard said. He picked up Elisabetha and walked back through the crowd toward his wife. He hated crowds.

&

Bernhard stood ready at third base. He had no glove. He reminded himself he should buy one or make one; he had forgotten how much he enjoyed the game. At the pitcher's mark, Joseph Eberle hurled another fastball. The batter, Andreas Stolz, swung at the pitch and like lightning the ball was flying toward Bernhard. He stepped to his right and cupped the bullet shot in his outstretched hands. Three out.

He tossed the ball to the pitcher's mark and walked back to the spattering of coats and blankets that was the team bench. Katherine smiled. "Good catch!"

"It was a hard one," he said. "My hands sting."

The congratulations and back patting continued as the other men returned from the field. A drink was offered, but he waved it away and took his seat next to Katherine and Elisabetha. He watched with curiosity as Katherine pulled the child close to her and began to braid her brown shoulder-length hair. Her hands moved with such speed and intention that the process seemed more machine than human, like one of those mechanical binders. He noticed Katherine's eyes survey the Sunday crowd as her hands worked the mane of hair; her attention moved to Mr. Harrison as he went to fetch the bat. A slight smile crossed her face when Harrison caught her glance. It was there and gone just as fast. That made it twice he'd caught them smiling at each other.

Katherine finished the braid and patted the girl's backside. "Now go show Papa."

The little girl spun around looking for her father. She turned one and a half revolutions before her eyes landed on Bernhard. "Papa," she said. "See." She pointed to her hair with a bent arm and upturned palm.

Bernhard laughed. "Oh, my little mouse, Momma made your hair so pretty."

The child nodded. Her eyes gleamed with pride.

The first pitch went wild and rolled off into the distance. Bernhard watched a pair of young children race for the runaway ball.

"Where's Frankie?" Katherine said excitedly, to no one in particular. She turned to Nels. "Have you seen Frankie?"

"He's over there with Lambert." Nels pointed to a group of kids playing kick the can some hundred yards away. "Don't worry, I told Lambert to keep an eye on him."

"Thank you," Katherine sighed, as she stared out into the distance.

The ball came in and Bernhard held Elisabetha tight as Harrison got ready for another pitch. Harrison hit the ball deep into right field and ran to first base. The crowd struck up a chorus of cheers, Katherine included. Bernhard spat. He was getting a sick feeling in his gut. He got to his feet, picked up Elisabetha and tossed her in the air. The child laughed and he squeezed her in his arms. He turned away from the game to watch Little Frank and the boys playing. Things were easier for kids, he thought. They didn't know what awaited them when they got older, only parts of it, small parts. He hadn't known these things when he was a child. Yet he doubted whether it would have changed anything if he had. He was weak. That hadn't changed. Katherine had helped him ease off the booze, but now he wasn't so sure. Booze couldn't hurt him like Katherine could.

The boys kept on chasing each other. Actually, it dawned on him, they weren't chasing each other; they were chasing Little Frank. The bigger kids—Lambert and Sebastian Feist's boy, Ignaz—were trying to catch him. Ignaz gained on Frank and gave him a two-handed push to the back that sent him sliding face first into the short prairie grass.

"Damn it!" said Bernhard. He set Elisabetha on the ground.

"What is it?" Katherine asked.

"Frank," he said, and he ran to the children. The other kids were standing over Frank when Bernhard got there. Ignaz and Lambert each grabbed one of Frank's arms and hoisted the boy up.

Bernhard looked Frank over; his hands were covered in fresh scrapes. He turned to Ignaz—the boy had more than a foot on Frank. Bernhard felt his insides boil. "You stupid kid." The boy stood there, frozen, looking like he didn't know whether to pee his pants or run off. Bernhard picked Ignaz up like a young calf, forced him over his knee, and spanked the boy on the buttocks three times. "Don't be pushing the little ones." Spittle shot from Bernhard's mouth.

Ignaz stood holding his backside while he held back his tears.

"You didn't have to do that," Frank said. "We were only playing a game."

Bernhard shook his head at the boy. "He's older than you. He should know better." Then he turned to Lambert. "And you! You have to stand up for your cousin next time someone pushes him."

Lambert looked down at the ground. "Yes, sir."

Another voice called from behind them. "Leave those boys alone!" It was Kaspar Feist. The old man was hobbling toward him as fast as his legs would go and looking as angry as a bull. Behind him Nels hurried to catch up.

"He pushed Frank," said Bernhard.

"You talk like you've never pushed another man in your life," Kaspar scoffed.

"Why do you care? This ain't your boy."

"He's my blood," Kaspar said. "That might not mean much to you, but it means something to me."

Nels made up the distance and stepped between Bernhard and Kaspar. Holding his arms up between them, Nels looked from one to the other as he spoke. "No sense turning this into part of the war between you two—this is just boys being boys."

"I don't have no problem here," Bernhard said. "The Feist boy just needed some straightening out."

Nels shook his head. "These boys are big enough to sort things out themselves."

Bernhard kicked the ground, tearing the mottled lichen and thin prairie grass from the dirt. If it'd been someone other than Nels talking to him like this he'd have knocked them back into their place. Still, maybe, Nels was helping him out. He could feel the weight of the folks watching in the distance. Bernhard spat at the dirt he'd laid bare; his bleak eyes narrowed in on the Feist boy, bidding him to wash the scowl from his face. The boy clenched his jaw and lowered his eyes to the mark Bernhard left in the sod.

"Now don't push so much," Nels said to the boys. "It's the Lord's day." Then he turned to Kaspar and Bernhard. "Let's go."

"Watch yourself," Kaspar warned Bernhard, and he followed Nels back to the diamond.

Bernhard shook his head in disgust. He'd heard enough of the old man's threats to last him a lifetime. Yet, it was Nels who'd disappointed him. He should stand up for his blood. Didn't he understand how important Little Frank was? He was the last link to his father—without the boy there was nothing but a dead man in a grave.

He walked back to the diamond thinking he needed a drink.

ᏟᎧ

Joseph was at the plate. He hit a fly ball to the infield that was easily caught by the shortstop, Jakob Feist. Joseph handed Bernhard the bat. "Go hit something," he said. "It'll make you feel better."

It wasn't a drink, but maybe Joseph was onto something. Bernhard took a practice swing and whipped the bat through the air; as he snapped his wrists a burning sensation shot up his forearm. He grimaced. There was always some annoyance. Tucking the bat under his armpit, he spat into his palms and rubbed them together, then walked to the plate.

Old Gutenberg was pitching. He threw a fastball inside; Bernhard swung and missed. The pain flashed through Bernhard's wrist and forearm and was gone just as fast. There was something in the pain that he liked. He took another swing between pitches just to feel it once more. The next pitch came and he tipped it foul. The feeling was there. It was good, almost like a drink, but not quite. Gutenberg wound up and the third pitch whizzed toward him. Bernhard swung and hit the ball deep into left field. He ran to first and caught sight of Harrison speeding past third base toward home. The ball was still in the outfield. Bernhard turned for second, making it without contest. He stopped there. Breathless. He looked back to the team and waved to Katherine. She waved back. Then Harrison approached her. Katherine said something that Bernhard couldn't quite make out; the two of them smiled. Harrison said something back to her and it seemed as though they were laughing. Bernhard could feel his anger burn.

"I have an old ox that moves faster than you," Jakob Feist said. "He's better looking too."

Bernhard shook his head. He couldn't get away from this

Feist family. He'd never meant to hurt Jakob all those years ago, but he couldn't fault the kid for growing up bitter. "Is that why you're still not married?" Bernhard returned.

Jakob kicked the dirt in the direction of third base and looked off toward the mishmash of folks sitting in the grass, where Harrison was flashing his easy-going smile in the direction of Katherine and Elisabetha. "Well, it looks like your wife has made a new friend."

Bernhard clenched his teeth. "I'll shut you up."

"I'd like to see you try," Jakob said. "I ain't some eleven-year-old boy."

The men stepped toward each other, pulled by invisible strings. Bernhard raised his fists, but Jakob struck first sending a hard right that caught Bernhard above the eye.

Bernhard shook off the punch and an expression of quiet amusement crept onto his face. He snickered. Bernhard could take a punch better than most men. There was something in the pain that eased him. It was as good as a drink, maybe better. He watched the fear creep into Jakob's eyes. This didn't surprise him. After all it was his special gift, his secret weapon; there weren't many men who knew how to fight against laughter. He drove a hard right into the kid's jaw sending him off balance; he followed with a left to the gut that knocked the air out of Feist and dropped him to the ground. Then they were on him, dragging him off the field toward the third base line.

He didn't struggle; he didn't resist; he let them take him. Words went flying into his ears. They were calling him all sorts of things, but he heard nothing new.

Nels and Christian met the group at the third baseline like guards meeting an arriving prisoner.

"We got him," Christian said.

Bernhard looked for Katherine. She was holding Elisabetha and Harrison stood behind her. He walked towards them. He had it all worked out. He softened his gaze so his eyes wouldn't betray the rage he was holding inside him. Then, when he was close enough that he knew no one could stop him, he broke loose from Nels and Christian, darted past Katherine, and tackled Harrison to the ground. Landing square on top of Harrison, Bernhard let loose a flurry of punches but Harrison raised his arms and shielded his face from the blows. Furious, Bernhard tore at Harrison's raised arms as Nels, Christian, and Joseph pulled him off Harrison and hauled him away towards the parked wagons.

Bernhard looked back to find Katherine consoling Elisabetha. Tears poured down the little girl's cheeks as she trembled in her mother's arms. Katherine stared back at him. Her face tense. Her brow knit and her bottom lip pulled tight. His heart sank. He'd never scared them or shown his anger in front of them like that before. Goddamn Harrison. He'd pay for this.

"What's going on?" Christian demanded. After they'd steered him far from the crowd.

"You shouldn't have stopped me."

"Why's that?"

Bernhard looked around to check who had followed them. He didn't want any gossiping ears, or Katherine, for that matter, listening in. "That Harrison fellow, he's been following Katherine around all day long." He turned to Nels. "You can't expect me to sit around and not do something about it."

Nels looked to Joseph and Christian, but they only shook their heads. Nels shrugged. "I hadn't noticed."

"Jakob Feist did."

"He's just trying to rile you," Christian said.

Bernhard huffed. This wasn't about the Feists. "What would you do?" The men were quiet. "Come on. You're all married."

Joseph looked back to the thinning crowd gathered around Harrison. "He's not one of us."

"I don't think that matters." Nels's brow knit tight. "I'd be lying if I said I wouldn't hit a man if he was trying to disgrace my wife. Still, I wouldn't be doing it in front of the town, no less Agatha and the children."

Bernhard nodded in agreement. Nels was right. Bernhard had often regretted not keeping a cooler head, but he could never seem to remind himself when the time came.

"What you have to do is talk to him." Joseph checked over his shoulder to see if anyone was close behind him. "Scare him. And bring others with you so he understands you're not alone—"

"And do it where no one's watching," Nels added.

"Let's do that," Bernhard agreed.

Christian folded his arms. "You're forgetting he's the grain buyer."

"There's more than one in this town," Bernhard replied. "And he needs us probably more than we need him."

Nels scratched his moustache. "I don't know about that."

"I need your help. If it's me alone with him—God forgive me for what I might do."

Christian kicked at the ground. "Don't be stupid."

Joseph looked to Nels. "He can't be alone."

Nels sighed. "Fine, I'll go with you, but don't you try to hit him."

"I won't touch him. He already knows what I can do with my fists. I'll just tell him what he can expect if he talks to her again."

"I don't like this," Christian said. "But I'll come."

Joseph agreed.

"Good. We'll do it today," Bernhard said. "Right after the moving-picture show and before the fireworks start."

"It'll have to be quick," Joseph said. "I'm in charge of the fireworks."

"Oh, we all know that," Nels teased.

"It'll only take a couple minutes," Bernhard replied. "Nels, if you can get him around the back side of the church, we'll have our words, and it's done."

Christian looked over Bernhard's shoulder. "Katherine's coming this way."

Bernhard turned. There she was. "Before the fireworks."

The men nodded.

Joseph fixed the belt around his waist. "I gotta get back to the farm and do my afternoon chores. I'll see you tonight."

"Me too," Christian said; and, the two of them walked off towards their wagons.

Nels and Bernhard watched Katherine approach. "She can't know," Nels said, under his breath.

Bernhard nodded.

"Nels, will you let us speak alone," Katherine said.

"Of course." He feigned a smile. "How about I take Little Elisabetha with me and let you two talk?" The little girl was standing next to Katherine, hiding in the folds of her mother's long dress.

"She can stay with us," Bernhard said.

Nels looked to his sister.

"It's fine."

Nels tipped his hat and headed back to the picnic.

"Why did you do that?"

Bernhard thought to ask her the same question but stopped. He was scared there might be a truth that lie underneath her answer. One he couldn't bear to know.

"Tell me."

"I didn't like the way he was looking at you," Bernhard said.

She closed her eyes for a moment, then opened them. "You can't do that. Not here. Not anywhere."

"Your brother just told me the same thing."

"We should go home," she said. Her body trembled in the warm July sun.

"And miss the moving pictures? No, it's too important for Frank and Elisabetha." He didn't want to be the reason the children missed something that the entire community had come out to see. "Everything will be fine. Go and help the other women with supper and I'll come find you when I get back."

"You're leaving?"

"It's time I go back and do the chores."

"Do you think I want to be here now, after what you've done?"

"I won't be long."

"You'll miss supper."

"Then save me some."

She shook her head. No.

Katherine had never been so cold toward him, but then they'd never had a day like this before. He picked up Elisabetha and gave her a kiss on the cheek. "I think she needs a nap." He handed their child to his wife.

"I know," Katherine said.

He watched them walk back to the picnic. He was happy to be leaving now. There were too many people; too many people that didn't like him. Better to get away and think, and maybe even have a drink at the house. He should've brought something with him.

He headed toward the wagon. The sun was still high. It wouldn't take much longer than three hours. He'd be back in time for the moving-picture show. Already there were a dozen fewer wagons than an hour ago. Everyone had the same idea. Gripping the lip of the wagon box with one hand, Bernhard sank down on his haunches to check the rear wagon wheel. He thought he'd seen a broken spoke. The next thing he heard was the sound of bone cracking behind his ears and echoing through his skull. Everything else was a buzz. There was no more sound. Only buzzing. He was aware his knees were no longer supporting him and then everything went dark.

III

She had noticed him in church—he was on the other side of the room, a row ahead of her—and he was the only thing she could think of. It was awful wasn't it, not only to have these covetous thoughts in church but also while standing next to one's own husband and children. Of course, she made every effort not to stare or draw attention to herself; a slight shift of the eyes was all that was needed to admire him. Yes, he was attractive—he was tall and young-looking with perfect teeth and a pleasant smile—but there was something more to him, a sort of confidence that didn't match the other men in Kaidenberg. It seemed silly. She barely knew him and perhaps that was it—she was making stories to fill the spaces between what was known and unknown about Mr. Harrison.

She had to get out of the church without speaking to him.

That much she knew. She'd follow Bernhard out and get lost in the crowd, then maybe she'd find one of the older women to chat with and they'd go on and on about something and everything would be fine. That'd work for the time. Maybe later in the afternoon it would be fine if they said hello, just once, casually, at some point when not much was happening or too much was happening for anyone else to notice. It'd be no particular moment, a moment just like any other, except for her it'd be the most important of the day.

Before she knew it, the choir was singing their closing hymn and the priest had returned to his sacristy. There seemed to be a race for the door as folks from both sides of the aisle piled in, shoulder to shoulder. Bernhard and Elisabetha were already thick in the pack more than a dozen feet ahead of her, and while they slowly advanced she seemed to be stuck where she was. None of this would have bothered her much, if she hadn't to worry about Mr. Harrison catching up with her as she walked out of the church. Oh, how the rumour mill would churn! She reached for her son's hand but Frankie pulled away from her and zigzagged through the stream of people. She moved with the rest of the crowd, smiling and saying hello to the people next to her as she went. Bernhard and Elisabetha were out of sight, beyond the tall boys and men that shuffled in front of her.

"Good morning, Mrs. Holtz."

She recognized the voice and shuddered. Although she wished she could ignore it, something compelled her to look over her shoulder. His smile radiated a life of optimism and laughter. "Good morning, Mr. Harrison," she replied and proceeded to step into Mr. Gutenberg's eldest son, bumping her chin on his shoulder. "Pardon me."

"Are you all right, Mrs. Holtz?" said Harrison.

"I'm fine, thank you," she said, blushing. She quickened her pace, trying to put a step between her and Mr. Harrison as they approached the church doors.

"Will you be around for the photograph?" he asked.

"Only if I can hide in the church," she joked, as she stepped into the sunshine.

He smiled. "Well, that would be a sad thing for all of us."

"That's kind of you to say." She returned his smile, then hurried down the church steps and disappeared into the crowd. She plucked a handkerchief from the sleeve of her dress and squeezed it in her palms. It was a mean thing, the way he made her feel: she wanted to run to him and from him in the same breath. Before she could do either, her sister-in-law, Agatha, grabbed her by the arm.

"Come with me," said Agatha. "We need help getting the food out. People have to eat. People always have to eat."

❧

She felt as though she were trapped in a dream that wasn't quite a nightmare and certainly wasn't a fantasy either. It was Mr. Harrison's doing. She had barely escaped him after church—had found some reprieve while she helped the other women with the meal service—but, now here he was playing ball with Bernhard and the other men. She wished he'd go somewhere else and leave her in peace, or was that only a lie she told herself in hope that she might come to believe it. In truth, she liked watching him, just not with Bernhard around. He'd been flooding her thoughts and dreams with sinful cravings for weeks now. She hadn't felt stirred like this in years; truly, she doubted whether she'd felt anything quite like this before. She wondered if it was possible that she might be in love with Mr. Harrison. He certainly wasn't like Bernhard and, while Harrison was handsome like her late husband, Frank, he didn't seem to have Frank's conceit or aggressiveness, which made her think it was possible. The only thing she could be certain of was that the way her body ruled her thoughts when she thought of him was surely sinful.

She knew hardly anything about Mr. Harrison. They'd met for the first time little more than a month ago, but it had been a remarkable meeting—with him coming to her aid on the evening of Markus Zerr and Anna Dudenhafer's wedding.

Katherine had stepped out from the celebration to take in the cool night air. Seeing the bride's joy and excitement as she danced with her new husband had reminded her too much of her wedding to Frank. It should have been a happier moment in her life, she thought, as she wandered toward the moonlight. It should have been a celebration like this one, but her fear had gotten in the way of her happiness. She had been happy to be married, but she worried about the wedding night. All the happiness it should hold had been stolen from her some years before. It still seemed too soon, but there was nothing to be done. No one she could tell. That said, there probably would never have been a good time for a wedding. She'd been ruined and that didn't just clean up.

Her eyes focused on the dark silhouettes cast by the row of horses and wagons lined in the farmyard, as she remembered the shame she felt that first night with Frank, her tears and his single-mindedness. It wasn't right. He hadn't been right. But could she blame him? It was their wedding night. She certainly couldn't tell him. That was another cruelty in the matter. Frank died not knowing her secret.

On a summer night much like this, someone had grabbed

her, slammed her to the ground and knocked her out. After that she remembered nothing. She woke in darkness, her mouth caked with the bitter taste of dirt and dried grass, like old sunshine decayed. She hurt inside—lower—between her legs. She felt sick, a sense of death clouded her mind, a piece of herself hadn't returned with her. Even now, she still feared night.

Now, tonight, she found herself beside one of the parked wagons. She ran her fingers along the dry, grainy flesh of the weather-beaten wagon box, then the stillness of the night exploded with the snapping bark of a spooked dog sounding close to her ear. Katherine jumped back from the wagon; tripping on the hem of her dress, she fell to the ground. The dog snarled and gnashed its teeth from its perch above her.

"Git! Git!" shouted a man from somewhere behind her. He approached them and for a moment it wasn't only the dog she feared. She crawled away from them both shielding herself behind a wagon wheel. The man spoke to the dog with a calm, commanding voice that slowly settled it. Then he turned to her. "It's safe," he said. He reached out to help her stand. She hesitated, but he was patient. When she took his hand she could tell that he was strong, although his hands were not as rough as Bernhard's.

"Are you hurt? Did it bite you?"

"No, it only startled me," she said, trying to remember how it was she ended up here in the first place.

"That's a relief." She could see his smile shining in the moonlight. "It's probably safer on the dance floor," he said. "Will you join me?"

She wanted to say "yes." His face was young and warm and she liked everything about him, even the strange way his German sounded. "I couldn't," she replied. He nodded politely and it seemed her slight rejection did little to dampen his good cheer. She smiled then looked back to the barn where the music from the wedding celebration continued to play. Two figures stepped out from it. "I must go," she said. "Thank you, Mister...?"

"Harrison. Charles Harrison."

"Mr. Harrison. Thank you. I'm Katherine... Mrs. Holtz."

Without any further words she walked back to the barn and the wedding celebration. Inside, she stood by the door and watched Frankie dance with the other children, while Bernhard joked along with a group of dirt farmers, and her sister-in-law Agatha bounced Little Elisabetha on her hip and twirled her daughter across the dance floor. She realized she was smiling, but whether she was smiling because of them or her new acquaintance, Mr. Harrison, she dared not ask herself.

❦

He was standing in front of her now with that winning smile holding up his cheeks as her fingers crisscrossed her young daughter's hair. He bent down and picked the bat off of the ground. His eyes focused in on her. She nearly blushed. The smile she yielded to him was, perhaps, the best and only recourse she could achieve without further revealing her secret desires. It was there in a moment and she put it away just as quickly. She could feel Bernhard's eyes on her; and, for a moment, she was angry with him. Angry that he loved her and forced himself into her world and made her feel something that wasn't quite love, but, perhaps, safer than love.

She finished Elisabetha's braids and passed the child to her father.

Elisabetha held her hands up to her head showing off her

braids. Bernhard smiled and Katherine's heart warmed. She couldn't count how many times she wished she had shared a moment like this with her late husband. If it had happened only once, Frank and his son together, it would be her most cherished memory. Instead, she felt like a fool. Always full of regret. She had a son who had his father's eyes, wasn't that the finest gift he could leave her? She had to cherish her son.

"Where's Frankie?" she cried out suddenly. She would never forgive herself if something happened to him while she indulged in her sinful thoughts. She turned to Nels and asked him if he'd seen her son. Nels pointed past the other spectators to where his son Lambert and Frankie were playing with some of the other kids, and assured her that Lambert was keeping a watchful eye on his younger cousin. She sighed her relief. Where would she be without Nels? He was always there when she needed him. She hoped Frankie and Elisabetha would become as close. Though sometimes she wondered if the two of them having different fathers might cause some sort of jealousy or division between them.

She let that thought slip away as she turned her attention back to the ball game. Mr. Harrison was still at the bat. Gutenberg's pitch whirled toward him. The hit was lightning quick. She cheered.

Then Bernhard jumped to his feet and a flash of fear shot up the back of her neck. "What is it?" she asked, fearful that he'd discovered her secret fantasy. She almost sighed with relief when he said, "Frank," and hurried off towards the boys, but it was fleeting. Her heart sped up when she spotted her son lying in the grass surrounded by the other boys. She prayed to God that Frankie wasn't hurt, asking Him not punish the boy for his mother's sins.

"Thank you, God!" she said under her breath when Frankie sat up. It seemed everything might be fine. She almost smiled, except she was afraid such an outward show of gratitude might work against her, and like that she saw Kaspar Feist hurry past her in pursuit of Bernhard. "They'll fight," she said to herself, but loud enough that it caught Nels's attention. Her eyes pleaded with him.

He shook his head and rushed to catch them.

Katherine brought Elisabetha to her lap, as Bernhard grabbed Ignaz Feist and bent him over his knee. She felt sick. Helpless. And she wasn't the only one: Elisabetha had squished up her face in a distressed manner, threatening tears. "Oh darling, do you want to sing the baker's song with me?"

The makings of a smile crept across the little girl's face as she nodded her head. Yes. They sang and clapped their hands in rhythm:

Backe, backe Kuchen,
der Bäcker hat gerufen:
If you want to bake good cake,
seven items you must take—
eggs and salt, lard and butter,
milk and flour,
saffron gives the yellow colour.

The song had eased her daughter, but looking up to find the men at a standstill, Katherine was still troubled. It seemed they might still square off. She pulled Elisabetha closer to her. "I love you, darling," she whispered. Then, almost without reason, the men were at ease. They walked away. Things had settled. And she felt a calm pass through her.

Bernhard took a seat on the grass a couple feet from her. She could feel his eyes on her. She turned to look at him and he met her with a sour stare.

"The boy needed some discipline," he said.

"Did you have to be the one to deal it out?"

Bernhard huffed. She closed her eyes and wished to be somewhere else.

ல

Katherine watched Bernhard take the bat from Joseph and give it a practice swing. She could read the anger in his movements. The white-knuckled grip. He swung hard on the first pitch and missed the ball. He looked stiff to her—like his chest, shoulders and belly were fused together—as though he were a big piece of wood. What was eating at him?

He took another powerful swing. This time he hit the ball; it flew behind them, and she heard someone shout, "Foul ball." The next swing took the ball far into the field, the farthest anyone had hit all day. She cheered as Bernhard ran the bases. Mr. Harrison was running too and much faster than she'd imagined him capable of. He ran all the way from first base. He did it. They both did it. She waved to Bernhard, who had made it to second base. He was out of breath, but that didn't surprise her. She had seen him run only twice before, when the pigs had broken free from their pen. She smiled thinking about it. Then she realized Mr. Harrison was approaching.

She fumbled for something to say. "Good work."

"Thank you. Bernhard had a good hit."

She giggled. She didn't know why. It felt as though he was complimenting her. It had something to do with the way he smiled when he looked at her. "I didn't know you could run so fast." She immediately regretted it. Why did she say that? She wished she could do better at keeping her thoughts to herself.

"Yes," he began and then his eyes were off of her. His face turned very serious. "Oh no," he said. "That's not good."

She looked in time to see Bernhard throw one then two punches that knocked Jakob Feist first one way then the next. She pulled Elisabetha toward her. "Stay close to Mommy," she whispered to the girl.

"Papa's mad," Elisabetha said.

"Not at you." Katherine got to her feet and picked up her daughter. She kissed the child's forehead. "Papa loves you."

The men grabbed Bernhard and pulled him away from Jakob Feist. She knew there was bad blood between Bernhard and the Feists, but why did Bernhard choose today to start up with them? Perhaps this was more to do with Bernhard disciplining Jakob Feist's nephew for pushing Frankie. Maybe.

"Did you see it start?" she asked Harrison.

"I saw Jakob Feist punch Bernhard, then Bernhard—"

She had never seen Bernhard act this way before, but she wasn't completely surprised. She'd always suspected there was a hot coal in him that smouldered under the ashes. That fire had even comforted her at first; a strong, powerful man could protect a woman and child, or so she had thought.

A man on either side of Bernhard, they were leading him toward her. She could tell something wasn't right. He wore an odd expression on his face. It seemed he was looking right through her. She held Elisabetha tight.

Then Bernhard broke free of the men; it happened so quickly, she didn't know what to do. She closed her eyes and buried Elisabetha's head into her chest. The air swept across her cheek, the right side of her body, as he rushed by her. She heard groans and the dull sounds of bodies hitting and crumbling to the ground. She looked around: he'd gone after Mr. Harrison. A wave of guilt washed over her.

They pulled the men apart.

Katherine hushed her crying child. Poor Elisabetha. She felt Bernhard's eyes on her as they took him away; she stared back at him. *Damn you, Bernhard*, she wanted to scream.

❧

Katherine felt a little lighter once Bernhard had gone home to do the chores. She retreated to the church, laid the sleeping child in her arms down on the pew beside her, and closed her eyes in prayer. The words spilled through her lips in a murmur.

Footsteps invaded the quiet church. She opened her eyes and saw a man standing in a pool of dusty sunlight. It was Harrison. She was in no condition to see him. She closed her eyes in hope that he'd be gone when she next opened them.

"I'm sorry," he said.

She didn't have to open her eyes to know that he'd taken a seat next to her. She wiped a stray hair off her cheek and tucked it behind her ear.

"I believe I've caused a scandal and made you the centre of it."

She held her eyes shut, daring herself not to look into his. It seemed the only defense. There was no trusting what she might say if she did.

He went on: "I feel the need to be truthful, here in this space, completely truthful."

She gulped.

"I think you are a very lovely woman. Charming and brave and—"

She opened her eyes. "You can't say that. You don't know who I am. This is my doing. It's my penance." The words had surprised her, but they were as true as any she had ever spoken. Why was it that men always saw her as something other than what she felt inside? What gave them the right to make her into something she wasn't? They'd all done it—Peter, Frank, Bernhard, now Mr. Harrison too.

She stared at him. It seemed her words had washed away his youthful optimism. And, for the first time, she saw him as she felt—sad and disheartened. It was only right. That's how life was. It was time he knew it too. It was time they all knew it.

She looked down to her work-worn hands. She needed peace. "I'm sorry, if I gave you some false belief."

"You couldn't—"

"No," she continued, and looked him directly in the eyes. "You're a nice man, Mr. Harrison. I'm sorry my husband went after you."

He cleared his throat and got to his feet. "Thank you, Mrs. Holtz. You have no need to apologize." He flashed a brave smile that washed from his face like chalk in the rain.

She wiped her eyes as his footsteps carried him away from her.

IV

Jakob lay on the ground, folded over in pain, upset that he had allowed Bernhard to get the better of him. He sure hadn't expected Bernhard to laugh. It was strange and twisted and sent Jakob's courage running. Rolling onto his belly, Jakob picked himself up onto his knees. He massaged the ache in his jaw. It probably wasn't too bad, he told himself. Bruised but not broken. He looked for Bernhard and saw that the others were taking him aside.

"Are you hurt bad?" Kaspar, his father, asked.

"I'm fine," he said. "I got one in."

Kaspar extended him an arm and Jakob got to his feet in time to see Bernhard tackle Harrison.

"There he goes again," Jakob said.

"What's that about?"

"I believe Mr. Harrison has an eye for Mrs. Holtz. I told Bernhard as much myself." He touched his jaw, noting the raw pain. "Perhaps that was a mistake." His eyes strayed from the wrangle, off toward the other sideline where Annaliese Reichert was sitting. He'd been watching her weave a crown of wildflowers and now she was placing it on her little sister's head. A smile crossed his face as the younger sister ran away to show off her new crown, leaving Annaliese to her flowers. She was as beautiful as any one of those flowers, thought Jakob. She was much younger than him, maybe 18 or 19 years old to his 28; and, like many her age, she wore a long blue dress with a white band tied at her midriff. Although it was a simple outfit, the band highlighted her shape in a very pleasant way, and the colours seemed to draw his eye to her honey-coloured hair and sun-freckled face. He shook himself from his trance and turned to his father before she could catch him staring.

"You shouldn't have done that," Kaspar said, referring to Jakob's words with Bernhard. "He's an animal and you stuck a thorn in his side. What'd you think was going to happen?"

"Well, it looks like Nels has reined him in," Jakob replied. He looked around the diamond. It appeared all the commotion had put an end to the ball game. The outfielders had migrated infield and the opposition was divided into two groups. One group was walking away from them, and the other group was huddled around Mr. Harrison. And, once again, Jakob's eyes were pulled to the sideline. This time the Reichert girl met his gaze. Jakob heeled the ground with his boot, embarrassed the girl had seen him get knocked around. He liked her but he hadn't dared talk to her. He turned away again. She was pretty and he was shy. And, perhaps, that was the simple truth as to why he was still single. He started off toward the outfield.

"Where are you going?" Kaspar said.

He ignored him. His father was rarely his best ally.

"If you want to be brave in life, you have to be brave in every way," Kaspar called after him. "Not only with your fists."

Jakob turned around. "I'm brave, but I'm not so sure about you."

"That's no way to talk to your father!"

Jakob eyed his father. The man didn't intimidate him the way he once had. Yes, he was taller and probably stronger than his father, but there was more than just that. His father's eyes were less fierce than they had been only a few years ago and his shoulders slumped forward like a man sapped of his honour. "I did more today than you've done in the last ten years to repay Bernhard for stealing your land."

Kaspar shook his head and stared off toward where Nels and his gang were hauling Bernhard. Jakob was happy to see him go. "What good would've come from some small revenge?" his father asked. "It wouldn't change what happened."

Respect. Honour. Weren't they worth something? He didn't say it. Instead, he rolled his eyes at his father and marched past him towards the beautiful Annaliese. He breathed out deeply as he tried to steady himself and let go of his anger. By no means did he want to scare her away. Indeed, he felt quite the opposite; he needed to talk to her. And if he couldn't do it now, he wasn't certain when he might find the strength, because even as he approached her he found his courage diminishing the closer he got. And, while his heart continued to race, it seemed his feet were growing heavier and heavier. Even his palms turned sticky. He stopped a few feet from her. Tongue-tied.

"Hello," she said.

"Hello," he returned. "You're Leo Reichert's daughter, Annaliese."

She smiled. "And you're Mr. Feist's son, Jakob."

He nodded unsure of what to make of this. It felt much different than talking to his sisters. He felt much more uncertain.

"So, we both know who the other person is," she continued, filling the silence.

"Yes." He paused briefly thinking what to say next. "I'm not really sure what to say. I only know that I wanted to talk to you."

"That's very nice of you to say." She smiled. "I wanted to talk to you as well."

He smiled too and wiped the palms of his hands, not quite casually, on the backside of his pants.

"Did he hurt you?" she asked. "I was worried he had."

"My jaw is sore, but I'll be fine. I'm sure I can still eat."

She laughed; he liked her laugh.

"Why did you hit him?"

"We have our differences."

"I've heard he can be a hard man."

Jakob nodded not knowing what else to say.

"That was a good catch you made in the field," continued Annaliese.

"Thank you." He smiled and folded his arms over his chest.

"You said you wanted to talk to me, but you don't say much."

She didn't understand. There was too much he wanted to say,

not too little. From the first time he had seen her in church he had constructed a secret world where he could go to be with her. They could hold hands and watch the sunset and talk until the stars came out, and in the winter they could sit by the fire and play cards. And she would smile the way she had smiled at him that day in the church. It wasn't a regular smile. It was a smile of joy and celebration and love for the world and everything in it. He knew that smile, but it had been years since he had shown it himself.

"What are you smiling about?" she asked.

"I was thinking of the first time I saw you in church."

"Tell me."

"You were singing. I didn't see you right away, but I could tell there was a new voice that day. Yours was so beautiful, it made me shiver—" he stopped. Best not to tell her everything.

"That's very nice of you to say."

"I remember your smile." He paused. She had turned quiet. "You don't come to church often. I don't see you and your family—"

"We live near Crane Hills."

"Are you staying for the moving-picture show?"

"Yes, Father wants to see it. Mother thinks it's the devil's work. She says she's only going because it's in the church."

"Maybe she thinks God will stop it from showing," he said, then wondered if he shouldn't have.

"Yes," she laughed. "I think she'd be happy if it didn't work."

He smiled. "And what do you think?"

"I don't know. I'm not scared if that's what you're wondering. I think it will be like looking at a photograph: it looks real enough, but it's only an imitation of the people it shows."

"I never thought about it like that." He paused. There was a feeling he had from what she said and it felt important to tell her. "It makes me feel sad to think about it like that... pictures, I mean. They should be a happy thing, but they're only another kind of memory."

"I suppose it is sad, especially because the picture can still be here when the memory and the person are gone."

Jakob gazed at Annaliese—a wave of sadness and fear rose from his heart when he looked into her eyes. How did she think like that? Her thoughts were like pieces of coloured glass—he wanted to see through them, to see the world as she did—they were precious, yet there was something sharp about them too. They could cut through his thoughts and feelings and make him bleed.

"Is something the matter?" she asked.

"No," he replied. He only felt like he didn't want to stop being with her. "Might I bother to ask if you'd sit with me for the moving-picture show?"

She smiled. "That would be very nice."

V

Little Frank wasn't angry with Ignaz for pushing him. It hadn't hurt much—only a few scrapes on his hands. All he had to do was spit in his palms and rub them together like the others had and they'd be fixed up. If he was mad at anyone it was his step-father, Bernhard; he shouldn't have spanked Ignaz. He'd ruined their game.

"Are you a little crybaby?" Ignaz said to Little Frank, after the adults had gone.

"No."

"Then why did your father come out here? Crybaby."

"Bernhard isn't even his real father," Lambert said. "His real father died before he was born."

"He can be my father, if I want him to."

"You don't get to pick your father," Ignaz argued.

"God does," said another boy.

"No, your mother does," Ignaz said.

"It's both," Lambert said.

"It doesn't matter. My cousin Jakob says your father is a drunk and a thief and he only married your mother so he could steal your real father's farm."

"That's not true," Little Frank said.

"How do you know?" Ignaz replied. "He already stole your mother, and when they have a baby boy he's going to give all your things to him."

"You're lying." Frank looked to Lambert with desperate eyes. "Tell him he's lying."

"I don't know. He might be right."

"Look!" Andreas Stolz's son, Stefan, pointed toward the baseball field. "They're fighting."

Frank turned to see Bernhard shake off Jakob Feist's punch.

"See," Ignaz said. "My cousin knows your stepfather's no good."

Frank was silent. He didn't know how to feel. He didn't want to see Bernhard hurt, but he was scared that if Bernhard kept hurting people then maybe they were right and he was just a bad guy.

"Shoot," Ignaz said, as Bernhard knocked Jakob Feist to the ground with two punches.

"He's going to kill him," Stefan said.

"No," Ignaz said. "My father will stop him."

Frank felt the closeness of the other boys around him—the skip of their heartbeats and the weight of their breath on his shoulders and the back of his neck. Every slight glance and stare they aimed at him closed him in more. He wished Bernhard would stop. Instead the other men, Ignaz's dad included, had to pull him away.

"I'm glad he's not my father," Ignaz said.

"Me too," said another boy.

Lambert clapped Frank on the shoulder. "It's okay. He's not your real father."

Frank nodded. Lambert was right. Bernhard wasn't his real father. He'd never met his real father nor did he have a picture of him, but his mother often told him he looked like his father. That she saw him every time she looked into his eyes. It didn't work the same for him. He couldn't see his father; he only saw his own eyes. Still, he had his father's name and that was something, although he called Bernhard 'Father'. He wondered if he was more like Bernhard than his real father. Did it work that way? Was it like catching a cold? He tried to think of all the ways he was different from Bernhard—like, his nose wasn't big and red like Bernhard's, and he didn't like to eat horseradish and drink coffee like Bernhard did, and he didn't fart and burp and laugh like Bernhard did. He had manners like his mother, although Bernhard's stinky farts and burps made him laugh, especially when Bernhard made him pull his finger. Was that catching? Did that mean he might turn mean and angry like Bernhard too?

"Let's play, already," Stefan said.

Away from them, the men were dragging Bernhard off the field, and Little Frank wanted nothing more than to get back to the game. He tried to hurry past Ignaz as casually as he could, but the older kid reached out and grabbed him by the collar. Frank's guts began to wrench; surely, Ignaz was going to throw him to the ground or punch him in the face.

"Look!" Ignaz spun Frank around to see Bernhard crash into the man who'd being talking to his mother outside the church.

"He's going to kill that guy," Stefan said.

Frank swallowed hard. Would Bernhard kill someone? He didn't know. He couldn't be sure what he knew about Bernhard anymore; maybe he was sick, or maybe the other men were all wrong about something and Bernhard was trying to stop them.

"You shouldn't watch this," Lambert said.

"Why's he doing that?" Frank asked.

"My father says he's a drinker," Ignaz said.

Frank had heard his mother say something like that before, a long time ago, when Elisabetha was only a baby. It was the day he'd poured Bernhard's jug of booze onto the ground. It had tasted so awful that Frank had thought it was best to pour it out so the baby didn't drink it. When Bernhard saw what he'd done, his eyes got big and he yelled, *"Dummkopf."* Then Bernhard pulled down his pants and spanked him. Little Frank had never felt so embarrassed, so ashamed. No one had ever struck him before. Each strike of his stepfather's hand seemed to cut him open. He cried; so did his mother.

"I wish I'd never married you," she said. And that's when Bernhard stopped. He pulled up Frank's pants and left the soddie. Frank was so sore he couldn't sit down. His mother made him lie belly down on the bed and she put a cool cloth on his backside; she stroked his hair and sang to him until he fell asleep.

Frank shook his head and snapped out of the memory. "Can we just play kick the can?"

"You can't play with us anymore," Ignaz said.

"Yeah," Stefan agreed.

"Why?" Frank asked.

"They're just scared. They don't want you to hurt them," Lambert said.

"We're not scared," Stefan said.

"It's because your father is a thief and a bully," Ignaz said.

"That's not fair," Frank said. "He's not my real dad."

"Yeah," Lambert agreed. "Let him play."

"Only if you do something first," Ignaz said.

"What?"

Ignaz crossed his arms and didn't say anything. Stefan sidled next to him and whispered something in his ear. Ignaz smirked. "I got it," he said. "You've gotta prove he's not your father."

"But his real father's dead," Lambert said. "How's he supposed to prove it?"

Ignaz puffed up his chest. "He's gotta knock him to the ground."

"That's stupid," Lambert said. "You don't have to do that, Frank."

"Fine," Ignaz said, "and you don't have to be our friend either."

"Let's get out of here." Lambert said to Frank, but Frank didn't move. "Come on, Frank."

"I want to stay."

Lambert threw up his arms. "Well, I'm going," he said and walked away.

"Go run to your mother," shouted one of the boys.

"Crybaby," shouted another. This set off a chorus of laughter among Ignaz's admirers.

Ignaz capped off the moment by kicking the can with all his might and sending it flying away from all of them. "Let's go," he said to the other boys. "This crybaby can play by himself." And he walked off toward the can; the other kids followed.

Frank wanted to cry. He wanted to run to his mother and bury his face in her dress. He'd only wanted to play with the other boys. It wasn't fair. This was supposed to be the best day of the summer but it wasn't. Bernhard had ruined it, and there was nothing Frank could do to change it. If he told his mother and the other parents, then the older boys would get mad and call him names and it would be worse than it was now. An idea came to him—he could run away. Leave. That would show them. He'd run where they could never find him.

He started there. He ran from the boys, Lambert, his mother, everyone. None of them were watching anyways. He ran toward the wagons. He saw his uncle Nels and Bernhard talking with Uncle Christian and cousin Joseph. He had a thought: maybe, he could live with his uncle Nels and aunt Aggie, Lambert, and the rest of them. But that probably wouldn't work. His mother would make him come home and live with them, and then things would be worse because Bernhard would know he didn't want to be there. If that happened, he'd have no choice but to go and live by the lake where no one could find him. He could hide in the coulees and ravines and find an old badger hole to sleep in; he was small enough to fit and it'd keep him warm at night. There'd be rabbits to hunt and he could make a fire at night and no one would call him a crybaby or a scaredy-cat.

Frank was close to their wagon now. All he had to do was take it and go.

He climbed into the wagon box—carefully, so no one would see him and try to stop him. Peeking over the sideboards, he saw his mother and Elisabetha walking towards Bernhard and his uncles. He ducked for cover before anyone could spot him.

He thought about his plans a little longer. He wasn't sure how long he'd have to live by the lake. Winter would be tough. He'd need a good coat and a fire to keep warm. That'd be too long really; he'd miss Christmas—the songs and the cakes, and the Christmas apple too. Things would have to get fixed by then. Would Bernhard leave? He could hear Bernhard talking with his mother. He peeked over the side of the wagon again.

He heard Bernhard say, "I didn't like the way he was looking at you."

He couldn't hear his mother's words, but he could tell by the way she was speaking, with her hands clenched tight, she wasn't happy.

Little Frank wondered who it was Bernhard was talking about. Who was looking at his mother? He dropped back behind the side of the wagon and, crouching, he hit his foot on a fieldstone that had been left in the corner. Frank turned around to see it. It was smooth like one of the rocks by the lakeshore and the same smoky grey colour as Bernhard's booze jug. He wished he had that jug now. He'd throw it at him; knock it over his head. That'd be fair. Ignaz would have to let him play with them if he did that.

Sitting with his back to the side boards of the wagon, Frank hooked his foot on the far side of the rock, and dragged it closer to him. He picked up the rock with both hands. It was too big for him to hold up for long. The sides of the rock wore against the scrapes in his palms and he set it in his lap. He listened for their voices, but he couldn't hear them...maybe, they'd gone. Then he heard footsteps. He listened carefully. It was Bernhard. He was sure of it. He knew the sound of his breathing. He could try to throw the rock at Bernhard or let it drop on his toe. Frank stood up, but Bernhard wasn't there—just four fingers clinging to the lip of the wagon box, including the ugly one that made Frank shudder when it touched him. His eyes followed the arm downward to where Bernhard sat squatting next to the wagon wheel.

Frank set the stone on the ledge and let it fall. He hadn't meant—no, maybe he had. Bernhard was getting up just as the stone went down. For a moment, he thought Bernhard would stand up and smack his backside black and blue, but he didn't. He just fell to the ground. It seemed to Frank that Bernhard was staring up at him wondering what he'd done. Then Bernhard's eyes rolled back in his head.

Frank jumped off the back of the wagon and ran as fast as his legs could take him, which didn't seem very fast at all. It felt like he'd been loaded down with sand from the waist of his pants all the way down to the tips of his boots. Keep running, he told himself. But he didn't know where to go. All he knew was he had to hide. Frank stopped behind another wagon and took a deep breath. He hadn't imagined that could happen—that he could knock Bernhard out, maybe even kill him. What if he killed him?

He had to find a good hiding spot. Maybe he should take the wagon and go to the lake. Whatever he was going to do, he should do it fast before someone found out what he'd done. He turned the corner on the wagon and ran straight into a man. He nearly fell over but the man caught him by the shoulder. Frank tried to run around him but the man held him back. There was no getting past him.

"Where are you going so fast, son?"

Frank looked up at the man: he was old; it was Ignaz's uncle, Kaspar Feist. He wasn't this man's son. He was no man's son. "I'm not your son."

"You're right." Kaspar studied the boy. "You look like you've just seen a ghost."

"It ain't my fault," Frank said.

"What ain't your fault?"

"Let me go." Frank tried to run, but the old man was too strong. "Please, just let me go." Frank sobbed. "I didn't mean to kill him."

"What?"

"I didn't. I only wanted to scare him."

"What are you talking about?"

The boy grabbed Kaspar around the waist and cried into his jacket pocket. Kaspar patted Frank on the back. "It'll be fine," he said. "Show me."

Frank choked back his tears and took Kaspar's hand and walked him to where his stepfather lay on the ground.

"You did this?"

Frank nodded.

Kaspar was quiet for a spell. He stared at Bernhard's crumpled body and shook his head. Then he got down on one knee and set a pair of fingers on Bernhard's wrist. "He ain't dead," Kaspar said.

Frank nodded gratefully.

Kaspar stared at the boy. "You got us in a mess of trouble."

"You're going to tell on me?"

Kaspar laughed. "Who'd believe me?"

"What are you going to do?"

"First thing we need to do is get him out of here before anyone else finds him. I need you to stay put and keep an eye on him while I go get my wagon." Kaspar picked himself up off his bad knee. "Now if someone comes while I'm gone you tell them I did this. They'll believe that."

Frank nodded.

"What did I say?"

"To watch him."

"What else?"

"You want me to lie."

"Just this once," Kaspar said. "Trust me. It's better this way."

Frank nodded.

"Good." Kaspar said, and he hobbled away as fast as he could.

It didn't take long for Kaspar to return with his team, yet it seemed like hours to young Frank. The old man set his wagon so that the end of it was only a few feet from where Bernhard was lying. They'd been lucky—Bernhard had parked the wagon toward the end of the row, and it hid them from prying eyes. Kaspar picked Bernhard up from under the arms and around the chest. "Grab his feet," he told Frank. "Help lift them up."

Frank grabbed his stepfather's boots and lifted them with all his might as Kaspar slid Bernhard onto the floor of the wagon.

"That's it," Kaspar said. He repositioned himself, grabbed Bernhard by the waist of his pants, and pushed him further into the wagon box, leaving only his legs hanging outside the wagon.

"Keep holding up his feet," Kaspar said as he climbed into the wagon.

It was getting harder and harder for Frank to hold up his stepfather's legs. He let the right leg drop so he could use all his strength to hold up the other one; and, just when Frank was thinking he'd have to drop it too, Kaspar grabbed Bernhard under the armpits pulling him all the way into the box.

Frank's arms dropped to his side—they were vibrating from the exertion. He noticed the old man's Sunday dress shirt was soaked with blood from Bernhard's wound. "Your shirt." He pointed to Kaspar.

Kaspar removed his jacket and the bloody shirt. He bunched up the ruined shirt and wiped his chest with it, before slipping it under Bernhard's head. "He's going to have a big goose egg. But it's done now. You get back to the others."

Frank nodded.

"And don't go around telling folks what we've done. This is our secret."

"Can I come with you?" Frank asked.

Kaspar slipped his jacket on over his bare chest. "No. You stay here and pray for him. Pray for us too."

Frank took a deep breath.

"It'll be all right, son," Kaspar said. "I know something about how you feel. We've all hurt people. I'll tell you a story about that some day, but for now I need you to get out of here so I can fix up your stepfather."

Frank turned to go back to the picnic. He tried to take a step but he froze. He wondered what kind of story the old man would tell him. Maybe it was a story about his real father. He turned to ask him, but the old man's horses had already kicked up the dust and the wagon wheels turned round and round.

VI

Jakob sat in the pew next to Annaliese; her brothers and sisters sat next to her, and her parents were at the end. At the front of the church Father Selz talked on about something of which Jakob was only vaguely aware. He was too anxious to notice anything more than Annaliese and the sweat from the palms of his hands. He was sure he had overcome his nervousness towards Annaliese, so it had to be her parents or the fact that everyone could see him sitting beside her that made him so nervous. It had to be one of those things, he thought.

He felt a cool breeze as Father Selz passed by him. Jakob wiped his hands on his trousers as the steady click, click, click of the projector took life. Light danced on the starched white sheet before them. The room sighed as the title frame appeared before them and switched to the black and white image of a man wearing a loose-fitting dark suit and a derby hat and carrying a walking stick and walking—waddling, one might argue—down a road. Behind him, a car sped his way; it barely missed him. My God. Jakob gasped in time with the rest of room. Then, a second car, this one from the opposite direction, raced past the unfortunate man, spinning him around and knocking him to the ground. Undaunted, the man in the derby hat picked himself up and proceeded to dust himself off in almost every way one could imagine. Jakob looked to Annaliese; she was smiling, her eyes were wide with pleasure. He watched her laugh, not really caring that he was missing the show; yet, he knew he ought to be watching it. It was impolite to stare. She glanced at him, smiled, and returned her eyes to the picture. Jakob blushed and quickly turned to see a ruffian threaten a young woman. The woman ran and found the man with the derby hat from earlier sitting under a tree; he saved her from the thug in his clumsy way. Jakob laughed. The man was about as lucky as he was. Then the whole room flooded with laughter as the man in the derby hat knocked out a much larger thug and sent him back to his gang's camp bruised and beaten.

ക

"It was like a dream," she said, plucking the words from his thoughts.

"A dream we all shared," he added.

"Yes, because we all know what happened."

"I thought he'd marry the girl."

"So did I. It made me sad, but I think he'll be fine."

Jakob laughed. "Yes, he's used to getting knocked around."

"Kind of like you," she teased.

He laughed. She was funny, smart, and pretty. He wanted to spend the rest of the evening with her—watching the fireworks, talking with her, and holding hands—and when she smiled at him, he thought, maybe she'd like that too.

They followed the last of the people out of the church. The sun was low in the sky.

"Annaliese," called her younger brother, "Father says for you to say good-bye to your friend because it's time for us to go. And, hurry." Then the kid ran off toward the wagons.

"You're not staying for the fireworks?" Jakob asked. It was a silly question. He already knew the answer.

"I wish I could."

His eyes bounced from the ground to her lips. "I hope I can see you again."

"I'd love nothing more," she said. Then she planted a soft kiss on his cheek before running off toward the wagons.

He watched her run and waited for her to turn back so he could wave good-bye. How could he be so happy and so sad at the same time, especially the sad part, he wondered. Because really everything that had happened to him this day seemed more like a dream than nearly any other day in his life.

Later, as he watched the fireworks burst red and green in the night sky, he decided he'd go see her. He'd ride out to her farm, although he didn't know where it was exactly. There were a lot of farms near Crane Hills, but he could ask old man Gutenberg where it was. Gutenberg knew his way around those parts. He'd bring something for the family and maybe they'd ask him to stay for supper. Yes, he'd do that. He'd do anything to feel like this again.

VII

Bernhard was going to miss the moving pictures. The church was filling up. Katherine had put some food aside for him but he wouldn't find it with them in the church. Had he planned this as part of some lesson he wanted to teach her? She couldn't imagine what point it served, nor could she wait any longer.

Elisabetha pulled at her arm. The child was strong for a three-year-old. "Let's go with the people."

"Yes, yes," Katherine hushed. She turned to Frankie. "Come on." She grabbed him by the arm; he seemed to wither in her grasp. The boy had been unusually quiet since the pushing and shoving at the ball game. "Frankie," she coaxed.

He stumbled towards her. "I'm sorry, Momma," he said, almost teary-eyed.

Whatever did he mean? The boy looked stricken. Had the older boys done something to hurt him? It was difficult being the young one in the group. Oh, did she want to give Bernhard a piece of her mind! If he'd only come back at a normal time, she could've spoken with Frankie away from this crowd. "It's all right, Frankie." She kissed him on the forehead. "I love you, my boy." Katherine pressed her lips together and smiled at him, pityingly.

A tear had stained his cheek. "Mother," he said, "I don't want you to call me Frankie anymore."

Katherine was taken aback by the boy's request; her shoulders had lifted to her ears. Why is this happening now? With everything else, she wondered. "Why?"

"Because it's a little kid's name. I want to be called by my real name. My father's name."

"I see," she nodded. He was a sweet boy and in such a rush to grow up and to do everything his father had done. "That's fine... Frank. It'd make your father proud." She smiled.

Frank nodded and wiped his eyes with his shirt sleeve. He looked at her with his dark eyes; they were somehow harder now, somehow more like his father's.

The smile washed from her face. "Now, let's go find your Aunt Aggie and cousin Lambert and go sit with them."

"Sure," said the boy, straight-faced as he took Katherine's hand.

They walked to the front of the church where Agatha and her children were seated; Agatha scooted her children down the bench to make room for them. Katherine managed a grateful smile as Frank pulled loose and snuck by Agatha, burying himself between his cousin Lambert and the wall. The church filled with a sort of quiet chatter—a mix of decorum and respect that befit the space and excitement for the event that was now so close at hand.

Katherine took a seat next to Agatha. "I don't know where he is. I'm so mad at him."

"He'll be back. He loves you like a dog; he can barely leave your side."

Katherine shook her head. The thought of Bernhard tied to her side like some loyal mutt only made her more upset. "He wanted to see the moving pictures. I don't know why he's late."

"Things happen—"

"Don't they? You'd never guess what Frankie, I mean, Little Frank told me just now."

"What's that?"

"He said he wanted me to stop calling him Frankie."

Agatha nodded. "Well, Lambert told me those boys were pretty hard on him today. I'd say that's part of it." Then she hushed the children as Father Selz approached the front. "He's such a kind-hearted man."

"Who?"

"Father Selz."

"Oh."

"The whole day is his doing. The kids have had so much fun."

Katherine nodded.

Father Selz approached the lectern and stopped. He smiled and looked over the congregation; Katherine felt his eyes on her for a moment. It was a good feeling, safe and warm, and when his gaze passed the feeling stayed just a little bit longer. Katherine looked to Agatha—her eyes were locked on the young priest and a smile beamed across her face—it seemed she was not the only one who'd been enchanted by Father Selz.

"Tonight I want to share with you a view onto the world. A world we see through the invention and imagination of men, but one that is ultimately inspired by God's will. It is certainly a marvel. Not only can we see faraway places and contemplate the stories of people who live a great distance from us, but also we see that the world is smaller for it. That we are closer to our fellow man than the distance that ships can sail or rail can haul," he paused. "And so, too, in Heaven will we know the stories of our brethren, their pains and misfortunes, their joys and triumphs. This is nothing to fear. We will celebrate each other as we've celebrated today." He bowed his head for a moment. "Well, then," he said, setting his gaze back on the congregation, "I hope you enjoy the splendour of the moving-picture show and take a moment to ponder the marvels and wonder that God himself has revealed to us and has yet to reveal."

A tingling sensation travelled down the nape of Katherine's

neck and for a moment she forgot everything else that had been on her mind.

"Now if everyone is ready, let's begin." Father Selz left them with one last smile and walked briskly to the back of the church. The place was silent except for a cough and the sound of Father Selz's equipment humming in the background.

She hoped that Bernhard would walk in the room now or not at all.

There was a clicking sound and a light appeared on the sheet in front of them. The light flickered and danced; then, after a few seconds, the sheet turned black and a design in white appeared. She recognized the words, 'THE TRAMP', and wondered if it was the same as the German, meaning 'hobo'. Then the image took her away to a country road someplace she had never seen before, far from where she was, and her thoughts turned to her cousin, Peter. She wondered if he had been there in his travels; maybe it was a place familiar to him.

She sighed. No, not just her, the whole room sighed in awe as the first picture moved before them. This was magic.

❧

Katherine hadn't enjoyed the moving picture after all. There were too many things on her mind—and, besides, the story seemed too much like her own life, beset with a series of misfortunes, some big and some small, but all of them caused by clumsy men wanting what wasn't theirs in the first place. And still she had no idea where Bernhard was. He could've walked to the farm and back in all of this time. He had to be drinking. There was no other explanation. After all these years, he'd gone back to his old ways.

"Have you seen Bernhard?" she asked Agatha when they met outside the church.

"No, I haven't."

She passed Agatha her daughter's hand. "Can you watch Elisabetha? I need to look for him."

"What's happening?" Nels asked.

"I can't find Bernhard and it's getting dark. He should be here by now."

"When was the last time you saw him?"

"Not since this afternoon by the wagons." She watched his face take on a fearful look.

"I'll ask Christian and Joseph," Nels said. Then he wormed his way through the crowd to find them.

Katherine grabbed Frank by the arm. "I want you to stay with your cousins and Aunt Aggie."

"Yes, Mother," the boy said. He looked scared, like he was about to cry.

"It'll be fine," Katherine said. "I need you to keep an eye on your sister."

"Yes, Mother." Frank looked down to the ground.

She paused for a moment. Thank God it wasn't Frankie—Frank—who was missing. She ran her hand through the boy's hair, then tilted his head up, so she could look into his eyes—those eyes always reminded her of his father.

"I love you." Frank sniffed back his runny nose.

She smiled and kissed him once more on the forehead. "I love you too, my son," she said. Then she shuffled through the crowd looking for Nels or Christian and hoping to find Bernhard. She spotted Mr. Harrison, who was talking with Mr. Stolz and Mr. Gutenberg near the church doors, and veered in the opposite direction.

"Katherine," Nels called. He was standing with Joseph. She hurried toward them. "Joseph tells me that Bernhard's horse and wagon are here. He must be close by."

"Are you sure it's our wagon? There must be over fifty of them out there."

"There's no mistaking that old quarter horse," Joseph said.

She clenched her fists. "If he's back, then why didn't he come find me."

"Maybe he's drinking?"

She noticed Nels raise an eye to Joseph. "Is there something you're not telling me?" she asked.

"Only he wouldn't be drinking," Nels said. "Listen. We're going to get Christian and we'll ask around, quietly. I don't want to get people in a fuss. He's probably off in a corner chatting away with some old-timer about one thing or another. Go back to the children and we'll figure this out." And he and Joseph made their way back into the crowd.

She shook her head. Something was going on; Nels was acting weird. And none of them were looking in the right places. It was only a feeling, but she had to check the wagons.

The sun had nearly set. Some of the crowd was already leaving. There were plenty of folks here that lived more than an hour away. They'd be travelling in the moonlight and trusting their horses to stay on course. She walked the row of wagons checking inside the boxes and hoping she wouldn't find Bernhard passed out drunk in someone else's wagon. Then she saw Bernhard's horse and realized the horse and the wagon hadn't moved since this morning. Her heart raced. She checked the ground next to the horse. Nothing. That was a relief. She checked the wagon.

"My God, Bernhard!"

He was lying on his back.

"Damn it." He must be drunk, she thought. She climbed into the box of the wagon and shook his shoulders to wake him. "Bernhard, get up. Get up, Bernhard." She gave him another shake. "I can't believe you'd do this. I thought you were done drinking. Bernhard—" There was no response. Dusk was falling and it was getting harder to see; she couldn't tell whether he was breathing or not. She put her cheek to his nose and could feel the slightest touch of air on her skin. He was alive, but she had never seen him this way before.

"Get up," she said again, this time it came as a whisper. A plea. Stroking his hair, she felt something wet. She touched the wetness to her tongue. It was blood.

"Help me, God!" She put her hand behind his head again and felt for the cut. She couldn't tell if the bleeding had stopped.

"Is something wrong?" said a voice, a man's voice. For an instant, she feared it was Mr. Harrison. Had he done this? Could he do such a thing?

"Yes," she said, "it's my husband. He's bleeding. He's not awake."

"Can you stop the bleeding?"

"I think so."

"I have something that might help him. I'll be back." And he ran off.

She pulled the handkerchief from the sleeve of her dress, folded it and placed it against the back of his head where she felt the wound. "Please God, don't take him now," she prayed. She shut her eyes. Somehow this was her doing, she knew it; God had spited her for her sins. For her selfishness. For having lustful thoughts for a man other than her husband. "God forgive me."

"I've got it," said the voice, straining for breath. He handed her a small dark bottle.

"Mr. Dudenhafer," she said, suddenly aware of her helper's name.

"Yes," he replied.

"What is it?"

"Smelling salts," said the old man, breathing heavily.

Katherine removed the cork from the bottle and placed it under Bernhard's nose.

VIII

The smell of ammonia rushed into his head and he wrenched forward, his eyes went wide and he knew he was going to hell.

"You're alive," she said. The words were like hammers in his head. He had never known the world to be so loud and so dark. He wanted to close his eyes again and not know this pain, and he might've but the light shot straight into the darkness.

BANG! And there was colour. Red. Green. White.

He shut his eyes and still he could see the splashes of light behind his eyelids. Was this hell? Maybe. Or maybe he was only dying, he thought. That explanation satisfied him.

"You must stay awake," said the woman's voice. Did he know her? It didn't really matter. Like everything else, it was too loud.

BANG!

"Why are they shooting guns?" said his own voice. It echoed in his head hurting his eyes, jaw, and every part of him above the shoulders.

"It's the fireworks," said the voice. "It's only the fireworks."

IX

Father Selz stood at the top of the church staircase looking out over his flock. As they tended to do, folks had gathered in their groups of friends and kinsmen to chat and share their thoughts. After such a very long day of games and activities, they were still a lively crowd. He, too, was filled with excitement, although there was still some time before dusk and the grand finale—the fireworks. He took a deep breath. The evening air was warm and he could smell the sweet scent of sage in the breeze. He smiled. It'd been a good day. Everything—the meals, the moving-picture show, the games—had, for the most part, gone according to plan. There had been the wrangle at the baseball game, some pushing and shoving, but even that might be expected of competitive men. Yes, it was definitely a fine celebration; and, his instincts about the moving-picture show had been right. Everyone, even the skeptics, had enjoyed it and wanted more. That was something. There was a genuine thirst for these stories and spectacles. Perhaps, someday the community might even make their own moving-picture shows; what a fine legacy that would be.

There was something else too, he remembered. He was sure the day had kindled at least one new love: Jakob Feist and the young woman with the sweet voice. Annaliese. They seemed like a nice pair. He smiled thinking of the marriages he might be performing months from now.

"Thank you, Father," said a young boy extending his hand to the priest.

He shook the boy's hand. "It's Lambert, right?"

"Yes," answered the boy.

"Thank you, Father," said another boy, his face sad and

worried looking. This was young Frank Weran. Father Selz recognized him.

"You're welcome," he said. He looked to Frank. "Is everything all right, son?"

Frank nodded.

"Tell me. What was your favourite part of the day?" the priest asked.

"The Orange Crush," Lambert said. "It was so fizzy."

"Yes, it was very fizzy, wasn't it. Good." He looked to the younger boy. Frank tensed. His mouth closed stiff. "Anything?"

"The moving-picture show," Frank mumbled.

Father Selz smiled.

"I want to see the fireworks," Lambert said, excitedly. "Uncle Joseph, he's really my cousin but I call him Uncle, said it'd be as loud as a cannon and prettier than a flower."

"Yes, well, he might be right about the cannon part," chuckled the priest, thinking that the sound was more like a few shotguns going off at once. "Where is your uncle? I should talk to him."

"I think he's that way." Lambert pointed past the side of the church. "He's talking with my dad and Mr. Holtz."

"Thank you boys," Father Selz said. He gave them both a clap on the shoulder. It was prudent that he find Joseph Eberle and inquire about the preparations, in case there was anything Mr. Eberle needed of him. He'd been so concerned about the moving pictures—the projector, the electrical generation, shading the windows—he'd entirely forgotten about the fireworks. As Father Selz approached the side of the church he heard what sounded like an argument coming from around the corner; he tiptoed a little closer and stopped. Yes, the voices were raised. He leaned up to the corner of the wall. He'd often wondered whether the confessional was a true indicator of the state of the lives of his parishioners or whether moments like these were more insightful.

"What'd you do to Bernhard?" said one of the men.

"You're joking. You saw it," said a man with an English accent. "He hit me. I didn't do anything." This had to be Mr. Harrison.

"Where is he?" said a third voice.

"I don't know. Last time I saw him he was on top of me. And that's the last I care to see of him."

"Stay away from my sister and that might help you some," said the first man again. That was Nels Eberle, thought the priest.

The priest's curiosity got the better of him and he peeked around the corner for a better look. It was a bit of guesswork to see in the shadow, but he could see that they were: Nels and Joseph Eberle, Christian Holtz, and Charles Harrison; and, Mr. Holtz had Mr. Harrison's back pinned to the wall of the church.

Harrison looked them in the eye, and said. "I intend to keep my distance."

"If you don't, then next time, we're not going to stop Bernhard from coming after you," Christian said.

· He'd seen enough. He'd given into temptation. Now he should intervene.

"But you won't help him either," Harrison said. He seemed to be looking at Nels and Joseph, in particular. "I can see it in your faces. You're tired of his games, aren't you?"

"Shut up," Christian said. "You disgraced him and his wife." He slugged Harrison in the gut. Harrison lurched back against the wall and Christian punched him again.

"Enough," Nels said.

Father Selz turned away from the squabble. He didn't want to be seen, not like this.

"I have to go," Joseph said. "I gotta get back to the fireworks before I can't see where the heck it was I set them."

"Go," Christian said.

Father Selz gave himself a shake and stepped out around the corner. "Ahem," he cleared his throat. "Excuse me, Mr. Eberle. Joseph. I was looking for you." He'd caught them by surprise. They certainly didn't look happy to see him, even Mr. Harrison who was doubled over in pain.

"Yes, Father. The fireworks," Joseph said. "I'm on my way." And he hurried past the priest.

Nels tipped his hat, and marched off in the same direction.

Then it was just Christian and Mr. Harrison left. Christian was silent. He didn't look at Father Selz; instead he clapped Mr. Harrison on the shoulder and followed the other men.

Father Selz approached Mr. Harrison. "Did they hurt you?"

"I'll be fine."

"What was that about?"

"Same old thing, Father. Same old thing."

"I don't understand."

"You know that moving-picture show, the one with the tramp and the lady, it's kind of like this place."

"Maybe a small reflection," said the priest.

Harrison sighed. "You know what goes on here, Father."

Father Selz looked to the ground; perhaps, he owed this man a moment to indulge his righteousness. The Parable of the Lost Sheep came to mind. If only one of his flock repented, wouldn't that be the most joyous thing! Indeed, amid the planning and celebrations, he'd forgotten his true purpose, as shepherd. "I'm sorry, Mr. Harrison. I should have stopped those men earlier when I had the chance." He paused, meaning to look Mr. Harrison directly in the eyes. He couldn't. He made it as far as his chin. "Please forgive me," he said.

"Isn't that something? A priest asking me for forgiveness." Charles Harrison laughed. "You're a good man, Father. Funny too." Harrison patted him on the shoulder and gingerly headed off in the opposite direction from the others.

Father Selz leaned against the wall of the church and slowly dropped to his haunches. He heard the first of the fireworks shoot out into the darkening night, as he let his legs slide out one at a time. He was alone for the first time since morning. It felt good to be alone. It'd been far too long a day.

WHISKEY AND FLU
1918

ERNHARD KISSED HIS daughter Elisabetha's forehead as the five-year old trembled in his arms. He shuddered to think that the worst might come. That she might shake loose from his hands and slip away to wherever it is that little angels go—alone.

The Spanish flu had invaded Saskatchewan in October 1918, striking first in the big cities and towns where the main railway lines ran. It took some time for the news to reach the small village of Kaidenberg—it seemed too foreign a thing to be real. For the flu to poke its head around Kaidenberg someone would have to visit first, was the joke among the villagers. Yet, someone did visit, or leave and return, because by mid-November the flu had struck Kaidenberg, hard.

Bernhard claimed it was Katherine's sister-in-law, Teresa Weran, who'd spread it to young Frank and Elisabetha when she'd stopped to visit on her way back from town. He'd been outside doing chores, and, not caring for Teresa or anyone that much, he'd kept his distance. But there was some part of him that doubted his guiltlessness. Only a day or two before her visit he'd been to town to check the mail and purchase supplies, including whiskey; the bootleggers were now flush with it as the prohibition of spirits had been temporarily suspended so folks could imbibe its curative properties. Yes, it had been a selfish thing to do. He could see that now. He hated that he'd done it. Hated a lot of other things he'd done too.

In the face of the flu, Bernhard felt useless. No, it was worse than that—he felt helpless. He'd grown accustomed to feeling useless since he'd been knocked on the head at last year's church picnic and had to rely on family to help him with the farm work. His wife, Katherine, had told him he should be grateful for the charity of others, but it had only hardened him. The do-gooders. They didn't seem to understand that their charity undermined him. Why hadn't they gone after Kaspar Feist if they wanted to help so much? After all, it was Feist who'd stolen his strength and his memories from him. Now that'd be charity he could accept.

When it came to nursing the sick, Bernhard didn't know where to begin. He was too rough for this work. Give him earth to plough or a horse he could whip, something he was good at; that'd be different. But this child, his child, was something he might likely break. He knew as much. Any softness he might've had had gone when Feist bashed his head. No, this was Katherine's business not his, but she was busy with young Frank. The boy was already in bed sick with the flu.

It had come on the boy fast, with aches and chills in the morning and the fever taking hold in the afternoon. Bernhard had watched it all from a distance; it bothered him to be too close with his guilt stirring inside of him. And Katherine had her rosary beads for comfort. They'd offer her more than he could. She'd only ask that he sit and pray with her. He'd rather not. All his prayers seemed to run against him in the end—like now, with his precious Elisabetha restless with the same aches and chills her brother suffered. Bernhard rocked her in his arms and when that didn't work he tried to hum her a tune, but the melody escaped him—another casualty of the attack—so he gave it up before he exploded in frustration, and waited for Katherine.

Katherine wiped the worry lines from her face as she returned from the children's room. She held her palm to Elisabetha's forehead. "Why is it the smallest always suffer first?"

"Why ask me? Why not ask God? What's He telling you?"

"Bernhard, this isn't the time to be cruel."

He felt the curl of his lip snap and release. "I didn't mean to—"

"You can help it," she said.

He knew she'd grown tired of his outbursts and his apologies. The outbursts were part of the change. He'd flare up in a thoughtless, filthy anger, and he had about as much control over how or where it landed as a pig flinging off its own muck, but that hadn't stopped her from thinking he could. Excuses, she had told him. Always the same excuse. Then he'd act kinder and she'd apologize for doubting him, and things would be fine until the next thing that pissed him off and caused her to question his ability to control his outbursts once more. Why now, Bernhard? You were doing so good.

Her questions caused him to doubt himself. His intentions. He didn't want to be cruel. He hoped she still believed it too; if not, how could she bear him? And her pregnant, again.

"I'll try," he said.

"I need you to do your best now," she said, wiping her puffy eyes. "What happens if I get sick? If we both get sick? They say this flu can take anyone."

"I'll try harder."

She went to the stove and put the kettle on. "We're running low on wood. Can you bring some in when you go outside?"

He nodded.

"You'll remember?"

"I'll tie a string around my finger."

"Good." She ladled the last of the broth from yesterday's soup into a cup. "Frank needs to eat something."

"It might come straight out again."

She shook her head as if to put the thought out of her mind. "A good broth is what we need."

"I'll butcher a chicken."

"First, can you bring Elisabetha into the room? No sense keeping them apart any longer."

He carried the girl to the bed where young Frank ached and moaned. The boy opened his eyes for a moment and they fell shut just as fast. Bernhard set Elisabetha on the other side of the bed and kissed the girl on her forehead. The boy too.

"I'm stepping out."

"Remember to bring in some wood."

He nodded and left the house.

Outside, the air was cool. Fresh. He felt drunk against its current. He'd been inside too long, with too much sickness and too many feelings of guilt and helplessness. He feared that Death had entered his home. That Death had set its black eyes on their children. While he filled the feed pails and hauled them to the troughs, his fear turned to anger as he added up the cruelties that God had visited upon him and his family. *Don't take them, God! Don't!* The words circled the air around him.

He went to the chicken coop and grabbed a fat hen. Something had to die. Something had to appease the darkness that surrounded them. He held the bird against the chopping block and sliced its throat with his knife. This wasn't Bernhard's usual butcher work; he hadn't the time or focus to be plucking feathers. So he tied the bird's legs together with some twine and hung it from a nail on the barn wall. The dog whined as the blood poured onto the thin white crust of November snow. "Git!" Bernhard kicked the air between him and the mutt. Pressing the knife into the skin around the bird's legs, he peeled the skin from the warm meat and pulled it down over the breast. He made small cuts around the trouble spots and tossed the skin and head in one hollow piece to where the dog sat ready for its spoils. He returned the chicken to the block and began to remove its innards but stopped and braced himself as he felt the world spinning beneath him. This was it. God wanted a larger sacrifice. Fine, he'd make that trade, so long as Katherine and the children weren't touched. After a few deep breaths, he pulled out the innards and tossed them to the hungry mutt.

He staggered back to the house. Inside, he rinsed the bird and tossed it in a pot of water and set it on the stove. He looked in the woodbox. It was running low. He had a vague notion that Katherine had asked him to get some wood; he looked at the string tied around his finger. Yeah, that seemed right. He went back outside and pulled an armful of wood from the stack along the west side of the house. He could feel the weight of it pulling him from this world down into a dream; or was this the dream —Katherine, the children, the chicken, the wood, the flu, all of it? Maybe he was somewhere else, lying in bed or in the back of a wagon looking up into a starry sky.

He grabbed another piece of wood and discovered a bottle of whiskey behind it. He had no recollection of this bottle or how it had come to be there; he suspected it was a gift of forgetfulness on his part. He set down the wood he'd gathered so he could more easily inspect its contents. Swirling the bottle, he could feel its precious weight. His thick fingers were suddenly nimble again as he uncorked the bottle and sniffed the pungent aroma of roasted grains and caramel. He took a swig. The liquid seemed to be everywhere at once: leaching through the cracks of his chapped lips and setting them on fire, while resting on his tongue and warming his gums and the underside of his tongue before it finally hit the back of his throat where the earthy flavours and caramel transformed to sparkles of mind-pleasing medicine. How good it was to find his old friend again. He slipped the bottle in his coat pocket and picked up the wood.

He fetched a few more armfuls of wood. That would have to do. It was all he could muster. Losing his strength, he dropped the last of the wood by the stove and staggered to their bedroom, where he fell onto the bed with his boots on. Nausea overcame him—the room began to spin, but unlike any spinning he'd known before. It was like a wave moving over and through his body. He turned over onto his back and let one foot drop to the ground to steady himself; maybe it would be enough.

He closed his eyes and prayed. *Take me, God, and spare them. I know You don't like me and I don't have much patience for You, but I'm no more good to this family. I can't even farm my own land without the neighbours or Katherine and her boy helping me. And the boy ain't even my own blood. I'm not fit to be their keeper; maybe, before —it's hard to remember. You save them, God, and take me instead.* The fever came over him, turning his eyelids heavy. Behind them, there were flashes of red in a haze of black vapour.

He thought he heard Katherine's voice talking to him: *Bernhard! I can't do this alone, Bernhard! The children are sick. I fear I may be next. I need you to be strong now. Remember how you cared for me all those years ago, how you made me love again despite myself. Show me that man again. Help me, Bernhard! Help me!* Then there was nothing but darkness, a darkness so deep it might be familiar, had he been able to notice it, but the light of awareness had gone out.

At some point there was a woman. She wiped his face clean and he felt both fear and love in her touch. Then more darkness. Later, he saw a man holding a cup to his lips. He tried to take the cup in his own hands, but he couldn't. "It's fine," said the man. "Just drink." And he fell back into the darkness once more. Until the voice of young Frank called his name: *Bernhard. Bernhard.* But when he looked up, the boy had turned into a man and he had a mad look about him. *You brought this on my family*, the man growled. *You and your whiskey. Why didn't you leave us alone?*

Bernhard shook his head. *No, I didn't mean for it—*

Frank, the man, put a knife to Bernhard's throat. *You brought nothin' but pain and death to us.* Frank thrust the knife and Bernhard woke with a gasp.

A frail boy stood over him when he woke next. The boy's lips and fingers were frosted blue. Where am I? thought Bernhard. And who was this child?

"We need to help Mother!" said the boy desperately. "She's sick. Really sick. And I don't know what to do."

Bernhard searched the room for something familiar. There was a chair with a coat tossed over it, a pair of boots set neatly on the floor, a dresser, and a woman's hairbrush on the nightstand, but there was no woman. "Where's your mother?"

"With Elisabetha," said the boy. "Uncle Christian was here yesterday. He said he'd be back today, but he hasn't come."

Christian? Elisabetha? The names had a familiarity, but he couldn't draw the faces from the darkness. As for the boy, he knew him. He'd seen him in his dream. He'd have to be careful; if it was a premonition, then death was still close at hand and the boy might be dangerous.

Bernhard tried to press himself up off the bed but was too weak to sit up. The boy reached his hand to him and on his second attempt he found the leverage he needed to sit. The boy held onto Bernhard's hand and led him out of the room. He could sense the desperation in the boy's weak but constant grip.

The woman lying in the bed was terribly sick. She looked cold, frozen—her skin was a dark hue of blue, not quite purple; he'd never seen anything like it. Yet there was something in the features, the strong chin and the high cheeks, that he recognized. He knew that he loved her, but her name was far from his grasp.

"How long has your mother been like this?"

"I don't know," said the boy. "She was like this yesterday, too."

Next to her, Bernhard saw the little girl. She was like something from a dream, a little angel that had visited him many years ago. This, he guessed, was the Elisabetha the boy had mentioned. She appeared to be better off than the woman; like the boy, the blush of blue was mainly around the girl's lips and at her finger tips. He reached down to pick up the child and was surprised to see that his own fingers were also a sickly blue. Feeling faint, Bernhard paused to collect himself before picking up Elizabetha. She was heavier than he'd imagined, or, rather, he was weaker than he'd thought. He took a deep breath and stepped toward the door; his forearms ached from the weight of the child, but he continued on to the other bedroom and laid her down on the bed. He covered her in the blankets. For a moment, the little girl looked at him. There was no message in the eyes, only a weariness, then they closed and the child was asleep. He wanted to stay with the dear thing, but Katherine—yes, that was her name—needed him.

He returned to the children's room. The boy was wiping

blood from Katherine's mouth. "What happened, Frank?" he blurted. The name had returned to him.

"I didn't do anything," Frank cried.

A wave of dizziness came over Bernhard as he stepped toward them. He reached out to brace himself and pulled the crucifix from its place on the wall. He clung to the crucifix as he found his feet.

"You have to help her, Bernhard," the boy wailed.

Bernhard set the crucifix on the bedside table and knelt down next to Katherine. He traced his finger under a loose piece of her dark hair and carefully set it over her ear. Then, taking the cloth rag from Frank, he wiped away the trail of blood from her nose. It continued to trickle.

"Why is she bleeding?" Frank asked.

"I don't know."

"Make it stop." The boy trembled like a tree in a cold wind.

Bernhard ran his hand through Katherine's hair. He held it close and breathed in her smell. It was all wrong. He'd expected vanilla and sugar; instead she smelled like rotten meat baked on a sheet of tin metal. How long had she been like this?

"Katherine," he whispered into her ear. "Can you hear me?"

She didn't respond.

"I need you, Katherine. Tell me what to do and I'll do it." He took her hand in his. This wasn't supposed to happen. He'd made a deal with God.

Katherine moaned, "Go away."

"It's me, Bernhard."

Her breathing quickened. "Don't! Get away from me."

Bernhard was confused. Was she speaking to him? Her eyes were squeezed shut, her face strained, gripped in pain.

He turned to the boy. "Get a wet cloth." The boy stood there, frozen. "What are you, useless?" Bernhard growled. The boy shook his head and hurried out of the room.

"Get off me," she said.

"I'm not on you."

Her breathing grew faster. It seemed she was fighting for each breath.

"Katherine, stay with us."

The boy returned to the room with a wet cloth in his limp hand and held it out to Bernhard, who took it and set it upon Katherine's forehead. Beads of cool water dripped from her brow and down the sides of her face.

"I know what you did," she mumbled.

He looked to young Frank. He felt ashamed. Had he hurt her? Of course he had. Was there anyone he hadn't hurt?

"It was you, Frank," she breathed out.

Bernhard looked to the boy. "No," he said. "It's me, Bernhard."

The trickle of blood from Katherine's nose began to run like a stream. Bunching up the wet cloth, he pressed it tight against her nose as he tried to staunch the flow. The cloth stained red, but it seemed to hold back the blood. He noticed Elisabetha's pillow beside Katherine; he slipped it under her head to help keep her from choking on her own blood.

"What does your mother mean?" Bernhard asked, desperately.

"I don't know," whispered Frank.

"Tell me."

Young Frank shook his head. There was fear in the boy's eyes. Bernhard reached out to pull the boy closer, but Frank took a step back.

"Get back here," Bernhard barked.

The boy shook his head fearfully. "I didn't do anything."

Bernhard heaved a great sigh and turned back to Katherine. Her breathing had become slower, shallower. He removed the blood-soaked cloth from her face, brought it to his side and squeezed it in his fist. Blood rained onto the bedroom floor. In that short time, the blood from her nose had poured down onto her nightgown. There was too much of it for the cloth. He pulled off his shirt and held it to her face. Then, quite suddenly, her head and chest heaved toward him.

"Get some water!" Bernhard shouted at Frank. "Bring the bucket. And another cloth."

Bernhard removed the blood-stained shirt from her face. The bleeding seemed to have stopped. He carefully wiped the blood from her dark blue skin as her convulsions weakened, then stopped. "Katherine, can you hear me?"

Blood bubbled from her nose and mouth. Her body lay slack.

"Katherine!" he shouted, but nothing happened. Her chest didn't rise; she didn't gasp one last final breath. She was gone.

Bernhard's heart pounded. He wanted to break something. God had cheated him. Had broken the rules. Bernhard stood up and turned around to find Frank had returned, struggling to carry the bucket. His face tightened. The boy looked back at him with sad, fearful eyes. Bernhard grabbed the crucifix from off the bedside table and stormed out of the room through to the kitchen and opened the door to the world. The daylight overcame him. He took two blind steps and threw the crucifix across the yard. "To hell with You!" he swore.

Returning to the house, he kicked at the first thing he saw, a child's stool, but his foot shot wide and he nearly fell to floor. "Goddamn it," he cursed. He went back to Frank, and to Katherine. The boy had hunched up on the floor next to the bed, sobbing. Everything was off balance. Murky. He was fogged in on all sides, the air heavy with the smell of sickness and death. He really needed a drink. In the kitchen, he began rifling through the pantry, tossing pots and pans from the shelves, looking for a bottle, but he found nothing. Then some other thought brought him to his bedroom, where Elisabetha slept, her tiny chest moving in shallow breaths. The poor child would wake up motherless. He felt the girl's forehead. It was cool. Bernhard covered her with the blanket, then sat down on the chair next to her. Dazed and tired, he stared at his stocking feet. He was never going to see Katherine's smile or hear her laugh again. It was as though his life with her had been a happy dream, and this was its end.

The boy's cries travelled from the other room and cleared the fog of Bernhard's mind. He stood up and, picking the coat up from the chair, felt a familiar heaviness in its weight. He reached inside the pocket and found the thing he'd been looking for. He pulled the cork and took a swallow. The liquid seemed to melt in his mouth and to settle the storm clouds in his mind. Then the sound of choked sobs reached him once more. He plugged the bottle, slipped the coat on over his bare chest, and went to the boy. "Frank," he said from the bedroom doorway.

The boy turned to him, his eyes red and full of salty tears. He said nothing.

"Come with me."

Bernhard led Frank into the kitchen and told the boy to take a seat as he picked a cup up from the kitchen floor and set it on the table. Bernhard poured a shot of whiskey into the cup while Frank stared at the table.

"I'm sorry," Bernhard said.

The boy sat, wiping away silent tears.

"How old are you now?"

"Nine. I'll be ten in spring."

Bernhard nodded and passed the boy the cup.

"This will help," Bernhard said. "Drink it."

The boy looked at him and Bernhard took a swig from the bottle.

"Go on," Bernhard said.

The boy picked up the cup with his two small hands and took a sip. Frank's face tightened. "It burns," he said, grimacing. "I don't want it."

"It'll make you right," returned Bernhard, and he took another swig to prove it. "It's time for you to be a man now."

The boy cried, "I want my mother!"

Bernhard poured another shot into the cup. "That's for you, for later. I need you to warm up the soup and watch your sister."

Frank nodded.

"You'll sleep with Elisabetha in your mother's and my room."

Frank nodded again.

Bernhard clapped him on the shoulder. "When your sister's better, we'll go see Uncle Nels and Aunt Aggie."

The boy looked up at Bernhard and said nothing. Bernhard lifted his hand off Frank's shoulder and returned to the children's room.

Bernhard gazed at Katherine's body lying on the bed: her long hair knotted and strewn about, her face stained red, and her nightgown soaked in blood. He knew there'd be no one to help with the body. There were no wakes, no funeral ceremonies, for the ones the flu had taken. Whatever needed to happen was his work now. He fetched a small knife from the kitchen, with which he pierced the cotton nightgown below the collar, and sliced it lengthwise from hem to hem. After he removed the gown from under her body, he tore it into a half-dozen pieces. It was strange seeing her this way. He knew her body in the darkness, a silhouette cast in dim moonlight creeping through the window. But this was improper. He focused his gaze on her face. He took a piece of her gown and dipped it into the bucket of water, then gently squeezed it. He dabbed the cloth on her brow and down the sides of her face, working carefully to remove the blood, to dignify her. And so he worked from head to toe. After he'd finished, he permitted himself one final look at her.

This was a different Katherine than the one he knew and loved: her skin too dark, the belly too small, and the child inside her either dead or dying. He turned his back to her, hoping he might cry, but there was nothing but anger and exhaustion inside him. A few coughs were all he could muster. He began to dress her in her Sunday clothes, working slowly as his strength continued to flounder; when he grew tired, he rested beside Katherine's body. Touching her face, he felt there was nothing left but cold emptiness where there had always been warmth and gentleness. At some point, he fell asleep beside her.

The next morning, he went out to do the chores. He was weak and moved slowly as he hauled water from the well and fed the animals. There was a ruckus among the hogs as they jostled for their turn at the trough. They had gone without food for a day or two. The boy had tried to feed them the day before, but didn't have the strength to carry a pail of chop. The horses and cattle had fared somewhat better with the extra hay someone— likely, his brother, Christian—had put out. It was the milk cow that was worst off. It bawled from the pain in its udders. The poor animal stomped and kicked its feet as Bernhard approached it. He fed the cow a pail of chop to help it settle but still it was a challenge to get close enough to pull on its red and hardened teats. *"Scheisse! Scheisse!"* he swore up and down. The poor thing. He'd have to keep an eye for infection or there'd be more death on his hands. Once he finished the milking, he left the sour milk for the dog and the barn cats.

The smell of burnt oatmeal greeted him when he entered the house.

Frank scraped the bottom of the pan onto a plate. He looked up to Bernhard in fear. "I burnt it. I didn't mean to."

"And what am I supposed to eat?"

"I hate you," said the boy.

Bernhard's jaw tightened and he raised his hand to the boy, but Frank didn't flinch. He looked at Bernhard straight on; his eyes willing Bernhard to strike him. Bernhard lowered his hand. Softened. "It's fine, Frank," he said. "I'll make something else."

The boy stared at him.

"Go watch your sister. Bring her a cup of water to drink."

A little while later he tiptoed into the room and found Elisabetha still sleeping; her forehead was now warm to the touch. The girl needed medicine. Sinking to his knees and bracing himself against the bed, Bernhard poured a spoonful of whiskey and, carefully, let it drip into the girl's mouth. The child winced and cried out.

"Shh." He hushed the child and held a cup of water to her mouth. "It's Papa. You need to eat. Can you eat?"

The girl shook her head.

He took another pull of whiskey—the wrong parent had died. He gave the bottle a swirl and downed the last of it.

"Frank," he hollered. "Get your things ready. I'm taking you and your sister to Uncle Nels and Aunt Aggie's." Bernhard went outside to hitch the team. When he returned to the house he bundled up Elisabetha, while Frank stuffed a pillowcase with his and Elisabetha's clothes. On the sleigh, holding Elisabetha in his arms, Bernhard passed the lines to Frank.

Bernhard opened his jacket, nestled the child closer to his chest, then wrapped his jacket around the bundle. Gazing at his small, sick daughter, he whispered, "God, protect them." He looked over to Frank and caught him staring back. The boy was still weak, but there was more than a little grit in him. He'd be a tough one someday. "Let them feel the lines, boy," Bernhard said, and Frank nodded.

A DEATH IN THE FAMILY
1919

PETER PULLED ON his end of the misery whip and the saw's teeth chewed through the giant Douglas Fir. He breathed in the sweet rainforest air as the saw travelled away from him and out on his return stroke. Deliberate. Disciplined. After the scaffolding and the undercut had been made, this was the routine. Just him and the kid, Henry, on opposite ends of the two-man saw. The kid, hidden from him behind the wall of tree. Their language unspoken—a vibration echoing through 12 feet of steel, meaning pull. The steel hummed through the wood. A smooth rhythm interrupted only by the need to place a pair of wedges to keep the saw moving. Around him, the other men chopped and sawed and the forest fell by their will.

It's here that Peter's mind can rest quietly. Free from the echoes of all the thoughts that haunted him in Kaidenberg and travelled with him those years he worked the Grand Trunk, stretching the railway west through the Yellowhead Pass. Yet, sometimes through the emptiness a picture of Katherine will shine through. Now, some ten years since he left home, there are only two pictures of her that remain: Katherine of the Steppe, 14 years old, with flowers in her dark hair skipping through the tall grass of the cherry orchard, her hands cupped hiding a secret she has to share with him; and, Katherine of Kaidenberg, as he last saw her, a mother with a child in her arms, her dark hair up, her sun-kissed face wearing a look of sad contentment. If he's lucky he'll be visited by the first memory. The second is a bad omen. With it comes other pictures; pictures of Katherine's deceased husband, Frank Weran. Frank growling and wild-eyed with his fist aimed straight for Peter's jaw; Frank, in the snow, broken and begging for help; and, lastly, Nels's bare hands cupped over Frank's mouth and nose, pressing tight, smothering the life from him.

But, for the most part, there's just a hollowness in his thoughts —memories pulled out by the roots. Everything else is action and words: eat; sleep; work; send money home; fish. And there is the forest, green, etching patterns in his mind as the feeble sunlight passes through rain-soaked moss and the bristled arms of these wooden giants.

Then, there's the kid, Henry, a brawny, 18-year-old with a widowed mother and pair of younger sisters in Vancouver. His eagerness reminds Peter of his brother Joseph at that age. Except where Joseph was eager to get married and do all the things married people do, Henry's hungry for adventure. Eager to prove himself to all the other men because the war in Europe was done before it was his turn to fight, and eager to send money home to his family. The kid's a good one. He's respectful. He doesn't call Peter, "Fritz", "Jerry", or "The Hun", not like the others. It doesn't happen as much any more, but Peter had more than his share of it during the Great War. More than once he'd been told how he didn't deserve to be making good money when Canadian boys were in the trenches dying for pennies in their pockets. In this sort of company, he was nothing but an outsider, a deviant, Canada's great enemy. There were times during those years when he wondered if he'd been better off in one of those camps for Germans, like the one where his friend Karl Ziegler was taken. They would've put him there if his birth certificate hadn't been issued by the Russian Empire. But it's better now that the war is over. Better too that Canada and Britain won.

This tree will be the last of the day. The last of the week for that matter. Later, the men will leave camp and travel the five miles to the town of Alberni. They'll eat and drink like machines. Some will play cards, others will pay for a fuck, and more will fight. Peter has done all three, but he'll settle for a good meal and a game of cards tonight. He's always been a reluctant fighter; as for sex, he's only ever paid for what he knows. He lost whatever handsomeness he'd possessed the night Frank Weran knocked out half his teeth. Since then, love has never been in the cards. In the morning, Peter will wake and go to church. In the afternoon, he'll fish the river. He will return to camp early Monday morning and the routine will start again.

The signal came and Peter and Henry hurried away from the tree as Cormac Gallagher, the crew's veteran lead topper, and Thomas Spence, the crew boss, pulled on a pair of line hooks that Cormac had rigged to the tree. The tree—half a tree, really, with its top already fallen—cracked somewhere deep in its core. *Pop.* The sound echoed through the forest. The tree was a tower. Five hundred years old.

"I love that sound," old Spence said.

"Uh huh," Peter said, under his breath.

Then, *pop-pop-pop*, the vertebrae of the tree broke and its massive body tilted away from them. For a moment, the tree held firm, like an arm-wrestler down but not out, then gravity's invisible hand reached up and pulled the tree to the forest floor. *Boom.* The ground around the men shook.

Henry flashed Peter a proud smile.

"Not so bad." Peter clapped Henry on the shoulder. The men walked carefully, like hunters coming upon their prey, as they returned to the fallen tree.

Later, the lumberjacks rode the supply wagons down the skid road back to camp. Five wagons each with nearly a dozen of them packed in like sardines as a late afternoon rain poured down on them. The March air was cool. Peter sat knees to chest with his back against the side boards of the wagon box. Henry was next to him. Cormac crouched at the back of the wagon, his long limbs and lean frame acting as a kind of end gate. He looked over to the latest recruit, Logan MacNair, and a mischievous grin shone upon his face. "I'm goin' to drink you under the table, MacNair."

MacNair was the newest topper on the crew and had become a minor distraction to Cormac since his arrival. MacNair was a war veteran, an RFC flyer who had been shot down and taken prisoner by the Germans. His story had captivated Cormac when they had met in the Alberni Hotel, and it was Cormac who had suggested to Logan that he come and try his hand at topping the giants. Since then, the two men were often busy trying to best each other in whatever pursuit they could think up.

MacNair peered at Cormac for a moment before sticking his head into his jacket. He revealed himself seconds later puffing on a cigarette. He passed the cigarette to Cormac, who took a pull and passed it back to MacNair. "I can't allow it, Gallagher. There's a lass in town I'm promised to, and I ain't one to break a promise."

Cormac huffed. "I've seen your girl; she's nothin' but a tart."

MacNair shook his head. "Not mine. She's an angel with emerald eyes and hair dark as night." He smiled and took another pull from the cigarette.

"You think you can mend her broken ways," Cormac continued.

"Aye, ye don't marry for money when ye can borrow it cheaper."

Cormac smiled at him. "Good enough, then." He looked around to the other men and his gaze set on Henry, who was telling Spence how he'd jump at the chance to top a big fir. "Kid," Cormac called out to Henry.

Henry turned to Cormac.

"You want be a topper?"

"Yeah."

"Then you gotta drink like a topper."

"Looks to me like his mother only just took him off the teat," MacNair teased.

Cormac laughed.

"I can drink," Henry said.

MacNair pressed his cigarette out on the wagon floor. "Ye drink like a virgin, kid. Nothing to be worried about though, we're all sure yer one of those too."

The wagon filled with laughter.

"Leave him alone, MacNair," Peter said.

"Come on, Smiles," Cormac said. "It's only a bit of fun. Why you got to be so Holy Joe serious all the time?"

"I don't mind, Peter," Henry said.

Peter shook his head.

"That's it, kid. Don't be putting yer trust in the Hun. He'd likely stick an axe in yer back—"

Peter burst towards MacNair. "You bastard." He reached for MacNair's shirt collar and cocked his fist ready to punch. It happened so quick that no one had a chance to stop him. A picture of Frank Weran falling to the ground, his spine snapped like a fallen tree, flashed in Peter's mind and stopped him from letting loose his punch. Henry pulled Peter away from MacNair, but MacNair swung at Peter, grazing his chin before Spence and another faller grabbed MacNair and stuffed him back in his spot.

"Enough," Spence shouted. "The war is over. Act like it."

The rain let up to a fine mist as the wagon rolled to a stop in front of a small two-room building that functioned as the main office; next to it stood the camp's mess hall with room enough for 100 men. And further along, past the rail siding and the steam donkey, were the bunkhouses. Peter was the last off the wagon. He followed the others toward the lean silhouette standing to the left of the setting sun that was Leahy, the owner of the operation. Leahy was a decent enough man in Peter's eyes. He'd given him a job when others had refused. Yet Leahy had a showiness about him that Peter didn't have much need for, and this ritual of appearing at the end of the week to distribute the men's hard-earned wages was part of it.

Peter fell in line behind Henry as the second wagon arrived and the rest of the crew joined the queue. At the front, Leahy handed the men their wages in small brown envelopes with whatever correspondence they might've received in the post. The line moved at a shuffling pace and from its mouth gurgled a spattering of thank yous.

Peter took his wages and nodded his thanks to Mr. Leahy.

"Wait a second," Leahy said. "You got a letter." Leahy shuffled through a bundle of letters he kept in his breast pocket and found the one addressed to Peter Eberle. He pressed it close to his bespectacled face then held it out to Peter. "Krautberg, Saskatchewan," frowned Leahy.

Peter took the letter without a word and walked away from the crowd toward the cover of the mess hall's overhang. The pit of his stomach dropped half an inch when he flipped the envelope and read his brother's name, Joseph. He'd hoped it might be from his cousin, Katherine.

The last correspondence he'd had from home arrived after Christmas. Actually, the New Year had already been well established when he'd received the Christmas letters, as there had been all sorts of delays with the mail in the wake of the flu outbreak. Both Joseph and Katherine had written to him. Katherine had written with news of her family. The children were healthy. Elisabetha had enjoyed her first season at the country school, while her son, Frank, continued to be heavy-hearted following the violent attack on Bernhard the previous summer. Although it seemed Frank was beginning to show signs of improvement. Possibly because Bernhard had begun to take on more of the farm work as the dizzy spells lessened and became more manageable. Yet, Peter couldn't help find another story between the lines—a maimed and frustrated husband with a weakness for booze. And, to add to matters, she was pregnant again. It would only be her third, but with Bernhard's temperament it would be a test. Peter feared for the family's circumstances and had been sending money to Joseph to give to Katherine ever since he'd learned of Bernhard's condition. He didn't risk sending it to Katherine and Bernhard directly in case Bernhard were to discover it. Peter knew he'd take offense at this charity. Kaidenberg folk were a stubborn, pride-filled lot.

Joseph's letter had followed Katherine's and, like her, Joseph had included updates on his family—Margaret and the children. However, Joseph's letter had included a sliver of information about folk in nearby Crane Hills contracting the flu. Joseph hadn't included any more details, leaving Peter to worry and pray that it was not an outbreak of the Spanish flu that seemed to be everywhere in the world. Peter had written back to Joseph and Katherine asking them both for news and this was his first response.

Peter's heart raced as he considered what news the letter might contain. Were Margaret and the children well? He said a silent prayer and unfolded the slip of paper.

February 11th, 1919

    My Dear Peter, I write to you with a heavy heart. Today, I received your letter of January 7th and I must relate to you the terrible news that your fears of the flu were well founded. The flu has taken our cousin, Katherine. I am sorry, Brother, I know you were very close to her long ago. It has been a difficult time in Kaidenberg. Katherine was not the only one of us lost. Ludwig Gerien and Teresa Weran, Katherine's sister-in-law, also passed and many are still recovering. You must forgive me for not writing to you earlier. Katherine passed in late November, then Margaret took ill and the children too. It saved me for last. Thank God, none of us were taken, I wouldn't know what to do had I lost Margaret or any of the children. It pains me to think of it.

    As for Frank and Elisabetha, well, Bernhard took them straight to cousin Nels's to be raised there. We are all grateful that Bernhard had the soundness of mind to know his limits and ask for help. I'm told it's hard for him to take care of himself no less two young children, although Frank will be turning 10 this spring. My God, 10 years. It's hard not to think of that trip to Battleford. I think of it most in the winter or when I pick up an axe. I pray for you, Peter. Must this be your penance? To wield the axe every day, so not to forget your sins? Please, stop. I think it's time you come home and be with your people. And meet the nephews and niece you've never seen. Steven, John, and Helen.

Your brother, Joseph.

P.S. I gave Nels the money you sent for Katherine and the family. He accepted it, kindly, and asked me to send you his greetings and thanks. He is still a rock, although I fear he's showing cracks.

Peter slumped to the ground as tears rolled from his eyes. Katherine dead. The baby too? It must be. "No," he mumbled. "No." Joseph must've gotten it wrong. He would've known if Katherine had died. In his guts, he would've known. How did this happen? She was still young. Now he'd never see her again. Not even on the other side. He'd be lucky to make purgatory for his sins: for his part in killing Frank, and for the women he'd had, the camp followers and prostitutes. All those times, he'd imagined it was Katherine in his arms. He'd tainted his memory of her with his lustful mind. It made him sick to think of it.

Peter fell to his knees and started to gag. His stomach found the back of his throat. He heaved and a thin line of liquid poured from his mouth; he coughed, wiping his mouth on his sleeve.

Henry came to Peter's side. "What is it?"

Peter wagged his head. No. He lurched and heaved again, a dry retching.

Henry lowered down next to him. "Peter?"

"Stay away." He coughed, and spat.

"What's wrong?"

Peter turned to Henry. "Go!"

Henry froze, staring at the miserable creature next to him.

"Leave me!"

Spence grabbed Henry by the shoulder and pulled him away from Peter. "Leave him," he told Henry. "Just leave him."

"He's lost someone," Henry said. "Hasn't he?"

Spence nodded.

ↄ

Peter didn't go to town that night. He stayed alone in the bunk-house and stared at his brother's letter illuminated by the flickering lamplight: '...*your fears of the flu were well founded. The flu has taken our cousin, Katherine.*' And wept.

Then something in him shifted, and he rose from his seat on the bottom bunk and crossed the room. He punched the wall, hitting an unforgiving wooden beam. "*Scheisse!*" he growled. Shaking his fist in pain, he returned to the lamplight to examine his hand. Yes, his middle finger was broken. Peter pressed the bone of his finger back into place and wrapped his hand in a handkerchief. The pain was sharp at first, then it softened to a dull throbbing pulse that calmed Peter's racing mind. He poured himself a whiskey and downed it quickly.

On Sunday morning, Peter woke to the same dull pain pulsing from his finger and down through his right hand. He rolled out of bed and set his bare, calloused feet on the cold wood floor. On the night table by his bed he found a cold dinner someone had left for him. He unwrapped the butcher paper and discovered a heap of cold beef and boiled potatoes. He fetched the knife he carried in a sheath on his belt and dug into the beef, eager to fill the hollowness in his gut. His thoughts were simple. Divisible. He needed to ease his hunger and tolerate the pain.

With his hunger gone, his mind began to clear. Katherine

was dead. God had cheated her and everyone she loved. Her poor children had no mother. The boy, Frank, was a true orphan now; Elisabetha might as well be.

Peter looked at the clock on the wall. Half past seven. It was early enough that if he started now he could walk to town in time for Mass. Instead, he grabbed his fishing rod and lures and a sack of apples and walked to his fishing spot on the Somass River. There was no one else on the river as he fixed a lure to his line and cast with his injured hand; the pain making him clench his jaw.

The air was still cool and steamy when Henry arrived, an hour or more later. Bleary-eyed, Henry nodded to Peter and took his place down river from him. The men fished quietly together for several hours, until the March sun peeked through the high tree tops and warmed their backs.

Before noon, Henry landed a good-sized rainbow trout, well over a foot in length. He clubbed the fish and set it in his creel. "That one's dinner," he called out to Peter.

Peter nodded, then turned back to his rod and his part of the river.

A short time later, Henry made his way through the bits of rock and forest that separated him from Peter. "I'm sorry," he said. "For your loss."

Peter was quiet.

"It's hard being so far from those we love," Henry continued, hesitating.

Peter reeled in his line and cast it out again.

"Did you do something to your hand?"

Peter stared off toward his fishing line. "Broke my finger."

"Can you work?"

"Have to."

Henry nodded, quietly, and kicked at the dirt. "Cormac challenged me to a drinking contest."

Peter shook his head.

"I knew I wasn't going to outdrink him," Henry said. Peter looked at him and nodded. A slight smile lit up the kid's face. "But I figured I might be able to drink faster than him."

"And did you?"

"Well, I thought we'd just do a glass of beer, but Cormac wanted to do whiskey. Spence settled it and set two glasses of beer in front of each of us. Anyway, I could see Cormac didn't want to be drinking beer; he still tried to get inside my head, but I didn't let him. And when Spence said 'Drink', I drank those beers down so fast Cormac didn't even bother finishing the second one." Henry smiled.

Peter looked at him. Somewhere inside he wanted to smile for the kid, but he couldn't pull the strings to turn his face right. He bit down and nodded. Henry was a good kid. He'd make a good man and a good father too someday. "So why do you want to be a topper?"

The kid shrugged. "To show them I can do it."

"I know you can," Peter said. "Why you care what they think?"

"I don't know, I just do. Why don't you care?"

Peter cast his line out once more. He could feel Henry's eyes on him. "It ain't any use to me what they think." Out of the corner of his eye, Peter saw the kid nod, then take a seat on an old cedar stump.

Henry was quiet for some time; at one point, Peter even turned to check and see if Henry was still there. When the kid finally spoke again, he said, "I'd like to have a boat someday. Then I'd go fishing whenever I wanted."

"Don't need a boat for that," Peter said.

"I mean for on the ocean. Could go between islands, to the mainland and fish the Georgia Strait. There's some really big ones out there."

"That would be good," Peter said. He felt a tug on his line and set the hook in what he figured might be a nice-sized trout. He reeled in the line and felt something on the other side of it pull away from him.

"You got something?"

"Steelhead." He brought the line in slowly, careful not to give the fish a chance to snap it. Peter stepped into the cold river water as the fish fought its way closer to shore. He grabbed the line with his hand and lifted the fish from the water. It flopped and shook itself in the air, throwing water off its silvery body.

"Nice fish," Henry said.

Removing the hook, Peter carried the fish back to shore. A faint smile, close-lipped, softened his face.

"It's a good one."

Peter nodded. Then a thought came to him—he turned back to the river and held the fish in the water until it stirred and kicked and fled his hands for darker water. Peter picked up his fishing rod and looked at Henry. He didn't offer an explanation.

"What'd the letter say, Peter?" Henry asked.

Peter swallowed. "Was it you who left me the food?"

Henry nodded.

"Thanks."

Peter fetched the flask from his inside coat pocket and took a pull from it. He offered it to Henry, but the kid shook his head. Peter took another drink and capped the flask.

"Katherine's dead," he murmured, trying the words.

"Your mother?" Henry asked.

Peter shook his head. "My cousin, Katherine."

"You were close?"

"I loved her."

"I'm sorry, Peter." Henry sighed. "What was it?"

"The flu." A tear spilled from his eye, and crawled down Peter's hollow face.

Henry kicked his boot heel into the cedar stump. "When did you see her last?"

"Ten years." Peter put the flask in his pocket and looked to the fishing rod in his hand. "I've been away too long."

"Do you want to go home?"

Peter didn't know the answer to that question, though he'd already begun pondering it. There was family there, some he didn't even know, but still he sensed if he went back to Kaidenberg he'd be just another ghost. Leaving had been its own kind of death. And then he'd waited too long to go back. If Katherine were still alive then, maybe, he'd have reason to return. He'd have gone in summer and brought boxes of peaches and plums for her and the kids, and she could've tasted their goodness and known something of the world they could've shared together. Peter shook his head. "I think I'd like to be alone." He turned back to the river.

"Sure," Henry said. "See you back at camp." And he walked away.

❧

It didn't matter if he swung the axe or pulled on the saw, the pain in his hand was there. Constant. Like the numbness in his jaw where his missing teeth should be. But he didn't wish this pain away. It served him. It distracted him just enough that

Katherine was not the sole focus of his thoughts. It kept him in the forest and in the work when his mind wanted him to be anywhere but. At times, Katherine was reduced to nothing but words, an echoed beat: *Katherine is dead; Katherine is dead.* It was afterward, when he put the tools away that the thoughts and the questions took over. Did she die alone? Had she thought of him as she departed this earth? Was there a funeral? Did they bury her next to Frank Weran?

The week passed. It ended like so many before it—a giant fir tree crashing to the ground and a wagon trip back to camp. He took his place in the front of the wagon and closed his eyes. He was tired. He wanted a drink. He wanted Katherine next to him. He didn't want to hear any more of Cormac and MacNair's plans for the evening or Henry's boot kissing. Leaning against the wagon box, he closed his mind to them and played out his fantasy—he imagined a night in Battleford where Frank never showed up. Where he kissed Katherine, as they both had wanted. And held her in his arms under the trees and neither of them were damaged. And when time moved on, it moved with him and Katherine together—not separated by the hurt they reminded each other of. Then, when he turned 19 and got his own land, he and Katherine made their plans. They went to their parents and asked for their blessings. It was no surprise. Their parents had seen with their own eyes how much the two loved and cared for one another. It was a small wedding—a family celebration —and children followed.

His imaginings even extended to Frank Weran, but there was no flip-flop of fate. He didn't wish Frank any suffering or have him go his own lonely way. No, in this world, Frank was alive and married to another woman. They lived a peaceful life, on a farm, miles from Katherine and him. And when Peter would see Frank at church or this or that gathering he'd nod his head and smile and be grateful that he'd awoken from his nightmares.

When they got to camp, Peter cleaned himself up and went into town with the others for their Saturday night meal at the hotel. He ate a plateful of roast beef—chewing it on the good side of his mouth, as he always did, like a cow chewing its cud. He washed the meat down with a beer. It was crisp and light like spring water and he drank another three glasses in short order.

"That's the pace, Smiles," Cormac called from the next table. He raised his glass to Peter. *"Slàinte!"* The others at the table followed Cormac's lead, even MacNair. Peter felt no ill will from them and raised his glass again and tipped it back. The room lifted in a chorus of hoorahs and the other men too drank their beers at a frenzied pace.

After one more beer Peter left the hotel. Outside, night was falling and a light rain had started to come down. He walked to the side of the building and took shelter under the overhang. He pulled his flask from his coat pocket. It was full. He took a swig. The whiskey tingled and warmed his insides. It was better out here. Quiet. There was room for his thoughts. He supposed other men needed to forget their thoughts, cover them up with chatter and games. That was fine for them. He'd done some of that himself. But, in that room, among them, he'd be no different than a piece of furniture or a painting, something to be talked about. There was no point to it. Nor did he care to pay someone for whiskey when he had his own on him.

He took another swig and decided to walk. He set his mind on Katherine—opening the door to old wounds and forgotten happiness. Each drink he took was a wedge that inched the door open wider. He could taste his anger and his disappointment, his complete sadness. How much he had wanted her. He remembered a time when they were both 12, maybe 13, and he had pressed himself against her while they were carving tunnels in the snow. She hadn't seemed to notice. She had even smiled when they were knitted up together as they raced through the snow-packed passageway toward the glow of sunlight at the mouth of the snow cave. Lust had moved him then, as well as pure affection, and he felt that same craving for her now. He'd give his soul to have her here with him.

Outside town, he realized he was walking to his fishing spot on the river. He stopped. Removing the flask from his pocket, he measured its weight in his hand—little more than half gone —took another swig. He breathed in its soothing warmth and sighed. He needed a woman, he decided—soft and warm, with long hair flowing to her bosom; the thought of it made him twitch, below. He knew that none of them would ever see him as Katherine had, as a handsome man. Or rather, as he was then, only a boy, like Henry, pretending to be a man.

Peter looked up to the rain-filled sky—a blanket of cloud and rain separated him from the starry night. He hated that he needed a woman so much. Part of him had the sense to make the long walk back to the bunkhouse and sleep off the booze and the cravings; another part of him wanted to walk back to town, to the brothel. He drank again from the flask and slipped it into his pocket. Pulling his coat tight around him, he walked back toward the dim light of town.

He walked the alleyway to the brothel, passing the shadowy silhouettes of other men coming and going in the darkness. Twenty yards ahead of him, a door opened and poured its light into the alley as a man stepped into the night. That was the door he wanted. It'd been months since he'd opened it.

Inside the brothel was a small parlour with a wood-burning stove, a table and few wooden chairs. Leading away from the room was a long hallway with several doors. The sounds of sex echoed out through the walls and down the hallway. From behind the table, a moustached man in his forties greeted Peter with a smile. "Looks like you took a swim in the river."

Peter nodded.

"Well, have a seat by the stove," the man said. "It'll be a while."

Peter stared at the wood chair. It was like any other he'd seen before, yet it was different. This place of business had changed it. He sat down onto the edge of the seat.

"You have a girl in mind?" the moustached man asked.

"I work with a Scotsman," Peter said. "He's got a girl..." The words left his mouth before Peter realized what he'd said.

"He's a faller?"

Peter nodded.

"And you want his girl?"

Peter shrugged. He supposed there was part of him that wanted MacNair's girl, wanted to know if she really was the beauty he'd talked so much about, dark hair and eyes. Dark hair like Katherine's? he wondered. "Yeah."

The man laughed. "Well, he's with her now. I figure they'll be a while longer."

Peter stood up. He didn't like sitting. He could feel the cold of his wet clothes press into his skin and bones. "You have a hot bath?"

"Two bits."

"For all, how much?"

"Let's call it two dollars fifty." The man turned his head down the hallway. "Hot bath, Florence."

Peter shook his head and pulled out his money. He laid out the dollar bills and dropped a handful of coins onto the table. He pulled away two dimes. It looked right.

"Not quite." The man grabbed one of Peter's dimes from him and handed him a nickel.

Peter slid the nickel in his pants pocket and brushed up against the wood stove. He felt a shiver run through him and he took another pull from his flask.

"You sure you want his girl?" The man paused. "I seen it happen before, one man getting the up on the other, then, next thing, one's got a knife in him."

"It's nothing about him," Peter said. "That bath ready?"

"Sure," the man said. "Follow me."

And Peter followed him down to the end of the hall.

The water was warm. Enough to stop his shivering. The old woman, Florence, had added two pots of boiling water to the metal tub. He'd asked her for a third, but she hadn't returned. He drank the last of his flask, leaned back in the tub and closed his eyes. His head lowered sleepily.

A knock at the door snapped him from his reverie. It was the old woman with the hot water. She entered the room slowly, eyes on the floor, carrying a kettle of steaming water with both hands on the wooden handle. Her bearing reminded Peter of a beaten dog. She set the kettle on the floor about arms reach from him and left as slowly as she'd entered. He poured some of the kettle water between his legs and scrubbed himself with soap.

Minutes later the door knocked again.

"Yeah," Peter said.

The door opened a crack. No face appeared. "Mister," said a soft, young voice. "I'm ready for you."

Peter wrapped himself in a towel and picked up his boots and wet clothes. The young woman was waiting for him as he opened the door.

"Hello," she smiled. She swept a piece of her dark hair back over her ear. The dark hair stopped him for a moment; he took her in—shoulder length hair, round face, white skin, too white, almost like an egg shell, and slightly turned up nose—only her dark hair and green eyes bore any similarity to Katherine, not much, in truth, but enough, and her age, 21, maybe 22, was about the same as Katherine's when he last saw her. Her dress was light green with short-sleeves, a low waist, and hem above the ankle. It was pretty. Katherine would wear it nicely. Then her smile faded and was replaced with something not far from pity as her eyes had settled on his sunken mouth and right cheek. "That must've hurt," she said.

"Yeah."

"Did a tree do that to you?"

"A horse," he said, choosing the easiest answer.

She nodded. "My name's Geraldine."

"Frank."

"Follow me, Frank," she said.

The room was like the others he'd been in, with a small vanity dresser, a chair, and a lamp on a nightstand next to the bed. The exception was the bouquet of wildflowers on the dresser and the pressed flowers adorning the vanity mirror.

"You can put your things there." She pointed to the chair.

Peter set his clothes on the chair and his boots on the floor. He felt dizzy from the whiskey and balanced himself against the chair as he took a deep breath. When he turned to the woman, she was still watching him but the look of pity was gone. It seemed to have been replaced by a mild curiosity.

"You asked for me," she said.

"I didn't know your name."

"But you know Mr. MacNair? Are you friends?" She slid her right dress-sleeve off her shoulder, then the left one. The top of her dress came loose around her bosom.

Peter licked his lips. "We both work for Leahy."

She stepped towards him and let the dress fall as her arms slipped from their sleeves. Her fingertips gently grazed his biceps muscle. "You're strong."

He nodded and looked to the dresser and the small bouquet of wildflowers.

"I'm over here," she said as she removed the top clasp of her longline corset.

He lowered his eyes and brought them back to her. She was a lean woman. Her breasts had the narrow rounded shape of pine cones. "Can I kiss you?" he asked.

"Not my lips," she said.

He touched his lips to her forehead and held them there. He felt her arms come to rest loosely around his waist as he lowered his head to her shoulder and buried his teary eyes in her dark hair.

"That's fine," she said, and patted the back of his head. "Come sit with me." She took his hand and led him to her bed. "You can sit if you like," she smiled at him. "It'd be nice if you did."

He took a seat next to her, making sure his towel still held around his waist.

She set her hand on his thigh. "There are other ways."

As he stared at the wildflowers, it seemed the whole room had begun to turn. And her offer to touch him with her hand made him feel sick. "I don't think I can," he mumbled. Then he leaned against her, burying his head in her chest.

⁊

The day's rest made some difference for Peter even though it had left him feeling more confused. It was the woman, Geraldine. He couldn't shake her from his mind. She was pretty, maybe even beautiful, but more than that she'd been kind to him. The generosity she'd shown him was heartfelt. She'd held him and made him feel known, even loved. He wondered if he could care for her or any woman, or whether he'd just be putting whatever feelings he had for Katherine, his hopes for love, onto them.

Another thought circled his mind: he'd told her his name was Frank. Why? He could blame the whiskey, but that wasn't a good reason. He didn't want to think about it too much, but not thinking about it only pushed it to the front of his mind. He decided he must've done it to keep MacNair guessing in case the girl said something to him. Of course, this made little sense. She'd only need to describe him and MacNair would know it was him. But it was answer enough to settle his mind, closing the circle on the motives of his drunken self.

Looking back, he probably shouldn't have asked for Mac-Nair's girl. The dark hair and the green eyes had been a small reflection of Katherine; perhaps, too much. When he closed his eyes and thought of Katherine, he couldn't be sure now of her face. Had her skin always been so snowy white? Her face soft and round? Wasn't there a blush in her cheeks? Freckles? Her face strong and angular? The picture was all too fuzzy now.

Back at the camp, there were slow changes about. It seemed at first that Henry was avoiding him. Peter'd been too much in his own thoughts to notice when the boy took off. It had started slow. A few minutes here and there, at lunch or in the morning before the toppers started up for the day, Henry would drift over to Cormac or MacNair to ask how they tied off their flipline when they started to top a big fir, or how to tell if the line hooks were fixed to get the right fall on the bottom half of the tree. When it was time to get to work, Henry would come back saying nothing, and Peter wouldn't ask. It was up to the kid to tell him. It wasn't his business otherwise, but it made Peter feel more distance between him and Henry than the 12 feet of saw that usually separated them.

The following week, Cormac and MacNair took a few minutes out from their breaks to show Henry the tools and tricks of the topper—how to use the spurred leg braces and carry an axe and saw behind you from a shoulder strap. He'd even begun to do some climbing, 20 or 30 feet, with borrowed leg braces and a flipline.

Peter did his best not to let on that he'd noticed Henry's training. He didn't want to upset the kid, but mostly he didn't want to lose Henry on the other side of the whip. His small little world had changed too much in too short a time. He wanted the kid to stay where he was. He was a good partner. He didn't complain much. It was sad the kid hadn't said any more about it. That probably disappointed Peter the most; he wondered if the kid felt it too.

That Saturday, Peter ate his lunch alone. He took it from the cook shack and sat in a patch of sunlight with his back against the trunk of a cedar tree. Eying Spence coming toward him, Peter tore off a piece of his sandwich and popped it in his mouth.

"You have a minute?" Spence asked. Peter nodded through his mouthful of sandwich, and Spence sank to his haunches. "I'm going to have you join the buckers for the afternoon." Spence picked a small stone from off the ground and rubbed it between his thumb and index finger. "We're giving the kid a chance to top a big one."

Peter finished chewing his food, then took a drink of water from the glass jar he carried with him. "I'd like to see him do it."

"Sure," Spence said, "if the kid doesn't mind an audience."

Peter nodded and Spence clapped him on the shoulder and walked back to the cook's wagon.

After he'd finished eating, Peter made his way over to where Cormac and MacNair were going over their instructions and last minute reminders with Henry. The kid was sure a different animal from Cormac and MacNair. He was broad shouldered and thick muscled, while they were taller, lean-muscled men. It might take him longer to get up there, thought Peter, but he'll be fast when it comes to the real work.

"You don't get scared any more?" Peter heard Henry ask.

"Things gets easier when ye know ye ain't supposed to be here," MacNair replied.

"Don't listen to him, kid," Cormac said. "It's good to have a little fear in you. Keeps you sharp. Makes the job fun."

Peter caught MacNair's glance. "Aye, these are the things a man does, if ye ain't a scunner like the Hun," MacNair said.

Cormac looked over to Peter who was still some ten feet away from them. "Enough, MacNair." Cormac turned to the kid. "Give those spurs a test, will you."

Henry nodded, then he looked to Peter and flashed him a weak smile. Henry took a step toward the tall standing fir and jabbed his left spur into the tree.

"That leg brace feel tight enough?" Cormac asked.

"It's good," Henry replied.

"Try the other one."

Henry pulled the left spur clean and heel-kicked the right spur into the wood. "It's good."

MacNair looked to Peter. "Ain't ye supposed to be cutting logs in twelves?"

Ignoring MacNair, Peter addressed Henry, "You mind if I watch you cut this in two?"

Henry smiled. "That'd be good."

"Now, kid, we want this one to fall to this side." Cormac waved his hand to the southwest. "You got plenty of space to make that happen."

Henry nodded.

"You ready?"

"I'm ready."

"Good," Cormac said.

Henry walked the flipline around the trunk of the fir tree, then tied it off around the belt harness. He strapped the belt harness around his waist and checked that the flipline and the belt straps were secure.

MacNair tied another rope to the back side of Henry's belt loop. "For the line hooks."

Henry tightened the shoulder strap from which his axe hung and gave the flipline a snap of his wrists, once then twice, so it hung about shoulder height on the opposite side of the tree trunk. He jabbed the right spur into the wood and stepped with his left. He stepped again, and flipped the line once more. He took a quick step with his right then left, and again, then flipped the line.

"Good," Cormac said. "Keep breathing."

The kid climbed on some 30 feet and took a look at his progress.

"Just keep looking up," Cormac called to him.

Henry nodded and kept moving, the flipline grabbing tight as he stepped higher and higher.

Sixty feet high.

"He's slowing," MacNair said to Cormac.

"He's good," Cormac said.

Peter nodded his head in agreement. Henry was slowing, but Peter knew that he could do it. The kid was moving steadily, checking his feet and the bite of his spurs, but he was still moving and that was the most important thing.

A few more minutes—a small eternity—passed before the kid stopped about 100 feet up and set his spurs into the wood and his flipline tight at waist level.

"He's a bit short," MacNair said.

"Ah, it's a smaller one," Cormac said.

Henry's first few swings of the axe looked soft to Peter, but soon the kid was really throwing some wood. A small smile crossed Peter's face, as Henry whittled the wood away to a point, like a sharpened pencil. Then the kid set up so his final strokes would steer the treetop to the southwest.

"A wee bit more," MacNair said.

"Stand clear."

The kid took another swing. There was a crack. Henry pulled the axe free and dropped down a foot as the top snapped and the tree swung like a pendulum. "Timber" came the shout, a moment too late.

The tree landed hard. Throwing branches and earth from the ground. The men had moved to a safe distance, but still they turned away or raised a hand to protect their faces from the flying debris.

"Woohoo!" Cormac shouted.

MacNair lifted his fingers to his mouth and sent a whistle up to the kid. Peter waved. And the kid smiled down at them.

Henry topped two more trees that afternoon. On the wagon

back to camp, Cormac and MacNair promised Henry a night to remember. Food. Drinks. Women. Peter hadn't the mind to drink. He was wrapped in his thoughts. The kid was moving on; Spence would have Henry topping trees when they were back at work Monday morning. As for himself, he'd have a new partner on the saw or he'd be on the bucking crew. Maybe it was time for a bigger change; he didn't know. He thought of Katherine, or was it Geraldine? He wanted to tell her about Katherine. How she reminded him of her. He hadn't told her anything of Katherine, and she hadn't asked. It'd be a silly thing to do, to tell her, but who else was there?

❧

Peter finished his supper and his second beer and left the others at the hotel. He had to see her. He had to sort his feelings. Things had changed and he was running out of reasons to be where he was.

He walked down the alleyway in the shadows of dusk. He asked the man for Geraldine.

"You want a bath too?"

"Not tonight," Peter said.

"Geraldine," called the man.

She came out of her room wearing the same dress as before. He tipped his hat to her.

"Frank, you returned." She seemed to smile.

Sober, the name hit him like a needle to the arm, pinching old muscles buried deep. He pursed his lips. "I've been thinking of you."

She nodded. "Follow me." And the corners of her mouth raised somewhat mechanically before she turned down the hallway.

In her room, his eyes landed on the bouquet of wildflowers. It had been freshened since he'd last been there. He recognized the pink and white lilies; as for the other flowers—some yellow and some white—he had no idea of their names.

"You like the flowers?"

"Yeah," he said.

"I collect them on my walks."

He nodded and turned to her.

"I didn't think I'd see you again. Maybe last week—"

He rubbed his jaw. She thinks I've come back to have what I missed, he thought.

"So, you're feeling better," she said.

He raised his eyes to her slowly. "I'm better."

She pressed herself against him. "You ain't smelling like a distillery this time. Would you do better with a drink? I want a drink." She turned to her nightstand, pulled out a slim flask, and offered it to Peter.

Peter shook his head.

"Suit yourself." She took a drink from the flask and let out a long breath. He watched, nervously, as she slid off her dress.

"Wait," he said.

"It's getting late, Frank." Her hand slipped open his pants button, then slid below. She took him in her hand.

He felt himself respond to her touch, but he pulled away from her. "No."

She shook her head and quickened her stroke. "What do you want? Do you want me to hold you like you were my little baby boy?"

He grabbed her by the wrist. "I made a mistake."

She let go of him. "Then go."

He looked at her, not understanding, as she slipped her arms through the sleeves of her dress.

"You heard me." Her voice raised. "Get out."

"Please, Geraldine—"

"You want something else?"

He nodded, sheepishly.

"I'm not your mother or whoever you're looking for—"

"Her name was Katherine. She wasn't—"

The door opened and the man from the front stood in its frame looking at Peter, then Geraldine. "Did he hurt you?"

She shook her head. "No, he's just playing games."

The man looked at her, then Peter, suspiciously.

"I'll be leaving," Peter said as he tucked his shirt into his pants. He took one last look at Geraldine. She looked more like Katherine than she ever had before—the Katherine of Kaidenberg, broken and filled with disappointment—and he was surprised he hadn't noticed earlier. Then he turned and left the brothel.

⁊

Sunday morning Peter was back fishing the river. He raised his fishing rod and watched the line lift through the water tracing a 'v' as it travelled its path. This always reminded him of a string of snow geese in flight. He slowly reeled in the line.

It was past noon when the kid arrived.

"I didn't think you would come," Peter said.

The kid looked hung-over—red-eyed and pale. "I didn't either." Henry stood there watching Peter cast his line into the river, its banks full, racing for the Pacific. "Are you mad at me?"

"No," Peter said. "You will be a good topper."

"I need to do it, Peter," Henry said. "Mother lost her job now that the soldiers are back and looking for work, and this'll be an extra five dollars a week."

Peter smiled close-lipped. "It's good you take care of your family." The kid was quiet, although Peter figured there was still plenty on the boy's mind. Peter took a step toward him and clapped him on the shoulder. "I'm proud of you, Henry."

The two fished together that afternoon for the last time. Peter was going home. There was no reason to be away any longer. He doubted that'd he'd stay in Kaidenberg for good, but long enough to see his family and see what else he'd been missing; and, of course, to say goodbye to Katherine.

He'd wait a week, maybe more, before telling Spence he was done. He didn't want Henry thinking it was because of him, because it wasn't.

❧

That Friday, April 18, 1919, Henry Sutherland died from a 110-foot fall down a 400-year-old Douglas Fir. None of the men saw what happened; he'd already begun topping the tree. It seemed that the spur on his left leg brace had broken, perhaps mid-swing, and the kid couldn't recover.

Peter gnawed his cheek as he helped Cormac load Henry's broken body onto the back of the wagon. He'd had to look away at the sight. Henry. The poor kid. This, for five more dollars a week. It made Peter sick.

"Back to work," Spence hollered at the men. "Nothing more we can do." And Peter watched as the men around him slowly picked up their axes and trudged off through the broken forest. "Go on, Peter," said Spence. "Don't make me dock your wages."

Peter stared back at Spence. "He wanted to get a boat one day," he said. "And fish on the ocean."

"I wish he could've, Peter."

"Me too," Peter rubbed his jaw. "I'm leaving, Spence. I'd planned to tell you later on, but now..." He shook his head. "You can dock my wages; it don't matter to me."

Spence sighed. "I ain't going to dock your wages, Peter. I just need the guys to work through it or it'll be harder tomorrow."

Peter nodded. "Let me take the kid back to his family."

"You'd do that?"

"I need to."

Saturday evening, Cormac and MacNair took up a collection from the men. Two hundred and seventy-two dollars from 54 men. Leahy added to it. Made it an even $300. Sunday morning, Peter accompanied Henry's casket aboard the train to Nanaimo, and from there onto the steamship to Vancouver. It was morning when the steamship docked.

Mrs. Sutherland lived in a small yellow house on Heatley Street. Peter took a deep breath, set his suitcase on the ground, and knocked on the door. He'd never done this sort of thing before, but he felt obliged to see her in person. The kid had been his friend, perhaps his only true friend since Karl Ziegler had been hauled away to the internment camp.

The door opened half-way and a woman with chestnut-coloured hair and dark-ringed eyes looked out from behind it. The woman wore a tight-faced expression and when she looked up at Peter, he could see there was anger in her eyes. He'd been told Leahy had sent a telegraph informing her of the accident and to expect someone. Yet he supposed he'd imagined Henry's mother reacting differently.

"Mrs. Sutherland?"

She nodded.

"Peter Eberle." He felt the woman's stare on his face and, for a moment, Peter thought he might lose his balance. There was something unsettling about this woman, Henry Sutherland's mother. "I am sorry," he said. "I worked with your son, Henry. He was a good man."

"Man?" She shook her head. "He was only eighteen."

Peter nodded.

She left the door open and walked into the shadows. "Close the door behind you."

Peter picked up his suitcase and stepped into the house. Mrs. Sutherland stood in the small kitchen wringing her hands in her stained apron. The room was dim, the curtains on the west-facing window offered only a fragmented patchwork of early morning light. She was alone: where were Henry's sisters? Peter wondered. She looked to the wood stove and the busy counter-top, then turned around to the small table, picked a potato sack off of it and set it on the floor. She looked at Peter and pointed to one of the mismatched chairs around the table. "Coffee?"

"Please." Peter took another step into the room, gripping his suitcase handle with both hands in front of him.

Mrs. Sutherland poured Peter a cup of coffee and set it on the table. Peter took a seat next to the coffee, then waited for Mrs. Sutherland to take her chair.

"Mr. Leahy's man made the arrangements. St. Paul's." She shook her head. "I ain't hardly taken a step west of Cambie Street since before the war started."

Peter took a sip of coffee. It was weak. Lukewarm. He set the cup down carefully. There were only a few things he'd wanted to say to her. He hadn't any real understanding of her world or this city; he knew as much about it as he did about crows' nests or bears' dens. He looked at Mrs. Sutherland. "Henry was a good worker. I liked working with him. We fished on Sundays."

The woman sat there silent. Peter waited for her to say something. He took another sip of the bad coffee and noticed a thin stream of tears tracing the woman's face.

"What are we going to do? There's no good work for us with the soldiers back and the Chinese working for cheap," Henry's mother cried.

Peter reached into his coat pocket and pulled out a thick envelope. "This is for you and the girls." He set it on the table halfway between him and Mrs. Sutherland. "We passed the hat."

Mrs. Sutherland reached for the envelope, then paused with her hand on it. She opened the envelope and flipped through the bills. Once she was done counting them, she tucked the envelope in her apron pocket. "I know it ain't proper to count it out in front of you," she said, almost defiantly, "but you can't put meat in front of a hungry dog and not expect it to eat."

"I know," he said.

He drank his coffee and tried to think of a polite way to leave. He almost wished he hadn't come. There was too much sadness here. Desperation. He missed the forest. The river. There was some peace there in the green world.

"Everything I hold onto leaves me," said the woman.

"I am sorry, Mrs. Sutherland," Peter said as he got up from his chair. "I have to go." He avoided looking at the woman, as he picked up his luggage and made for the door, fearing, if he did, something about her might hold him there. Then, not being able to hold back any longer, he stopped and turned to the woman. "I am sorry for you and Henry." He swallowed and stepped out the door.

Outside, he took a deep breath. What was it that people

wanted? He shook his head. How could he answer that when he didn't even know what it was he himself wanted?

Peter turned on Union Street and walked toward Main. The day was warm. There were people about on the street. Automobiles puffing out smoke. And, to the south, there was the rail yard and the clang of steel on steel. He made his way to the rail station. His path was straightforward now: he was going east. Riding the steel rails through the Rockies and over the prairie back to Kaidenberg. Back to Katherine.

TELLING STORIES
1919

FOLKS WEREN'T so kind toward me or mine following the attack on Bernhard. The rumour mill had passed its judgment and settled on me, Kaspar Feist, and Charles Harrison as its main suspects. And, again, it felt as though Bernhard was heaping his revenge upon me. This time without the slightest bit of effort. Not that I envied him. From what I was hearing he was in a bad way. But when it comes to sorting the wheat from the chaff once a story has had its way around Kaidenberg, I'll take my chances on finding a needle in a haystack. Zahn, the shopkeeper, told my wife, Margaret, that Bernhard had gone deaf, dumb, and blind. I'd heard from Andreas Stolz that Bernhard was right as rain, but had developed a mean streak to rival the devil—something about him ripping off chickens' heads and plotting his revenge on me and on Harrison. While Stolz's story seemed more in tune with the Bernhard I'd known, I doubted very much that he would ever be the man he was before. I'd done all I could that day to stop his bleeding and to revive him. It was the reviving that worried me the most. When I returned him to his wagon box, I would've wagered his chances of waking near even—either he would or he wouldn't. The fact he did tells me either God ain't finished with him or he ain't finished telling God what's what.

Truth be told, I'd say there's something about taking care of a man you've spent a good part of your life hating, fixing up his wounds and such. It changes your heart and your heart changes your mind. It's a funny thing how that works. So, I guess after all that hate, it finally ended up that I genuinely pitied Bernhard and wished well for him.

I'd be lying if I said I hadn't given some thought as to whether a righting might be coming my way, especially early on when Bernhard showed little sign of ever running a plough again, much less tying his boot laces. I figured if someone would be making amends it'd be Bernhard's brother, Christian, and maybe his brother-in-law, Nels. Seeing that they didn't, I reckon some common sense prevailed. They probably figured that had I wanted to seek my revenge on Bernhard I would've found a better place in the past ten years than the church picnic to do it. But that didn't mean we all just magically got along. There was plenty of talk behind our backs and nasty looks, especially in that first year. Going to church became a hurtful thing. I'd never seen so many scowling faces eyeballing me as I did when Margaret and I would walk to our pew on Sunday morning. Eventually, things got better, but only because so much else changed—Father Selz leaving for Alberta, the flu epidemic, automobiles and everything moving fast—maybe it got easier to let go. There were little things that helped too, like the boys working things out, Frank Jr., Lambert, and my nephew, Ignaz. I helped a little with that. It made a big difference for young Frank, and I was happy to help him. We had talked a bit. I suppose I was the only one he could talk to at that time.

It was a few weeks after the picnic that I noticed Frank—young Frank, I mean—lurking around the farm. He was about eight, I believe. The first time, I was going off to feed the milk cows when I saw him out of the corner of my eye, about 100 yards away, on the side of the road, ducking behind the wheat crop. I took a double look and saw him peek his head out again and just as quickly he was gone. I didn't give him much mind. I figured if he wanted to talk he'd come find me. I spotted him again a few days later. He was in our pasture hiding among the cattle. He was a sneaky little guy, keeping an eye on me as he moved from one cow to the other. I watched him from my blacksmith shop, off and on for nearly half an hour before I finally got to my work. After that I suppose he must've figured our little dance was done, because when I walked into the blacksmith shop the next day he was there waiting for me, looking over my forge and hand tools from a distance.

I wasn't too sure what to say to the boy. Those who know me know I'm not the most welcoming of others in my work space— just ask my son, Jakob—but I had no intention of telling this young fella to go. The last time we'd spoken I was setting off to help mend his stepfather's head after he'd dropped that rock on him. The boy had been about ready to run away and never come back, and seeing him like this got me wondering if those thoughts weren't back in his head. He wore a sad-puppy look on his face and for some reason seeing him there reminded me some of my own little boy, Anton, who might've been just a few years older than Frank was then when he died. Anyhow, I just gave the boy a nod of my cap and sat down at my grindstone. I had it rigged like a bicycle with two foot levers to get it spinning.

"Pass me that axe." I pointed to my work bench about halfway between the two of us. He looked at the axe and then fetched it for me. I took the axe from him. "I'm going to put a new edge on this. If you watch how I do it, then you can work on the next one."

He nodded, and I got to pedaling and honing that axe blade on the spinning grindstone. The boy watched with a keen focus. His dark eyes narrowed and his jaw relaxed enough that I could make out a little space between his thick lips. He didn't make a sound. After I finished, I got up and found an old hatchet and told the boy to take a seat. The seat plate was made of cast iron and I had set an old piece of sheepskin on there to provide a little comfort, but the boy, being a runt of a man, couldn't push both pedals at once; still, we made it work. And he showed plenty of patience as we put a nice fine edge on that old hatchet.

"Now put a new handle on it," I said, "and it'll be just like new."

I could feel there was a smile inside him somewhere, maybe it was in his eyes since his mouth didn't quite show it, but it was a start.

"You're a ways from home, huh?" I continued. My farm was three miles from Bernhard's, a little less by the way the crow flies, but this time of year, with the crops standing tall, there were no shortcuts.

He stood there shy and quiet and staring at his feet.

"You hungry? Let's go see what's in the garden," I said. He seemed to like the idea, so I walked him over to the garden patch and let him pick at the peas while I dug up a few fresh carrots about the size of my fingers. As I dusted off the carrots, I watched Frank shell the four or five pea pods he'd picked into the palm of his hand; he lowered his face down to his palm and ate them up like a hog eating from the trough. Watching him munch up those peas put a smile on my face.

"It was nice of you to pay me a visit." I handed him a carrot. "Any particular reason you come by?"

He looked down at his feet again. I remember thinking this

boy must be a fearful, scared type, but when I look back at it now I think he had more courage than most his age. It's something, to reach out to another person; it's not light work. It's easier to bury things, or so I'd say from my own experience. It might've been a half-minute or so before the boy chirped up and answered me. "I wanted to hear your story," he mumbled.

"What story would that be?"

"You told me you had a story," he said, with a shy kind of desperation.

"I did?"

"Is it about my father? My real father?"

"I'm sorry, I don't know much about your father," I said, before I fully gathered what it was the boy wanted to hear. "He seemed to be as good a man as any," I continued, trying to make amends. "He kept a good farm and worked hard. I remember he liked talking about your mother, he was proud of her, proud to be married to her. I suppose that's something I know."

The boy nodded. There wasn't too much shine in his eyes. I felt a whole lot of sadness for the little fella. I hadn't realized he had his mind set on hearing a story about his father. I don't know what made me do it, but as soon as I started speaking again the words came straight out my mouth without my head's knowing.

"Well, there was that one time your father...he helped me out of a bad situation."

"How did he do that?" asked the boy.

"Well, I'll tell you." I gave him another carrot. He took a bite and chewed on it, just as I was chewing on how best to tell this one.

"It happened in the fall just before the year you were born, but he knew you were coming. He was on his way back home from town, probably went to check in on the priest. Your father was good for doing that kind of thing.

"Anyway, like I said, I was in a bad situation. I'd gone out to do... some hunting. I used to hunt back then, not so much these days. I wanted to get a deer, so we'd have some deer meat to mix with pork and make some good sausage for over the winter.

"So, I was out there on the land and I'd been out there most of the day. I was getting cold and I was making my way home. As I did, well, I saw the biggest deer I ever did see, and I think it made me a bit careless because I forgot which horse I was riding that day. She was a jumpy one, especially at the sound of a gun. Had I been smart I'd have gotten down off my horse, led her away and maybe tied her to something nearby. But, like I said, I was excited and pulled my rifle out of my saddle holster and took aim. It was a long shot, but I wanted that deer. So, I took my shot. And BANG! My horse reared up on its hind legs as scared as can be and I went falling back, nearly went head over heels, and I landed hard on the ground. Knocked the wind right out of me. And my horse took off.

"Now, somehow my horse ran nearly straight toward your father, and, true I wasn't there to see it, but I know that horse was mighty upset and there was no stopping it, for him or no one. But, your father, he must've seen it coming off in the distance and he must've seen a chance to do some good. So, what he'd done was, he unhitched one of his horses from the wagon, and I'm guessing he picked the fastest of the two—"

"That'd be Dusty," said the boy, who I could see was now wearing a big smile, full of excitement.

"I think you're right. I think he said his horse's name was Dusty." I smiled back at the boy. "Well, he rode his horse, Dusty, bareback right up to my own and when he got there he did a fancy thing and went straight from riding Dusty onto the back of my horse and he rode her till she got used to his feel and he got her calmed down—"

"What was your horse's name?"

"Oh that, that was Juniper. She's still out there." I pointed to the pasture. "We'll go see her later and get her hitched up to the wagon, and I'll take you on back toward your place. How does that sound?"

"I don't have to go," the boy said.

"Sure, not now," I said. "Later on. We ain't finished the story. Anyway, where was I... Oh yeah, well, your father he did all that without knowing who he was doing it for and I thought that was awful nice. And he rode Juniper all the way back to his wagon with his good horse, Dusty, following right behind them. Now I think that'd be where most people would stop, you know, they'd probably see the brand on the horse and take the horse over the next day. But your father, he knew something was wrong and that someone might be hurt, so he hitched his horse back up and tied my Juniper to the end of the wagon and rode out in the direction she'd come from.

"Thing is, I was hurt bad and hadn't even got to my feet. I was just lying in pain and moaning and praying to God that someone might find me. It was darn near dusk by then and I was worried I'd be spending the night under some cold stars, but when I heard the teetering sound of that wagon coming over the prairie I got so happy I might've danced if I could've, but I couldn't, so I shouted for help. And, well, it was your father who came to my rescue and I was so happy to see him, let me tell you. He got me standing and when I saw he'd found Juniper too, I swore to him I'd do what I could to help him someday. I even offered to give him some money for what he'd done, but he just said, 'Kaspar, you keep your money, and just you keep an eye out for me and my family, 'cause my wife and I got a little baby coming, and I'll do the same for yours, because that's all that matters.' And I said I would... I reckon that's the story I meant to tell you when I said I had a story to share with you."

I looked down at that boy and damn it if he wasn't crying, and I just got so that it made me cry too—thinking about that boy never knowing his real dad and wishing I'd seen my Little Anton once more. And thinking about him in that little box when we buried him back in North Dakota, some five hundred miles away. Well, I got choked up. And he just wrapped his arms around my waist and we had ourselves a cry. Then I walked him on over to where Juniper was and he noticed my bad limp and asked if I'd gotten that when I fell off the back of Juniper. Well, I didn't see the harm in it, so I told him that's when it happened. I think he liked that. It made me smile when we got her hitched to the wagon and he offered to help me up. "Oh, just like your father did," I said. That brought another big smile to his face. We talked a little more on the ride back. He wanted to know what happened to the deer. "I must've clean missed it," I told him. And he figured maybe his father went back the next day and got it, because he'd heard his grandpa tell him his father was a good hunter. And it seemed fine to me, so I told Frank, "I think I heard he did get that big deer."

Then, as we got closer to his home, well, we both turned a little quiet and I could tell he wasn't so happy to be leaving just then, so I told him he could sneak by every now and again, but not to do it too often or his mother would get worried. I told him his father would want him to be helping her as much as he could and that seemed to settle him some and he put on as brave and proud a face as I'd ever seen any boy wear.

I'm ashamed to say I didn't ride him all the way back to his yard. I didn't think Bernhard would take too kindly to me coming by without no invitation. So I dropped Frank off about a half-mile from the yard and headed on toward my son Jakob's farm. I guess that was another thing about that boy, his visiting brought me and Jakob back together some. I know I surprised Jakob when I showed up like that, without his mother or saying so much as a word beforehand.

Things had never been easy between me and Jakob. I was hard on him even before Bernhard took that land from underneath my nose. It was just the way we rubbed up against each other and those early days in the Dakotas were hard on all of us. So I didn't take it so bad when the first words out of his mouth were, "What's wrong, Father?"

"I wanted to see you," I said, climbing down from the wagon.

"That's it?"

"I'd been thinking about you. Your mother tells me you and the Reichert girl hit it off at the picnic."

After I mentioned the picnic, I could see the thoughts change behind his eyes. "There's a lot of people saying you're the one who hurt Bernhard."

"And you think I did?"

He shook his head. "Wouldn't upset me if you did. If folks didn't know what kind of man he was before the picnic, they had some picture of it by the end. I just don't understand why you'd wait so long to do it."

"You think I did it?"

"Well, it wasn't me," Jakob countered.

I laughed. What was I to tell Jakob? That it was an eight-year-old boy who'd done it. That poor kid already had enough misfortune, being born half orphan, and the idea of passing the buck to him—I don't think I'd ever have slept another peaceful night had I let that slip.

"It was your mother," I told him. "She finally had enough of all my talk."

Well that put a smile on his face, and he told me he visited the Reichert family and had coffee with them and had been invited back for a Sunday meal. It was happy news. A blessed day. And it all started with young Frank walking into my yard. The boy reminded me so much of Anton; I wished I could've shared that with Jakob, but I wasn't so sure he'd see it the way I did. He still had plenty of anger to direct at Bernhard and that extended to just about anything Bernhard cared for. Of course, that was my doing, setting Jakob up on that farm right next door to him. That's another one I've added to the list of the things I ain't so proud of in my days. Anyhow, those are other stories, and this is about Frank.

So young Frank took me on my word and paid me a couple more visits that year. He slowly started talking to me, telling me the things that were on his mind. Of course, he wanted to know more about his father. I tried to help him where I could without inventing more than I could remember. For the most part, they were innocent little stories, like the one where his father caught a hawk and trained him to land on his arm. I told him that one happened back when his father was a little boy on the steppe. I figured it was harmless enough. The one that worried me some was the one I'd made up about his father being asked to leave choir because he was so good he made all the other singers sound like mooing cows. It sure made the little fella laugh when I told him that one.

There were other things he wanted to know about too, like coyotes. He wanted to know what they liked to eat, if they'd eat a boy, if they could see in the dark, and what would happen if they found him crawled up inside one of their dens. Badgers too. Some of the questions he asked were harder for me since I didn't really know most of the answers myself. Nor was it something I wanted to make up fancy stories about; I was getting the feeling the boy might be thinking about running off, but I didn't say nothing. Then winter came and I didn't see him around except for church, and only a few times the next summer. I took that as a good thing. The times he did come around, he'd taken an interest in blacksmith work, heating the metal, bending and shaping it into the things a man could use.

Things pretty much went to pot for young Frank that winter when the Spanish flu hit and took his mother with it. Him and his sister Elisabetha went to live with their uncle Nels and aunt Aggie. I guess, things could've been worse. He could've stayed with Bernhard. How that would've worked I don't know. From what I'd gleaned from the boy, the accident at the church picnic had changed Bernhard. He forgot things like whether he'd done the chores or not. He'd yell and get upset real quick. And there was drinking too. More since Katherine's passing.

It must've been November 1918 when his mother passed, and I think it was late May or early June of the following year when Frank paid us a visit. He'd gone quiet again and it wasn't stories he was looking for, it was the forge and the hammer he wanted. He had a hurt inside him he needed to work out. All I could do for him was heat up some iron and let him hammer that metal against the anvil.

It went on like that for a while. It seemed he was here nearly every other day that summer, though it probably wasn't that often. I don't know how he got away from the farm so much without his cousin Lambert or his uncle and aunt getting curious about it. Well, eventually they did. I understand now that he'd been telling them that he was going off to visit Bernhard. That worked up until Nels checked in on Bernhard himself and didn't find Frank there. Well that must've set Nels's mind turning. That Nels is a cool one. He didn't show his cards straight away. He just waited until the next time Frank told him he was going off to visit Bernhard and let Frank have his start and then followed the boy the mile and a half to my farm.

That's how it happened that Nels come by my farm that July day in 1919. I was in the house when Nels rode up on his horse. Not one of those big Belgians he owned, this was a smaller quarter horse. I hadn't yet seen Frank that morning, though sometimes he went straight out to the blacksmith shop.

It didn't take much for me to put two and two together. I guess I'd always suspected this day would come. Still, I'd be lying if I didn't tell you I had an uneasy feeling in my gut when I looked out the window and saw Nels Eberle riding up to the house.

So, I set my coffee down and went out to meet him. "Nels," I said. "What brings you here?"

He didn't say nothing straight away. Instead he just leaned back in his saddle, looked at me for a moment or two like he was studying me, like he could learn something from the way I was standing there waiting for him to talk.

"Why don't you come on down and have a coffee with me and Margaret? I was in the middle—"

"Sorry to bother you, Kaspar. I'm looking for Katherine's boy, Frank. Have you seen him around here?"

That was it. There was no fancy story I could tell to get me and the boy out of this one.

"He's probably around somewhere."

"What's he doing here?"

"He comes here every once in a while. He likes to help me blacksmith."

Nels's eyes turned to the shop and, like he and his horse were of one mind, the horse turned straight for the door of the shop.

I hurried over to the shop as fast as my bad knee would take me. I was worried for the boy; he'd been lying to Nels for a while. There was no question in my mind that Nels would be wanting to teach him a lesson, and if I had to guess about it I figured he'd do it right there and then, just to show me he was the authority. "Frank," I hollered, as Nels stepped down off his horse. "Frank, are you there?"

Young Frank stepped out from the door right in time for Nels to grab him by the shoulder and give him a slap to the backside that made him jump off the ground.

"Whoa!" I shouted. I was within spitting distance of Nels. "Best you hold up on that boy!"

"Keep your nose of out of this, Kaspar," Nels said. "You've done enough against this boy with your revenge on Bernhard." Nels paused. It was as though his mind were suddenly stuck on the thought—why Frank would even be at my place. "What sort of lies has he been feeding you?" he shouted at the boy.

"He ain't been feeding me nothing," Frank said. He sniveled and held his hand to his backside.

"Nels, the boy's been helping me is all. I was meaning to get around to telling you. That's my fault, not the boy's."

"Don't lie to me, Kaspar. It doesn't suit you." He let loose his grip on the boy and turned his anger on me. "Is this your way of getting back at Bernhard? I used to think you were a decent man."

"You mind how you speak to me on my own land," I said. I

took another step closer to him. I could feel my blood boiling. Sure, it might all be a misunderstanding, but I didn't take to being insulted on my own farm.

We were nearly standing toe to toe—it was a staring match if I'd ever been in one—and I wanted to push him. Send him right back where he came from. We must've both been thinking the same thought because suddenly we had each other by the arms in a pushing match. And, just as I could feel my bad knee wanting to give way, the young fella shouted out, "He didn't do it."

Nels grunted and turned to the boy. He'd eased up just enough that I got my arms free of his and hobbled a half-step to the side. From the corner of my eye, I spotted Margaret standing by the house with a worried look on her face. I shook my head and waved her away.

"Didn't do what?" Nels said.

"That's between me and Frank," I said.

"He didn't hurt Bernhard... I did."

"Don't lie to me." Nels grabbed the boy again.

"Don't," I said to the both of them.

"I'm not lying," the boy said. "I dropped the rock."

Nels paused; his mouth fell open. "You put him up to this," he said to me. There was spit hanging from his lip and I suspected he was about ready to continue our pushing match. As for myself, I was smiling inside. I was so proud of the boy for telling the truth and standing up for himself and for me.

"No," I said. "I only helped him keep it a secret."

"What the hell, Kaspar! Why?"

"He's just a boy. He didn't know what he'd done... Ain't you ever been on the wrong side of something like that?" I said. And from the way Nels looked—his eyes lowered for the first time since he'd stepped onto my farm—I figured he had. "I have. It's a heavy enough cross for a man to carry, let alone for a boy all by his lonesome."

Nels's eyes were still lowered. He was thinking hard. Then he looked straight at young Frank once more. "Why'd you drop a rock on Bernhard?"

The boy was quiet. I wanted to speak for him, but I knew Nels wanted those words from Frank.

"You can tell me," he said, his voice softening just a little.

"I don't know."

"You do know."

"He made me mad," the boy said.

"How'd he make you mad?"

"He hit my friends and he scared Mother...and I didn't want him to be my father any more."

Nels sighed. We all just stood there.

"What am I to do with you, Frank?" The words hung in the air for some time.

"He's a good boy," I said. "He's been a big help for me, Nels."

Nels nodded, then he kicked the dirt with the ball of his foot and walked back to his horse. "He's too big to ride back with me on this horse," he said. "Can you bring him back to the farm when you two are done?"

"Sure," I said. I watched Nels climb up on his horse. It turned its head towards the boy in a pretty way, like it was giving Frank a kiss on the cheek. Then, as quick as that, Nels and the horse were headed back from where they'd come.

Frank and I spent some more afternoons together that summer. We never did talk too much more about that day. But there was a change in the boy; after he made his confession a load had come off him, and his anger seemed to cool. He was less interested in pounding the iron, drawing and spreading it. Instead, he wanted me to teach him new things, like how to twist iron to make a fancy cross like I did for Anton or bend it into a perfect circle. He visited some the next summer, and he's come a few times again this year, but I got a feeling he doesn't need me like he did before. I know I should be happy for him, but I miss him and our visits. And I miss my Anton too.

THE CARD GAME
1928

I CROSSED PATHS with young Frank Weran today; caught him on his way back from Bernhard's old farm. He's no longer the little boy getting pushed around at the church picnic. He's grown up, a big broad-chested 19-year-old, not much younger than his father was when he passed. Damn. It's hard to look at him and not see his father, especially around the eyes. They're Weran eyes: dark and kind of sunken in under the brow. When Katherine was around he still looked plenty like his mother; nowadays, all I see are those deep-set eyes and my mind plays tricks on me and takes me back to that winter day when my brother, Peter, killed Frank's father.

Anyhow, Frank and me got to talking, and while half my mind was stuck reliving that horrible day, I managed to blather on as I do. "Checking on the old farm?" I asked from my wagon perch; forgetting it wasn't Frank's to be checking on. "I mean...I know it ain't yours—"

"I've got some dealings with Jakob Feist," Frank said from his saddle, "which might change all that."

Those words put a chill down my spine, and the half of my mind watching my brother slam the axe in the older Frank Weran's back stopped, and another memory took its place.

✌

It was last October, 1928. There were four of us playing the regular Friday afternoon card game above Zahn's Hardware & Lumber Supply in Kaidenberg. It was a small room with two card tables and maybe a dozen chairs, a scrap of carpet on the floor to dull the noise of shifting table legs and tapping feet, an east-facing window draped with a sun-bleached blue sheet, and an electric light hanging from the plaster ceiling. We sat at the table nearest the door and the electric light. None of us were expecting Bernhard to show up, but it was an open game and anyone with a few bits in their pocket was welcome to play.

"I got another letter from Margaret's brother-in-law in Argentina," I told the others as I tossed a couple of pennies into the pot.

Jakob Feist leaned back in his chair. "They need money?"

Andreas Stolz stroked his thick beard, pulling it to a point at the base of his chin. "Lots worse off than us."

I nodded. "Their son's got TB. I have a stack of a dozen or more letters all asking for whatever we can spare to help with his treatments."

"You sent them money before," Frederich Gerein said. Unlike Stolz, he'd shaved his harvest beard some days earlier. Gerein dealt us each another card face up. It was stud poker. Seven cards.

"I did. But just the once. I got thinking it might be a swindle so I ignored the others. I've never met them. Margaret says her sister would never do such a thing." I sighed. "She also says she ain't ever going to see her sister again except in heaven and she wants to be in her good graces when the meeting comes, and now with this new letter she says I'd better pay up."

"So, you're going to give them more." Jakob folded his long

arms behind his head. He looked relaxed; he'd had a good year on the farm and had treated himself to a new coat and hat.

I shook my head. "I don't have much of a choice. I sent two dollars in the last letter and now they're asking for three." The three of them laughed at that and I smiled too. "But I sure ain't giving them three dollars."

Stolz smiled. "And now you're playing poker with us."

"I told Margaret I believe in her sister; I'm guessing the husband is a drunk but Margaret doesn't care. She just took a dollar from the keeping place, wrote her letter, and sent me to mail it." They all laughed again, but I just shook my head.

"That's it, Joseph," Stolz said, between laughs. "Keep your wife happy." The crow's feet around his eyes cut deep into his leathery skin. You'd have to figure he spent most of his days smiling and laughing in the sun. He eyed up the pile of coins in front of me. "Was that the dollar?" I smiled at him and tossed a nickel into the pot; Stolz laughed and tossed in his nickel.

Jakob shook his head. "I'm out."

Gerein slid a nickel into the pot. He had a dangerous hand showing: a chance at a straight or a spade flush. I had a pair of sevens on the table and another seven in my hand—enough to run me into a bit of trouble. Gerein tossed out the cards, face down this time.

I looked at mine. Not what I wanted. Gerein huffed when he picked up his card; I couldn't be sure if it was just show, so I tossed in another nickel. "I'm betting you guys don't want to take any more money from my poor brother-in-law," I joked.

"Your brother-in-law doesn't have to worry about me." Stolz said, folding.

"If you're giving money away to hopeless causes," Gerein said, "you might as well throw some my way." He put down his nickel and laid out his cards—spade flush.

I tossed my cards onto the table for them all to see. "Beats me." Stolz passed me his bottle of whiskey. "To losing," I said. Then I raised the bottle and took my swallow.

Money crisscrossed the table over the next few hands, but our easy ways were interrupted by the slow mechanical clomp of boot heels echoing through the floorboards and up the stairwell. It was followed by a duller sound, a breathy "pa-pa-pa" of a weary soul. I stalled the dealing and kept shuffling the cards waiting for our visitor to show.

"We can get another hand in before this one makes it up the stairs," Gerein said.

"Thought a greedy pig like you'd want more feed in the trough," I teased.

"I'm the butcher, not the pig," Gerein said. And, the way he said it, a little too seriously, made us all laugh again. Then the clomp-clomp stopped and all I could hear was the sound of puffy breathing from behind me.

"Speaking of pigs," Jakob said. His expression turned cold and dull as he looked to the door. "Look what the cat dragged in."

Bernhard Holtz stood leaning one hand against the wall at the top of the stairs—his nose was red from years of booze and his beard patchy with tufts of grey hair curled around the jaw line. He wore a miserable look on his face. The kind of look a man gets when he has a broken tooth shooting pain through his head and body. I don't know if Bernhard had a toothache, but I knew he had plenty to be miserable about—there was the beating he took at the church picnic that could've killed him, then Katherine dying and having to send the children to live with

Nels and Agatha, and living all alone again ever since. It's more than I'd wish on my worst enemy.

"Feist," Bernhard said, "I knew there was a reason my head was beginning to ache."

Jakob Feist grinned in a mean-looking way. "You've just seen through to the bottom of a few too many bottles."

Bernhard didn't say anything back. He just puffed himself up; his silence did the talking for him. He hobbled to the table, pulled out the extra chair between Gerein and me, and sat down.

"You look rough," Stolz said. "Like you've been sleeping in the livery."

"I heard old man Weninger's been sleeping in the livery," Gerein said.

"Ha! Sleeping? Zahn told me he caught the old man lying with the horses." Stolz snickered.

The bunch of us laughed. Old man Weninger was a scrawny fellow no higher than a country fence pole and probably just as thin. A genuine bachelor all his life. It seemed his mind had been causing him more and more trouble in his later years. Another sad story.

"I'm not surprised," Gerein said. "Ever since Gutenberg butchered the last of his sheep, he's had nowhere to sow his seed."

"Ugh." Jakob made a disgusted look. "Enough of that. Let's get on with the card game. You got money to play?" he asked Bernhard.

Bernhard reached deep into his coat pocket. He fished out a rust-coloured flask, removed the plug, and took a nip. Capping the flask, he returned to his pocket and pulled out a wad of grimy paper and coin mixed with bits of grain and straw.

"He's got money," Gerein said. "Deal the cards, Joseph."

There were five of us at the game now and I dealt us each two cards and a third face up as I told Bernhard the rules. Gerein set his pocket cards face down on the table. "Low card pays a penny. That's you, Stolz."

Stolz flicked a penny toward the centre of the table. "That's just on the first round," he said to Bernhard. "High card leads after that."

The rest of us followed along and put a penny in the pot. I dealt each player another card. The ace of diamonds, the high card, went to Gerein, and he tossed a pair of pennies into the pot. Bernhard called and so did the rest of us.

Another round passed. Everyone checked. It seemed no one had much of anything. Bernhard took another nip from his bottle. I got a whiff of it. It was a fierce drink.

On the next round, I paired my eight and raised the pot a nickel. Stolz folded, then Jakob. Gerein called with an ace-king showing; Bernhard called too. He had a mess of cards; I put him down for a head full of moonshine and a pocket pair.

"That's a lot of money, Bernhard," Jakob said. "Maybe you should save some for your daughter." It was a low blow, but I figured he wasn't the only one who'd thought it.

"I'll do as I please," Bernhard said. "Just like any other man."

"Leave him alone, Feist," Gerein chirped. "At least until the hand is done." Stolz and I smiled; it was typical form for Gerein. Jakob huffed and pushed his chair back from the table, while Bernhard took another pull from his flask.

I tossed one last card to Gerein, Bernhard, and myself. Face down. I looked to my card. King of clubs. It paired my king in the hole, leaving me with two pair—kings and eights. I tossed another nickel into the pot.

Gerein called my nickel and raised his bid a dime.

Bernhard grunted. "I don't know what I got here." He looked to Gerein and then to me. "I get so I don't remember the last thing I looked at sometimes," he said. Then he pushed his cards in. "I fold."

Jakob snickered. He seemed to be enjoying Bernhard's misfortune.

"All right, Gerein. What'd you get?" I mumbled to myself. I was pretty sure he didn't make his straight, he might've paired his ace, but mostly I figured he was trying to bluff me. So, I called his raise.

He laughed a sad kind of laugh. "I was hoping I could scare you off." He turned over his cards. He had nothing but the ace-king high.

I flipped over my pair of kings and raked in the pot.

"Did you get that on the last card?" asked Stolz as he collected the cards.

"Maybe I did." I smiled.

Jakob pulled his chair up to the table. "I was going to say earlier," he looked over to Bernhard, "before we got distracted, you aren't the only one getting letters from distant family. We've been getting some from Annaliese's family too, now that her father's died."

"Where are they?" Gerein asked.

"Back on the steppe."

"They want money?" I asked.

"They're not so fussy. They'll take money, old clothes, whatever we can send them."

"It's hard everywhere." Stolz pursed his lips and shuffled the cards.

"Yeah, but these Bolsheviks steal land from hard-working farmers," Jakob added.

"I should've stayed in the old country," Bernhard said. "I was old enough."

"I wish you would've," Jakob muttered.

"What's that?" Bernhard said, raising his voice. "You gotta speak up to me. I got this ringing in my ears ever since your father took a baseball bat to the back of my head."

"Shut your rotten lying mouth," Jakob said, firing spittle from his mouth. "My father ain't the one who harmed you."

Bernhard groaned. "You expect me to believe that."

"He told me so. On his deathbed."

Bernhard shook his head. "He had the opportunity."

I looked around the table: Stolz was fixed on the cards; Gerein was shaking his head, staring at the table; Jakob huffed and stared right back at Bernhard. I knew what they were thinking. Bernhard might've forgotten, but no one else who was there that day could forget the fireworks that Bernhard had started that afternoon. I prefer to think of the other fireworks show that day; the ones I set off and painted the evening sky with. Anyhow, Bernhard looked to me and said, "You were there, Joseph. Didn't you see something? I don't remember none of it."

"You upset a lot of people that day."

"See?" Jakob said.

"Can we stop reliving the past and get back to our game already," Gerein said.

"Yeah, yeah." Stolz started shooting cards out like a smooth machine, each one stopping just where you wanted it to be. The cards went out two down and one up, just as neat as anyone could make them.

Gerein threw in his penny and Bernhard matched it, so did Jakob and me.

Stolz folded. "This ain't my hand."

"You just keep tossing them pretty like you do," I told him.

He gave me a wink and tossed out the next round. It was an ugly mess. I checked, although my jack was the highest card showing. Then Jakob tossed in a pair of pennies.

"Feeling rich," Gerein said. "T call."

Bernhard threw in his coin. I looked at his cards. He had a five of diamonds and a two of spades. I had to wonder if he knew well enough how to play or if he was just going along with the rest of them. Apart from the odd flash, there wasn't much of his old spirited self. That knock to the head changed him, but it seemed there was more than just the effects of the injury haunting him. He looked tired to me. Worn out.

I threw in my pair of pennies and Stolz dealt us each a card.

"Have you seen Elisabetha lately?" I asked Bernhard.

He sat quiet.

Stolz looked around the table at the cards he'd dealt. "Four spades." I looked around and it was as he called it—he'd dealt us each a spade. "And for my next trick, I'll deal you each an ace." He laughed.

"Your bet, Feist," Gerein said, trying to hurry up the game. Jakob raised a pair of pennies, and Gerein folded.

"Don't you believe me? I'm going to deal you an ace," Stolz teased.

"No, I don't," Gerein replied.

Bernhard called Jakob's raise. "I ain't seen her in a month... maybe two," he said, slowly like he was trying to think each word out. "It's hard to remember time. Besides I ain't much good to her right now." He took another pull from his bottle.

I shook my head at his words. It was a pitiful shame to hear a father talk like that. I looked over at Jakob Feist. He was shaking his head and I could tell he was biting his tongue. I figured he might believe the guy was owed some hardship, but I knew he wasn't one to go on beating a dead horse.

"It's your play, Joseph," Stolz said.

"Yeah, yeah," I said. "I was just thinking." And tossed two pennies in the pot.

Stolz dealt again. The first card to Jakob was an ace of hearts. "What did I say?" said Stolz, laughing. "Shoulda stayed in the game, Gerein."

"Ah, that's just one."

He threw a queen of spades to Bernhard.

"See?" Gerein said.

"Sorry Bernhard, but maybe that lady's better for you. Chasing the flush?" Bernhard grunted noncommittal-like, and Stolz sent me an ace of clubs. "Ha," he said. "Damn near."

Jakob looked at his cards. He had an ace-king high on the table. *"Scheisse,"* he said. I figured, he was worried about that spade flush Bernhard was chasing. "I check."

"Check," Bernhard said.

I checked too.

Stolz dealt us the final card face down. Jakob snickered when he picked up his card. I couldn't tell by that snicker if he'd made something or missed it by a fraction; as for Bernhard, I couldn't see any light in his eyes when he picked up his card. There was no telling what he might be thinking. I wondered whether he was still with us, or maybe floating in a dream somewhere. As for myself, I picked up the nine of clubs, which paired the nine I had on the table. It was something.

It was Jakob's bet. He tossed his nickel without saying a word. Bernhard looked at him and tossed a nickel. It clanged with the other coins. Then he tossed in another.

"One of you has something more than me," I said. "I fold."

"You going to call?" Stolz asked Jakob.

Jakob sat there looking at Bernhard while Bernhard stared at his cards. "For some reason, I can't help to think you're fooling with me." He eyed Bernhard a moment longer. "Maybe I'm wrong..."

But Bernhard just kept staring at his hand. It was heavy on spades. Apart from the one off suit, he had the queen, the two, and the seven of spades on the board.

"I'll pay to know," Jakob said. He tossed another nickel into the pot and flipped his cards. "Aces over eights."

Bernhard turned over an ace and nine of spades. "Flush," he said. Then he took a nip from his flask and pushed his cards away.

"Good hand," Gerein said.

"Did you make it on the river?" Jakob asked.

"I can't hardly remember," Bernhard said. "Probably."

"Do you believe him?" Jakob said. He wasn't smiling.

"I don't think he's lying if that's what you're getting at." Gerein grinned mischievously.

Bernhard sat there not paying attention to Jakob or any of us, really. I pushed the pot toward him.

"Frank had a good year farming that quarter you left him," I said to Bernhard, trying to engage him. It was like talking to an old deaf aunt. "He's going to drill a new well and build a wood-frame house in the spring."

"I didn't leave him no quarter," Bernhard said. "Just gave him what was his."

"Ha, that's funny," Jakob scoffed. "To hear you talking like that."

Bernhard slammed his beaten old fist on the table. "You think I'm some lying cheating thief, but your father egged me on."

"You always had a choice," Jakob growled at Bernhard. "We

didn't. You put a burden on my family, split us apart, embarrassed us. My father wanted to get you back but he didn't have the stomach for it. I wish I'd hit you over the head myself, wish I would've thought of it earlier."

Bernhard closed his eyes. "Your blathering makes my head ring." He shook his head, and when he finally opened his eyes he stared long and cold at Jakob. "You talk about a burden, but I got a curse on my head from you folk. Anything I ever wanted or loved is gone from me: my wife, my children, my memories, even my unborn child." He paused as the tiredness came back to him. It seemed he only had enough fire left for the odd spark; he'd burned too much of it away. "I just want it to be over between us," he said. "I'd have preferred to finish it with Kaspar, but he ain't around no more to lift this damn curse, so you'll have to do it."

"Curse?" Jakob wagged his head.

"I say curse because that's what's it's been to me."

"You want me to wave my hands and lift your curse?"

"Play me for it," Bernhard said.

Jakob laughed nervously. "Play you for a curse? You've been drinking too much, Holtz."

"You win and I'll give you that quarter of land your father wanted."

I looked to Jakob and it seemed like those words hit him clean across the face and wiped away any smug thinking that had stained his mug.

"And if I win," Bernhard continued, "you set me free from the curse."

"That's it?" Jakob asked. He sat back in his chair and played with his hat, twirling it on his finger as a slow and easy smile raised his cheeks. "I don't even know how I'd go about lifting a curse."

"You write it out," Bernhard said. "And make it so the curse doesn't pass on to anyone else, especially my Elisabetha."

"That's all you want?" Gerein interrupted. "Get him to throw in something—a hundred dollars, a bred mare—something."

"Now you just stay out of it, Gerein," Jakob said.

"Put in something," Stolz encouraged.

"I don't know if I trust him is the thing."

"I don't take no pride in the pain I caused you or your family, Jakob. It's been on my shoulders for 20 years and I'm tired of living with it. I want it gone," Bernhard said, then he turned to me. "Write it out, will ya, Joseph?"

There was a desperation in his eyes. I found a piece of paper and put down the words: *I, Bernhard Holtz, do sign my quarter section of land to Jakob Feist.*

"And I'll sign it if you win," he told Jakob. "But I expect as much from you."

Jakob nodded. "Well, you get Joseph to write it up how you want it and I'll sign it, if you win."

"One hand?" Gerein asked.

Jakob looked to Bernhard. "Your choice."

"One hand," Bernhard said. "I win, the curse is gone."

"You don't want anything else?" I asked Bernhard. He was liable to forget such things.

"Don't need no horse. Just keep it simple."

"You agree?" I asked Jakob.

Jakob Feist looked at me and everyone else. "It's always been about the land," he said. And he handed the cards to Stolz to do the dealing.

I took another piece of paper and wrote: *I, Jakob Feist, do relieve Bernhard Holtz and all his kin from the curse that was set upon him many years ago.* And then I read it out loud. "How's that sound?"

"It works," Bernhard said.

"No one 'set' a curse," Jakob said. "Scratch that out."

"For what?" I asked.

"I don't know. Something different."

"Fell upon him," Stolz said as he shuffled the cards.

"'The curse that fell upon him many years ago'," I said.

"That'll do," Jakob said.

"Bernhard?"

"It don't matter."

So I wrote it down as Stolz dealt them each two cards face down in that fancy way of his and tossed them each one more face up: a jack of clubs for Jakob and an eight of diamonds for Bernhard.

"You can flip them up," Gerein said. "It won't make no difference."

Jakob stood up and flipped over his cards: four of spades and five of hearts. Bernhard turned his over too. Seven of hearts. Queen of hearts.

"This is going to be interesting," Gerein said.

Stolz flipped two more cards. Jakob got the four of clubs and Bernhard the five of spades. Jakob clapped his hands.

"That's a pair," Gerein said.

"For him," Bernhard said, sounding unsure of what had just happened.

"Yeah," I said.

Next came a ten of hearts for Jakob and king of diamonds for Bernhard. Bernhard had the highest cards but was still behind that low pair. Then came a six of spades for Jakob and the queen of clubs for Bernhard pairing his queen of hearts.

"Wooee!" Gerein shouted. "Pair of queens, Bernhard."

Jakob kicked the floor and shook his head.

"One more card," Stolz said.

The room went quiet as an empty church. Stolz picked a card off the deck and tossed it to Jakob—the six of hearts.

"Yes," Jakob said. "That's two pair for me."

"Woo!" Gerein said. He was sweating over the cards more than the rest of us. We were all on pins and needles waiting to see what might happen. My guts were tied in knots. I was hoping Bernhard would win. All he needed was one to make another pair and his queens would win the hand. I had a soft spot for him and the suffering he'd endured. I couldn't have imagined surviving it myself.

Bernhard stood up from his chair and slid it towards the table resting his weight on its back. The room took a breath as Stolz flipped the last card: two of clubs. Silence.

"Ain't that something," Stolz said.

"Yippee!" Jakob shouted.

"Sorry, Bernhard." I said, and patted him on the shoulder.

"It's fine," he said. "Hand me the paper and I'll make my mark." I gave him the paper and he signed it. Then he extended his hand out to Jakob Feist. "I'd be pleased if you shook my hand."

Jakob looked at that big calloused hand, the one that had done more than its share of punching and emptying bottles of liquor, and gave it a firm shake. Then Bernhard took his bottle and hobbled his way down the stairs.

The room vibrated quietly as we waited for the sound of the door to close below us.

"Ain't that the strangest thing," Jakob said, once the door swung shut.

"What's he going to do now?" Stolz asked.

"I don't know," I said. And I grabbed Bernhard's money from off the table and hurried to catch him.

I caught him outside, across the street, taking a drink from his flask. Behind him the sun was lowering over the town, bathing the world in soft pink. It was like staring into a wild rose. I waited for him to finish his drink.

"What are you doing, Bernhard? Where are you going?"

"Yonder." He nodded toward Main Street. "Eat something."

"What are you going to do without your farm?"

"I'll get by," he said. "I'm glad to be rid of it."

"I don't understand."

"No, you don't, I suppose." He looked hard into the sun then back at me. "I got a ringing in my ears and a headache I can't even drink away." He tapped his chest over his heart. "I got one lasting picture of my wife and daughter and it's taken over every memory I've had of them. There ain't nothing I remember of their faces but what I see in that picture."

I shook my head not understanding what he was telling me. Not understanding how truly tired this man was.

"I'm glad to be free of that land. It was a curse to me and now it's gone. You see?"

"You wanted him to win?"

"Either way," he said. "I didn't lose in there. I was counting on I'd be free of it. Elisabetha too."

"And Frank?"

"I don't see it having a hold over him. Things are good for him now. His mother's watching over him."

"Where are you going to sleep?"

He shook his head. "I'll probably stumble over to the livery. Zahn don't care if I'm in there. He says I scare Weninger away."

"Here," I said, and I put the coins in his hands. "Your winnings."

He looked at the handful. "Winnings?" He sighed, then stuffed the coins in his coat pockets and walked away.

Inside the card room the others were still talking. I heard their voices as I climbed the stairs.

"I tell you, he has to be drunk or crazy. Why else would he gamble his land away?" Stolz said.

"I think he knew what he was doing," Gerein said.

"I should give it back to him," Jakob said.

"After all those years? Kaspar would be rolling in his grave."

The men turned quiet as I entered the room and took my place at the table.

"Did you speak to him?" Stolz asked me. "What'd he say?"

"I'm going to give the land note back," Jakob said, before I could get a word out. He was wound up in a way I'd never seen before, pacing the room and waving around those notes. "I even signed the other note," he continued. "He can have it too. I don't want it."

"It's fine," I said. "He doesn't want any of it."

"Really?" Jakob said. He stopped pacing, picked up his chair, and held it up six inches off the ground.

"Feel free to take a seat," Stolz teased.

"He's happy to be rid of it," I told them.

"I don't understand," Jakob said, still holding the chair. He was all stirred up. I knew how he felt. I'd been that way myself more than once. The whole world unfolding in a way that is so strange and twisted it makes you want to run; at the same time it holds you—pulling you back with its reins, because you're at the centre of it and it's waiting till you let go of the bit, settle out and calm down before anything else might happen—otherwise, you'd just be jumping and kicking and going nowhere.

"He truly believes it's cursed," I continued.

Stolz laughed. "You were right, Gerein, he did know what he was doing."

"Strange as that seems," Gerein said.

"I think you should keep it," I told Jakob.

"How's he going to get by?"

"He's going to drink," I said. "Probably drink himself dead."

The men just shook their heads.

"He should stay there through the winter," Jakob said. "Any of you see him, you tell him I said so."

"I don't think he'd listen," Gerein said.

I nodded in agreement and the room went quiet again. It suddenly felt too small for the four of us and our thoughts. Gerein shuffled the deck. It ruffled like a flurry of grouse taking wing from some grassy cover. "Kaiser game?" he asked.

"The light's getting low," Jakob said. "I should be going." He stuffed the paper in his pocket, collected his coins and his hat and hurried down the stairs.

"How about the rest of you?" Gerein asked.

"One more game," Stolz said. "It'll help to set your mind on other things."

He was right. I didn't want to leave like Jakob, with my mind racing off the tracks. That's when mistakes happen. So I sat down with the boys and we played a game of Rummy. The cards were a blur of red and black numbers and faces. I couldn't make sense of them. More footsteps came up the stairs. It was Zerr. Stolz told him the story and I filled in the other parts when Gerein wasn't interrupting. Later, Gerein's brother, Peter, showed. By then, I'd had my fill of cards and talk, so I excused myself from the table. I wanted to find Bernhard. I wanted to offer him something: a meal, a bed for the night, something. I wondered if Jakob had found him and told him to go back to the farm and get some rest. I left the others to the game and went to find Bernhard.

I walked past my horse and grabbed a lantern from the back of my wagon, then walked down to the livery where I figured he might be drinking or sleeping it off. I opened the livery door and raised the lamp in front of me.

"Bernhard?" I called. To my left, a horse grunted and snorted hot heat through its nostrils. "Easy, boy. Easy."

Further down, I heard a kick and thrashing from inside a stall. The beast was upset. Frightened. I closed the livery door behind me. A bad feeling crept inside me and pulled on my guts. "Easy," I repeated. The horse whined and kicked at the boards. I heard a dull sound like a sack of grain hitting the floor and the creaking of the rafters as a piece of rope rubbed a groove in the wood. Then a hoof came up over the edge of the stall and I jumped back. Scared the shit out of me.

"Shhh," I hushed the horse. Trying to hush my beating heart. "Shhh!" I lifted the lantern shoulder height and the horse reeled on its hind legs casting monsterish shadows in the darkness. I heard another dull thud from inside the stall. When the horse dropped to all fours, I saw the rope shifting on the rafter and Bernhard, as big as a door, dead and bug-eyed, came swinging toward me. It was a horrible sight. It made me shrivel and I was sick right there on my boots. I couldn't say how long I was like that, I just remember shaking like a leaf, trying to spit the bitter taste from my mouth. Once I'd straightened up, I cast the light back into the stall to check my eyes on what I'd seen.

They hadn't lied. Bernhard was hanging by the end of the rope and it was cutting into his neck from all the kicking and commotion of that awful-frightened horse. I had to get Bernhard down before that rope sawed through his neck. I waited until the horse had backed off some and I slid the stall door open. It didn't take much for that horse to dart for the open door. I had to jump quickly so as not to be in its path. It ran for the other end of the barn, but stopped and reeled itself up in the darkness before it got close to the outer door. I let it be for the moment and ducked into the stall and slid the door closed behind me.

I had a hell of a time getting him down. I ended up cutting the rope just behind the noose. It was as high as I could reach. I don't care to think much more about how he landed and the sight of his neck and face or the other things that happen to the dead. I kept the stall door closed and got that poor horse settled in another stall before I ran back out into the night to get some help. I fetched the livery owner, Mr. Zahn, from next door and we took care of the body and he gave me a place to stay for the night.

I rode out to Nels's the next morning. He was in the middle of his chores when I got there. He seemed to have an idea that something had happened, said he could see it on my face, so I told him the story as I knew it. It wasn't much of a surprise to Nels. "The man had no luck," he said. That was the best approximation of it, I supposed; so I left Nels to the job of telling Elisabetha and Frank, and I carried on to Christian's farm to tell him the story before he found out some other way. He came out of the house when the dogs started barking, and I recounted the events of the card game and how I'd come upon Bernhard in that the terrible way, making sure he understood it was Bernhard's doing and no fault of Jakob Feist.

"Where is he now?" asked Christian.

"In the tack room at the livery," I said. "We couldn't think of nowhere else to put him."

Christian nodded. "The priest won't want him in the cemetery, I suppose."

"Probably not," I answered.

"Well, I better make a box."

"Yeah." I nodded, staring at the ground.

"Probably need more wood."

"Yeah."

It was noon when I made it back to the farm. Margaret ran out of the house looking tired and all shades of worried and angry. "Where have you been?" she shouted to me before I was even off the wagon.

I shook my head. I didn't want to talk about it all over again, but I owed her something. "Bernhard's dead."

She covered her eyes and a string of tears ran down her cheeks. I stopped the wagon and handed the lines to my boy, John, and went to Margaret and held her in my arms.

"I had an awful feeling," she said. "I thought something might've happened to you," she sobbed into my ear. "I was worried all night long."

"It's fine," I said. "I'm here." I held her tight for a while longer; neither one of us wanted to let go.

A few days later, I was in town and ran into Jakob Feist. We talked some. He wasn't looking too good.

"It's all too much at once," he said. "The way some people look at me like I might be Death himself or something." He had a worried expression. "You think he meant to do this?" he asked. "To get to me? So people would think him a martyr and make me and my family look like we did something evil."

"I doubt he thought beyond himself," I said.

"You think?" He rubbed the creases in his forehead. "I know he out-thought me, maybe even the whole bunch of us."

"You have to be pretty lost to go down that path of thinking."

Jakob nodded as he chewed on that thought. "I'd have given him back the land."

"I know."

"There ain't nobody who'll take it now."

The wind was blowing cold. I needed to be going. "You'll make some good of it," I said.

"Yeah," he said, and he turned up his collar.

I gave him a pat on the shoulder, and we went our separate ways.

‽

Until today, I thought the whole thing with that land had been settled. But Frank told me Jakob Feist seeded Bernhard's quarter to grass, and Frank had been helping Jakob mend the old barbwire fences. In return, Jakob was going to let Frank pasture his cattle on the quarter.

"Jakob Feist's basically a good man," I told him. "He'll always do the right thing in the end."

Frank nodded. "I think he feels bad about how he got that quarter—he's offered to sell it to me. Cheap."

Those words made my neck hairs stand on end. "You sure you wanna do that? Bernhard figured there was a curse on that land."

Frank half-smiled and looked at me with those ghostly eyes. "I don't put much stock in curses, Uncle. Far as I can tell, there's been one over me since before I was born."

Acknowledgements

Thank you to my parents, Dan and Georgeline Heit, for supporting and encouraging my work on this book. To Emmanuel and Veronica Bertsch for sharing your memories and answering my questions about those early settler days. And to Joseph S. Height whose research and writing grounds these stories.

With respect to craft, I need to thank my friend and mentor, Dave Margoshes, who pushed me to listen to and learn from my characters. Dave is a tough old dude, and he's one of the most generous I know. Thank you for believing in me. It's made the journey less wearisome.

Also thanks to Alissa York for her comments on earlier drafts of many of these stories; Leona Theis for very carefully reading my manuscript and providing me with helpful feedback; and, James McNulty for digging deep into "The Horse Accident" with me. Big thanks to my editor, J. Jill Robinson, for being tough, thoughtful and tireless in her work. You've helped me to enrich these stories.

Many thanks to Mary K Renwick, Karl Tischler, Sean Renwick, Dianne Peacock, Inge Gowans, and Chris Volk.

Finally, I would like to thank the Saskatchewan Arts Board for their financial support.

An excerpt from "Fireworks Over Kaidenberg" appeared in *Prairie Messenger*, Vol. 94, No. 6, June 22, 2016.

About the Author

Jason Heit was raised on his family's farm in west central Saskatchewan. Growing up in a rural community that struggled to thrive inspired him to study rural issues and work in the area of community economic development in Canada, Latin America, and Mongolia.

He holds a Master's of Arts in Interdisciplinary Studies with a focus on co-operative organizations from the University of Saskatchewan, and continues to work in economic development as a policy analyst with the federal government.

Heit's writing often reflects his interest in rural communities and people, their issues and stories. His short stories have appeared in *Event* and *Coffin Bell. Kaidenberg's Best Sons* is his first book.